WIND CHIME WEDDING

A WIND CHIME NOVEL

SOPHIE MOSS

Dear Claire,

Merry Christmas!
Hope you get lots of down time
for pleasure reading :)

♡
Sophie Moss

Sea Rose
Publishing

Published by Sea Rose Publishing

ISBN-13: 978-0692470978

For the memory of my grandmother
Frances M. Nace
1917-2004

ONE

*M*iss Haddaway?"

Standing in the doorway to her classroom, Becca Haddaway glanced down at eight-year-old, Luke Faulkner. He was clutching a piece of paper in his hands and shifting self-consciously from one foot to the other. "Hey, Luke. Is your mom running late again?"

"I don't know." He looked down and pushed the paper toward her. "This is for you."

Becca's heart melted when she unfolded a pencil drawing of a bunny with big floppy ears in a field of clover. "This is so sweet. Thank you, Luke... But wouldn't you rather give this to your mom? I'm sure she'd love to have it."

He shook his head. "I want you to have it."

Becca scanned the crowded hallway filled with parents and students heading out for the long weekend. She didn't see his mother anywhere. "Why don't you stay and hang out for a while? I picked up some colored pencils at the store the other day. You could do another drawing for your mom, and then I could walk you home afterwards."

"That's okay." He dug the toe of his sneaker into the tile. "She'll be here."

Becca frowned when she spotted the holes in his shoes. His grass stained jeans looked like they could use another spin through the washing machine, and she was pretty sure he was wearing the same sweatshirt he'd worn yesterday.

Bending down to untangle the frayed laces of one of his shoes that had come untied, she glanced back up at his face, watching him for a reaction. "You've been quiet in class this week."

His small mouth thinned, his hands tightening around the straps of his backpack.

"I know things have been hard at home since you lost your father," Becca said gently, leaning back on her heels after she finished tying his shoe. "I'm always here if you want to talk, even outside school hours. You know I only live a few houses down from you. If you ever need anything, all you have to do is knock."

He nodded, avoiding her eyes.

Most schools would caution teachers to not get so involved in their students' personal lives, but this was Heron Island—less than three miles wide, with a population of only eight hundred year-round residents. People made it their business to know what was going on in their neighbors' lives, as much to look out for one another as for the gossip. More than one person had mentioned being concerned about how Luke might be getting on at home these days. It was her responsibility to make sure none of her students slipped through the cracks.

The sound of a rattling muffler drew her gaze out to the parking lot. A small, beat-up sedan pulled up to the entrance of the elementary school and Luke's mother jumped out of the driver's seat, rushing toward the glass doors.

"I have to go," Luke said, already jogging down the hallway to meet her. "Happy Easter," he called back over his shoulder.

"You too," Becca said, rising slowly back to her feet.

Courtney Faulkner pushed through the entrance. Her face was pale. Her dark blond hair was piled in a messy knot on top of her head. And she was still wearing her black hairdresser apron. She caught Becca's eye and mouthed, "*I'm sorry,*" as she grabbed Luke's hand and pulled him back toward the car.

Becca watched them drive away. She knew Courtney was doing her best. She was probably in a hurry to get Luke home and fed and shuttled over to her brother's house so she could race off to her second job, where she worked as a night shift housekeeper at one of the hotels a few towns over.

Looking back down at the paper in her hand, she wondered if Luke had given her the drawing because he thought his mother was too busy to appreciate it. She knew Courtney was far too proud to ask for help. And as much as Becca respected her independence and determination to pick up the pieces after her husband's death, everybody needed to lean on someone now and then.

Walking back over to her desk, she slipped the drawing into her purse and surveyed the mess from the surprise party she'd thrown for her class that afternoon. The tables and chairs had been pushed into a haphazard circle. The floor was covered in plastic eggs and candy wrappers. A questionable sticky substance was smeared across several flat surfaces, which she could only hope was leftover from the marshmallow bunnies that had almost incited a riot when she'd passed them out earlier.

Smiling at the memory of her students' excited squeals when she'd announced that instead of practicing double-digit subtraction they were going to have an Easter party, she spotted Shelley Needham walking down the hall. "Shelley," she called out to the Heron Island Elementary School principal. "I've hardly seen you around all week. Where have you been?"

Shelley paused in the doorway. Her short, curly gray hair was slightly mussed. Her hazel eyes were distant and troubled. "Meeting with the board."

"Why?" Becca asked. "What's wrong?"

"Nothing." Shelley offered a ghost of a smile. "Routine stuff. Planning for next year." She reached down, snagging a pink plastic egg off the floor. "I'm surprised you had time to throw a party today. Don't you have enough on your plate with the wedding and the move?"

Becca ignored the sudden twinge of apprehension. She was getting married to her high school sweetheart, Tom Jacobson, in three weeks and moving to D.C. after their honeymoon. She should feel excited about her new life...not anxious. Reaching for the broom propped against the wall, she started to sweep up the sparkly bits of green plastic grass. "I found time."

"That reminds me..." Shelley fished out a piece of dark chocolate from inside the egg. "I still haven't gotten your letter of resignation."

"Oh, right." Becca's gaze landed on the envelope that had been burning a hole through her desk for two weeks now. She had given Shelley plenty of advance notice, but she hadn't made it official yet. Taking a deep breath, she picked up the letter. What was the point in putting it off any longer? Crossing the room, she handed the envelope to Shelley. "I keep forgetting to give it to you."

Shelley took it, slipping it into her pocket. "Thanks."

Becca paused when she noticed the dark circles under the other woman's eyes. "You look tired."

Shelley forced another smile. "I'm fine."

"Are you sure?" Becca set the broom down, gesturing for her to come further into the classroom. Shelley had been like a second mother to her since she was sixteen. She could usually tell when something was wrong.

Shelley's gaze drifted out to the playing fields. "I really didn't want to burden you with this."

Becca closed the door behind them. "What's going on?"

Shelley sighed, running her hands down the front of her wrinkled suit jacket. "I guess I'm going to have to tell everyone on Monday anyway. I might as well tell you now." She looked back at Becca. "The board is thinking of shutting us down."

"What?" Becca's eyes widened. "Why?"

"The state cut the education budget for next year."

"But we've survived plenty of budget cuts in the past. Our district always finds a way to come up with the money."

"This time it's different," Shelley said. "A few of the board members have been pushing to shut us down for a while now. They're convinced that the county could save a lot of money by consolidating. The governor's decision to reallocate the funding for next year has motivated them to explore their options."

No way, Becca thought. There was no way the board would actually shut down the school. Heron Island Elementary had been open for over sixty years. She had gone to school here. Her father had gone to school here. Almost every person on this island had gone to school here. There had to be another way to balance the budget. "What about the renovations the board approved for the gym—the ones that were supposed to happen this summer? Can't they be pushed back?"

"I've spent the past six months convincing the board that those renovations had to happen. They think the gym won't be safe for the kids if we don't get the work done this summer. And even if we did try to delay it, it still wouldn't make up even a fraction of the cost that it would save by shutting us down."

"Where will all the kids go?" Becca asked.

"St. Michaels Elementary."

"But those classrooms are already overcrowded."

"I know," Shelley said. "I wish I had a better solution. I've been trying to talk them out of it, but it's not looking good."

Becca sat down in one of the kids-sized chairs, staring at the sticky marshmallow goo smeared across the table.

"I know it's a small consolation," Shelley said after a long pause, "but you picked a good time to leave."

A good time to leave? Becca lifted her gaze to the wall covered in construction paper bunnies that her students had made that day. It was one thing to leave her job as a teacher, but the thought of the school closing down completely...?

This classroom had been her mother's classroom when she was a second grade teacher. All Becca had ever wanted was to follow in her mother's footsteps. She would have been happy to teach at this school for the rest of her life. She had agreed to move to D.C. to be with Tom because that's where his job was now, but she had secretly hoped that he might want to move back here one day, that he might tire of the city after a while and want to work at one of the smaller firms in Easton or St. Michaels. She had hoped that, maybe, after a few years, she might be able to come back and teach at this school again.

Becca looked up at Shelley. "I might be leaving, but this island is still my home. I wish you had told me what was happening. I could have been doing something to help. Why don't you let me talk to the board? If nothing else, I could raise the issue of Taylor."

"I already have." Shelley pulled out the chair across from her and sat down. "Dozens of times. They said they're planning to hire more counselors next year, that it would be good for her to get used to the structure of how the larger schools work for when—"

"For when *what*?" Becca cut in. "When she has to go to middle school? That's three years from now. Taylor will be in third grade next year. She still has a long way to go before she's ready to face a classroom of thirty-plus kids. She needs to be here, where we can give her the attention she deserves. Where she can be taken care of, and where all the teachers care about her progress, not just one counselor who might be able to fit her in between all her other appointments."

"Becca," Shelley said softly. "I know. Believe me, I've said all the same things to the board."

Becca met Shelley's gaze across the table. It wasn't just Taylor who would be affected. If this school shut down, Shelley and all the other teachers would lose their jobs. "What will happen to you?"

Shelley picked at the yellow sugar stuck to the marshmallow goo with her fingernail. "I've started putting out feelers to some of the other schools in the area, but no one's hiring right now. It might be time for me to retire, or find something else to do..."

"Are you ready to retire?"

"No, but neither was Della when she got laid off last year. She worked as a receptionist in that law firm in Easton for thirty years and now she's a chef at the café. I've never seen her so happy."

"That's not the same," Becca argued. "Della loves to cook. She didn't want to answer phones and manage calendars for the rest of her life. This is your passion, Shelley—kids and teaching. You've been working here your whole life. You can't just let that go."

Shelley smiled sadly, covering Becca's hand with her own. "We always knew this could happen one day. I'm just glad you decided to leave before it happened to both of us."

A MILE DOWN THE ISLAND, Colin Foley stood inside the waterfront inn his friend, Will Dozier, had inherited from his grandparents last year. Pulling his gaze from the thin crack snaking through the wall beside the fireplace in the family room, he glanced over at the contractor. "How much is this going to set us back?"

"We need to replace the drywall and repair the damage to the foundation," Jimmy Faulkner answered. "Two weeks worth of labor. Maybe a few extra grand, probably closer to five."

Colin ran a hand through his hair. He wasn't worried so much about the money. He was worried about the delay. He'd already told several key donors that they would be open by Memorial Day.

He couldn't go back on his word to the first people who'd invested in him, or to the families of his former SEAL teammates who'd already made plans to travel out to the island for the opening.

It would be the first time they'd all gotten together since the devastating mission in Afghanistan that had ended with two of their youngest team members being flown home in body bags and an extended stay at Walter Reed National Military Medical Center for him.

When he'd returned home from that career-ending deployment over a year ago with the lower half of his left leg blown off by a grenade, he'd struggled for months to figure out what to do with his life. It was a trip to Heron Island last November to visit his former team leader that had sparked the idea to open a rehab center for wounded warriors on the island.

Colin had managed to convince Will to go into business with him, and as soon as his friend's contract with the Navy was up in a few weeks, he'd be moving back to Maryland to help run the place.

This inn had been in Will's family for generations, but at the moment, it was Colin's responsibility. He didn't take that responsibility lightly. "If you need to hire more men to get the job done faster, hire more men. We need to open by Memorial Day."

Jimmy removed his red trucker hat, rubbing the heel of his palm over his scalp. "What about Becca's wedding?"

Becca's wedding? Crap. He'd completely forgotten about that. Will had promised Becca that she could hold her wedding here the week before they opened. They couldn't go back on their word now. "We need to have everything finished and cleaned up before then."

"It's going to be tight," Jimmy warned.

Reaching into his pocket for his phone when it buzzed, Colin glanced down at the screen, then back up at Jimmy. "Whatever you need to do, just do it."

Jimmy nodded and Colin turned, picking up the call. "Hey, Dad."

"Colin," his father's deep voice came through the line. "I understand you cancelled your seat at the Victory PAC fundraiser in Baltimore tonight."

"I had to make a last minute trip down to the island." Colin stepped over a pile of paint cans on his way out to the porch. "Something came up at the inn."

"Is everything okay?"

"Just a minor setback, nothing we can't handle."

"Good," Nick Foley said. There was a pause and Colin heard a muffled voice in the background, most likely his campaign manager or one of his assistants. As the Governor of Maryland, his father rarely went anywhere without an entourage of assistants.

When his father came back on the line, his tone was rushed. "Are you still planning to attend the dinner at The Dockside in Annapolis on Saturday night?"

Colin looked out at the wide sloping green lawn that led down to the Chesapeake Bay. The last thing he wanted to do was sit through another fundraiser dinner, but part of the agreement he'd made with his parents when he'd committed to work on his father's campaign through May was attending at least two social events per week. "I'll be there."

"Natalie wants to know who you're bringing."

"I'm sure she does."

"Colin—"

"Put her on, Dad."

"What?"

"Put her on," Colin repeated, leaning his shoulder against the unpainted doorframe. "I know she's sitting right next to you."

There was another long pause before his stepmother's smooth, cultured voice drifted through the line. "Colin, honey, I need to know who you're bringing to the dinner Saturday night."

"Hi, Natalie."

His stepmother sighed. "Why do you insist on making this difficult for me?"

Colin smiled. "Because I don't need you to set me up."

"But I have so many friends with nice *single* daughters."

"I don't need you to set me up," he repeated.

"But what about Priscilla Davenport's daughter, Julie— remember her? Your father said you two went to pre-school together."

"Oh?" Colin said. "Were we an item back then?"

"Please be serious, Colin. Julie just moved back to the area and she's recently divorced. I think you two would really hit it off." She added a note of hope into her voice. "I could arrange for you to sit together on Saturday night..."

"Natalie." Colin pushed off the doorframe. The woman was relentless. "I'm bringing someone."

"Who?" she asked, surprised.

"You'll meet her on Saturday."

"Won't you at least tell me her name?"

"No."

His stepmother lowered her voice to a whisper. "She's not one of those women you pick up at the bars, is she?"

Colin choked out a laugh. "What?"

"I know what goes on in downtown Annapolis on the weekends," she huffed. "I hear things."

Colin rolled his eyes. "I'm not bringing a woman I picked up at a bar."

"Then who is she?"

"Someone you've never met before."

"How...mysterious."

Yes, Colin thought. She was. She was so mysterious she didn't even exist yet.

"You'd better not be making this up," Natalie warned. "Last time you told me you were bringing a date, you came alone, and there was an empty seat beside you all night. We had to put your father's jacket on the back of your chair so it didn't look like you'd been stood up."

Colin shook his head, smiling. No one at that party had thought he'd been stood up. But appearances were everything to his stepmother. And ever since she'd taken it on as her life's mission to find him a wife, he hadn't had a moment's peace. If he had to spend one more night talking to a woman who made him want to claw his eyes out from boredom, he'd lose it. "There won't be an empty seat this time, I promise."

"I wish you would tell me who you're bringing," she said. "What if I forget her name when I'm introducing her to people?"

"You won't forget her name," Colin said. Natalie Foley never forgot a name. "I'll see you on Saturday." Ending the call, he slipped his phone back in his pocket.

Jimmy walked out to the porch, unscrewing the cap off a tarnished silver flask. "I made a few calls. Looks like I can get a bigger crew here to start on Monday."

"Thanks," Colin said.

Jimmy handed him the flask.

Colin took it, walking down the steps to where a pile of raw lumber sat under a blue tarp. He lifted the tarp with the toe of his boot, inspecting the quality of the wood.

"I saw your picture in the paper last weekend," Jimmy said.

"Yeah?" Colin said distractedly.

"Who was that woman you were with?"

"Last weekend?" They were all starting to run together at this point. Letting the tarp fall back into place, he glanced back at Jimmy. "Christy Caraway, maybe?"

"Christy Caraway of Caraway's Crab House? The heir to the biggest chain of seafood restaurants in the Mid-Atlantic?"

Colin nodded, taking a sip from the flask.

Jimmy whistled. "I'm impressed." Leaning back against the house, the contractor dipped his hands in his pockets. "Nice rack, too. Have you seen her naked?"

Colin smiled. "She's easy on the eyes, but that's about all she's got going for her."

Jimmy grinned. "She looked pretty good in that picture."

They all looked good in the pictures, Colin thought. Every woman his stepmother set him up with was the same: attractive, wealthy, well connected, and only interested in him for one reason—because he was the governor's son.

He'd been engaged to a woman who'd only wanted him for his status before—for being a SEAL. He hadn't realized it at the time, but his ex-fiancée had made it perfectly clear when she'd broken up with him a week after he'd returned from Afghanistan without his leg, saying she couldn't marry an amputee.

Gazing out at the wide expanse of water, he watched the late afternoon sunlight glint over the surface. He could hear the water lapping against the rocks along the shoreline, the wind whipping at the layers of plastic covering the gaps in the walls where a few of the downstairs windows were being replaced.

There was no going back, no point in remembering what he'd lost or who he'd once been. This place was his future. And the first step was opening by Memorial Day.

Nothing was going to get in the way of that.

Screwing the cap back on the flask, he tossed it to Jimmy.

Now, all he needed was to find a date for Saturday night.

TWO

*I*t was close to four o'clock when Becca walked out of the elementary school. The parking lot was empty except for the few cars that belonged to the teachers who hadn't left yet—teachers who were going to find out next week that they would soon be out of a job.

Unlocking her Toyota Corolla, she set her purse in the back seat, and looked across the street at Magnolia Harbor. April winds whipped at the sailboats in the slips. Halyards clanged against metal masts and white caps chopped over the surface of the Chesapeake Bay. She could hear the gravelly voices of several watermen talking to each other as they prepped their lines and traps for the morning.

The teachers weren't the only ones who would be out of jobs soon. The watermen on this island had been struggling to make ends meet for years now. Many of them, including her father, had already taken on second and third jobs on the mainland.

Their hearts might still be out on the water, but deep down, they all knew that their way of life was slowly dying.

You picked a good time to leave.

Opening her driver's side door, Becca slid behind the wheel. How was it a good time to leave when everything was falling apart? It felt like a betrayal, escaping just in time. Like she was turning her back on her friends.

She pulled her phone out to see if Tom had called her back since she'd left him a message an hour ago, but there was only a single text message from Jimmy Faulkner, the contractor in charge of renovating the waterfront inn where her wedding would be held in three weeks.

Ran into a setback. Call me.

Fantastic, she thought, dropping the phone onto the seat beside her and easing out of the spot. What else could go wrong today?

Turning right out of the parking lot onto the long flat road leading toward the inn, she watched a lone osprey glide over the thin fingers of water that snaked in and out of the marshes. She still couldn't believe Shelley hadn't told her the school was in danger of being shut down. Up until an hour ago, she'd thought they told each other everything.

Was this the beginning of what her new life was going to be like—her friends hiding their problems from her because she was leaving?

She didn't want to be cut off from her community, from being a part of this island.

It wasn't like she was moving across the country.

D.C. was only two hours away.

Dodging a pothole, she fought back another wave of uneasiness as a thick hedge of hollies and blackberry bushes gave way to a private stretch of land surrounded on three sides by water. A pale yellow inn with white shutters and a wide front porch sat at the end of a curved oyster shell driveway. Two trucks were parked outside: Jimmy Faulkner's red Ford and Colin Foley's dark blue Chevy.

Her heart did a funny little flip flop in her chest at the thought of running into Colin. She hadn't seen much of him over the past several months. He spent most of his time in Annapolis and only came down to the island on the weekends, while she spent most of her weekends in D.C. with Tom.

As far as she knew, he was still working on his father's reelection campaign.

She paused, her eyes widening. Maybe Colin could help them. It might be too late to make any changes to the education budget for next year, but if the governor could promise an increase for the following year, maybe it would be enough to convince the board to keep the school open.

Stepping out of the car with a renewed sense of hope, she saw the sheen of wet paint on the front porch steps and headed around the side of the house to the backyard. The faint scent of viburnums, sweet and spicy, filled the air when she spied the man down at the dock talking on his cell phone. Colin Foley's back was to her, but there was no mistaking those broad shoulders, that tall commanding frame, that thick shock of black hair that had grown even longer since the fall.

When he turned, and their eyes met across the long stretch of lawn, she felt the punch of heat roll all the way through her.

"Enjoying the view?" a deep voice drawled.

Becca jumped and spotted Jimmy leaning against the side of the house for the first time. "I didn't even see you there."

"Clearly." Jimmy chuckled, lifting a flask to his lips and taking a long sip.

Becca narrowed her eyes, picking her way through the piles of raw lumber to where he stood. She watched him lower the flask until it dangled loosely from his fingertips, almost like an extension of the rest of his arm.

No one should look that natural holding a flask.

Jimmy had always been a drinker, but after his younger brother—Luke's father—had passed away in January, things had taken a turn for the worse. A few of the islanders had talked about confronting him, but so far he hadn't done anything to hurt anyone besides himself.

Becca wasn't crazy about the idea of waiting around for that to happen. She knew far too well the effects alcoholism could have if left unchecked. She held her hand out for the flask, intending to pour the contents onto the grass as soon as he gave it to her.

Jimmy grinned, slipping it into his back pocket. "Why don't you join me at Rusty's tonight? Let me buy you a real drink?"

"No, thanks."

"Why not?" He pushed off the side of the house, looking her up and down suggestively. "You're still single for three more weeks."

Becca took in his red rimmed eyes, unshaven face and unwashed flannel shirt. Part of her wished she could say something to convince him to clean up his act, if not for himself, at least for his sister-in-law. Courtney and Luke both needed him right now. But she knew better than to have that conversation when he'd been drinking. "I'm engaged. That doesn't exactly make me single."

He took a step closer. "As far as I'm concerned, you're still single until you walk down that aisle."

Becca felt a prick of irritation. Jimmy had always been a flirt, but lately his advances had gotten more persistent. "It's not going to happen, Jimmy."

He reached up, picking a piece of Easter grass out of her hair. "I like it when you try to be stern."

She caught the sharp stench of whiskey on his breath and took a step back, putting more distance between them. "I got your text message," she said, changing the subject. "You mentioned something about a setback."

He let the piece of plastic grass drop to the ground. "We found a crack in the foundation this morning. It's going to push everything back a couple of weeks."

"A couple of weeks?" Becca's brows shot up. "That only leaves one week to finish the rest of the renovations before the wedding."

Jimmy nodded.

Becca looked back down at the man on the dock. "I think I'll walk down and see if I can do anything to help."

"Suit yourself." Jimmy pulled his flask back out of his pocket. "If you change your mind about tonight, you know where to find me."

"I'm not going to change my mind." She turned, bristling at the sound of his low laugh as it followed her across the yard. She didn't like the thought of Luke staying at his uncle's house when Jimmy was drinking this much. She knew what it was like to watch someone drink to the point of blacking out each night. She knew what it was like to try to help them stumbling and staggering into bed only to find them passed out on the floor the next morning, still cradling the bottle from the night before.

She knew how helpless it could make you feel, wondering if it would ever stop, wondering what you had done to cause it, wondering if one morning you would try to wake them up and find that you couldn't.

She made a mental note to talk to Courtney this weekend. She knew Luke's mother was busy, but if she had to schedule a haircut to get some time with her, she would. Things couldn't go on like this. If no one else was going to intervene, she would take matters into her own hands.

Passing the old swing hanging from the branches of the black walnut tree, she let her fingers trail over the weathered ropes before stepping onto the wooden planks of the dock. "Hey," she said, just as Colin ended his call.

"Hey, yourself," he said, smiling and pocketing his phone. "Long time no see."

She nodded, trying not to notice the way his thin gray T-shirt stretched across his broad shoulders and muscular chest. A pair of worn jeans hung from his narrow hips and his work boots made a dull thudding sound against the wood as his long legs ate up the pier.

If it weren't for the subtle difference in the drape of the denim against his left leg, she would never know there was a prosthesis hidden beneath his jeans. Not that the loss of a limb seemed to be affecting his love life in any way. His picture had been in the newspaper several times over the winter and a different gorgeous woman had been hanging on his arm in every shot.

Annie and Della had started taking bets at the café on which one he'd end up with.

When he paused in front of her, she had to tilt her face to look up at him. At five-foot-two, she was short compared to most people, but Colin towered over her by more than a foot. "How've you been?"

"Good." He shifted a little to the left, so he was blocking the sun. His features came into view even sharper—that strong chiseled jaw, those wide slashing cheekbones, that full, sensual mouth. "Busy. You?"

"Yeah, me too," she said, suddenly at a loss for words. She had forgotten she tended to get a little tongue-tied around Colin. There was something about those cool blue eyes that unnerved her...and made her feel things she really shouldn't be feeling when she was engaged to another man.

Her gaze shifted away from his face and she struggled to think of something else normal and natural to say.

"I just got off the phone with Will," Colin said. "He said to say, hi."

She brightened slightly. "How's he doing?"

"Anxious to get back to the island."

Anxious to get back to Annie was more like it, Becca thought. Will had fallen head over heels for the single mother when he'd come back to the island on temporary leave last fall. The two of them were engaged now. In a few weeks, they, along with Annie's eight-year-old daughter, would be moving into the private wing that had been added onto the inn over the winter.

Jimmy and his crew had managed to build a brand new addition that fit perfectly with the historic structure. The contractor might be teetering on the edge of alcoholism, but no one would ever question his ability to get the job done, and get it done right.

Getting it done *on time* was another matter entirely.

"Jimmy told me about the crack in the foundation."

"Yeah." Colin rubbed a hand over his jaw. "The timing's unfortunate. We'll have to hire a bigger crew to get the place ready in time, but it's either that or push back the opening, and we're not pushing back the opening."

She'd figured he'd say that. "Can I do anything to help?"

He shook his head. "We've got it covered."

"Are you sure?" she asked, surprised by the confident tone of his voice. "Because Jimmy said—"

"Let me handle Jimmy."

Becca's gaze flickered down to the long, lean muscles of his forearms where he'd rolled up his sleeves and the big, wide-palmed hands that had earned him the reputation of being one of the Navy's deadliest snipers before his career had been cut short.

She had no doubt the former SEAL could handle their small town contractor.

"So," she said, forcing the thought of what other skills those hands might have out of her mind, "how's the campaign going?"

"Pretty good. My father's not thrilled that I'm cutting out early, but he'll get over it."

Becca nodded, remembering that when Colin had first raised the idea of the rehab center to Will, he had suggested they open by the fall. But once Will had signed on and Colin had started rounding up funding, things had picked up speed fast. The two men had pushed the opening date up to Memorial Day.

Colin gazed out at the water, watching a pair of ducks paddle toward the marshes. "I'm just happy not to think about it when I'm down here."

Of course he would want to escape the campaign when he came to the island, Becca thought. According to Annie and Will, Colin had never wanted to work on his father's campaign. He had only agreed to it because it would mean that he'd get to spend six months rubbing shoulders with some of the wealthiest and most powerful people in Maryland—people who might be interested in investing in the veterans' center.

Unfortunately, she really wanted to talk to him about politics right now.

"I always feel like a weight has lifted when I cross the Bay Bridge. Like all that"—Colin gestured behind him toward the Western Shore, which was home to the cities of Baltimore, Annapolis, and the sprawling outskirts of D.C.—"is worlds away. I can't wait to move here full time in a few weeks."

A few weeks.

In a few weeks, Colin would be moving to the island...and she would be leaving.

Whenever she voiced her concerns about leaving the island to Tom, he accused her of being afraid of living in the city, of finding a new job, of fitting in with his friends. Maybe he was right. Maybe she was afraid.

He'd been telling her for years that it would be good for her to leave the island. That people needed to leave their hometowns to change and grow, to become the people they were meant to be. It was just that sometimes, late at night, when she lay awake, she knew without a doubt that *this* was all she had ever wanted to be.

But marriage was all about sacrifices, right?

Glancing over her shoulder, she looked back at the picturesque farmhouse. Six months ago, when Will had inherited this inn from his grandparents, he had almost turned it over to a developer who'd planned to tear it down. Thanks, in large part to Colin, Will had changed his mind at the last minute and decided to keep it.

Becca couldn't imagine the island without this inn, anymore than she could imagine it without the elementary school. If they had found a way to save this inn, surely they could find a way to save the school.

"Colin," she said, turning back to face the man who might be their only hope. "I need to ask you a favor."

"Sure," Colin said, wondering why she looked so nervous all of a sudden. Whatever she needed probably had something to do with the wedding, and while he wasn't a big fan of weddings at the moment, he was always happy to help out a friend. "What's up?"

The wind pushed a few strands of brown hair into her eyes. She attempted to force them into the clip that held the rest of her hair back, but pieces kept falling loose, framing her pretty, heart-shaped face.

The sharp tug of attraction took him by surprise, just as it had the first night they'd met almost six months ago. With her shy smile and expressive brown eyes, she was more of a girl next door type of pretty—not the type he usually went for—but there was something about her that pulled at him.

He had noticed her immediately, even before Will had introduced them that first night back in November, but he'd backed off as soon as he'd spotted the rock on her finger.

It was still there, catching the sparks of sunlight that bounced off the water—a glaring reminder of the promise he'd once made to a different woman, back when he'd still had his leg, his career, and a foolish belief that no matter what happened to him overseas he would always be enough for her.

"I know you have a million other things to do and I completely understand why you don't want to think about your father's campaign while you're down here," she began, jolting him back from his thoughts.

His father's campaign? That was the last thing Colin had expected her to say.

She tugged on the single charm that hung from a gold chain around her neck. "You know that I work at the elementary school, right?"

He nodded.

"I just found out that we might get shut down at the end of the year."

"Shut down?" Colin stared back at her. "Why?"

"The board has been threatening to do it for years. I never thought they'd actually go through with it, but now, with the budget cuts coming..."

Budget cuts?

Shit.

She meant *his father's* budget cuts.

In a few days, the governor was planning to announce a brand new fully funded program to help Maryland veterans find jobs. It was a program Colin had worked tirelessly on for the past six months. If it became a success, it would act as a model for similar types of programs all over the country. But to fund the program, they'd had to borrow money from several other sectors.

After weeks of analysis, they had determined that since Maryland already had one of the best school systems in the country—thanks to an increase in national funding and hefty donations flowing in from individuals and private businesses over the past several years—it could handle a slight cut.

But Colin hadn't considered how that decision would affect some of the smallest schools in their state's most rural communities. And he sure as hell hadn't considered how that decision might affect eight-year-old Taylor Malone, the future step-daughter of his best friend and business partner.

If he had known there was even a chance that this island school might close, he would never have pushed so hard for those cuts.

"How many people know about this?" Colin asked.

"Right now, only you, me and Shelley. The board will probably make a formal announcement at the end of next week, but Shelley's planning to tell the teachers on Monday."

"Will and Annie don't know yet?"

"No."

"Will's going to lose it when he finds out."

"I know." Becca moved the tiny charm back and forth on the chain. "Actually, that's what I wanted to talk to you about." She glanced back up at him, her doe-brown eyes hopeful. "I know it's a lot to ask, but is there any chance you or your father might be willing to make a few calls to some of the board members over the weekend? It might go a long way toward changing their minds."

"Of course," Colin said quickly. There was no way he was going to let the board take Taylor's school away from her, not after everything she'd been through. "Let me see what I can do."

Becca let out a sigh of relief. "Thank you."

"No problem," he said, far more confidently than he actually felt. "Would you mind if we kept this between us for a few more days?"

Becca nodded. "Do you need me to do anything? I could type up an email to your father about how well Taylor's doing. About how important this school is for her. Offer some specifics, as her teacher."

He was about to tell her that wasn't necessary, then he paused, reconsidering. "Would you like to tell him in person?"

"In person?" Becca asked, surprised.

Colin nodded. This could be perfect. He still needed a date for the event on Saturday night and it couldn't hurt for his father to hear from Taylor's teacher, to get a better grasp on the situation before he reached out to the board members. "There's a fundraiser for the campaign in Annapolis on Saturday night. Why don't you come with me and I'll make sure you get some time with my father to talk about the school?"

Becca hesitated. "Aren't there guest lists for things like that?"

"Yes," Colin admitted. "But I already told my stepmother I was bringing someone, and I don't have time to find a date. You'd actually be doing me a favor."

Becca looked up at him doubtfully. "I have a hard time believing you have trouble finding a date."

Colin's brows rose.

"I mean..." Becca blushed, looking away. "You know what I mean."

"No." He smiled, enjoying himself. "I'm not sure I do."

"I just meant..." Becca's hand fluttered out in front of her, trying to wave him off. "Everyone knows you've been dating a lot of women lately."

"Everyone?"

"Everyone on the island," she said quickly. "You know how fast word spreads around here."

Colin watched a telltale shade of pink spread across her cheeks. She was trying to play it off like she'd heard the gossip in passing, but he had a feeling she wouldn't be blushing like that if she hadn't been keeping track on her own.

He would have thought, with her upcoming wedding and impending move, his love life would have been the last thing on her mind.

Apparently not...

Becca picked at a piece of construction paper stuck to the sleeve of her purple sweater. "What kind of event is it?"

"It's a dinner." He leaned back against the piling. For someone who was getting married in three weeks, she seemed awfully distracted.

"Is it fancy or casual?"

"Casual."

"How casual?" Her gaze flickered back up to his. "I mean... should I wear jeans or a cocktail dress?"

Colin's lips curved as his gaze combed down the front of her crewneck sweater, ankle length chinos, and black ballet flats, then all the way back up. He was beginning to think Saturday was going to turn into a very interesting evening. "Wear something red."

ear something red?

Becca walked into her house, dropped her purse on the floor, and leaned back against the door. What was she doing letting Colin flirt with her? And what was she thinking telling him she had a hard time believing he had trouble finding a date?

She might as well have a sign stamped to her forehead saying she was attracted to him. Scrubbing her hands over her face, she felt the cool band of her engagement ring brush against her skin. Her hands dropped quickly back to her sides.

A rush of guilt swept over her as she took in the half-finished wedding projects scattered throughout the living room—material and thread for the ring bearer pillow she'd insisted on sewing by hand, spools of lavender ribbon that still needed to be cut and tied around the dozens of glass jars that would line the aisle to the altar, a growing collection of classic love poems that she was hoping to draw inspiration from to write her vows.

Reaching down, she picked up a crocheted afghan that had

fallen off the sofa and draped it back over the piece of furniture. She should call Colin and tell him that something had come up, that she had just remembered a previous commitment, and that she wasn't free after all.

The sound of her neighbors' voices drifted in from the street. Their muffled conversations were punctuated by the faint hiss of a hose as Gladys Schaefer watered her flowerbeds and the low growl of Randy Cole's diesel engine as he eased his truck into the driveway next door.

Randy's oldest child was supposed to start kindergarten at Heron Island Elementary next year. How many times had his wife, Kate, come over worried about how their painfully shy daughter was going to fit in?

She would be eaten alive in a bigger class.

Didn't Becca owe it to her friends and neighbors to do everything she could to try to save the school before she left?

It wasn't like she was going to get another invitation to meet the governor face-to-face.

Taking a deep breath, she pushed off the door and made her way through the cluttered living room to her first floor bedroom. She was going to that dinner on Saturday. She was going to talk to the governor. And she was going to find a way to convince him to help them save the school.

She opened the door to her closet, catching a few sweaters as they tumbled down from the overstuffed top shelf. At some point over the next few weeks, she really needed to go through all the clothes in this closet and decide which ones she wanted to keep. Her best friend, Grace Callahan, had been threatening to stage an intervention for years.

Snagging the sleeve of her favorite Salisbury University sweatshirt off the floor, she lifted it up and looped it over a hook on the back of the door.

She had never been very good at getting rid of things.

She wasn't a hoarder...just sentimental.

Satisfied that nothing else was going to fall out of the closet, at least for the next few minutes, she started pulling possible outfits off the hanging rack and tossing them onto the bed. When she found what she was looking for—a pale yellow wrap dress with the tag still on—she laid it over her arm and knelt down to search for a pair of shoes.

She spotted a pair of wedge sandals buried beneath a rubber boot in the back and started to reach for them, but paused when a pair of red heels caught her eye.

Wear something red.

Her pulse skittered at the memory of those cool blue eyes combing down her body.

It didn't mean anything, she told herself. He probably looked at all women that way.

Her hand hovered over the wedge sandals. The safe choice. The right choice. But those red heels were brand new. She hadn't even worn them yet. And they would look great with this dress.

Her fingers inched toward the red heels.

They were just *shoes*, she rationalized. Colin probably wouldn't even notice if she wore them. And if he did...well, then they could get a good laugh out of it.

It wasn't like she was wearing them for him.

She needed to look her best for the governor. Definitely not for—

"Becca?"

Becca jerked her hand back. She twisted around, snagging the strap of a purse and the hanger it was attached to, and bringing them both toppling down onto her head. "Dad," she said, relieved when she spotted the man in the doorway. "I didn't even hear you come in."

He walked over and untangled the wire hanger from her hair. "You're jumpy today."

"It's been a long week."

He set the hanger down and held out his hand, helping her to her feet. "I ran into Shelley out in the street. She seemed distracted, too. Is everything okay at work?"

Becca hesitated. She didn't like keeping secrets from her father. He lived across the street and they saw each other almost every day, so even when she tried to keep something from him, he found out eventually. But she didn't want to upset him with the news about the school. That building represented one of the last physical connections he still had to his wife, and she really didn't want to reopen the old wound.

Besides, Colin had seemed fairly confident that the governor would be able to help them. There was no reason to worry her father yet. "Everything's fine," she assured him.

He glanced down at the dress in her arm and then looked over at the pile of clothes on the bed. "What's all this?"

"I'm cleaning out my closet," she said, opting for a half-truth. "I'm trying to decide what to keep and what to get rid of."

He walked over, picking up a dress that had fallen on the floor. "Are you getting rid of all these?"

"No." She took the dress from his hands and laid it back on the pile. "I'm just going through them."

He picked up a delicate cream-colored wrap with tiny pink flowers embroidered into the edges. His weathered waterman's hands held it gently, lovingly, like it would disappear if he let it go.

"I'm not getting rid of that, Dad," Becca said softly. "I would never get rid of anything of Mom's."

He looked up at her. Even after all these years, she could still see the grief reflected in his light brown eyes. "You know I have room in my house if you need to store anything."

"I know." She took the wrap gently from his hands and hung it back up in the closet. Neither of them had ever been very good at getting rid of things. "Are you hungry?" she asked, changing the subject. "I think there's some leftover fried chicken in the fridge."

He nodded and she let out a breath as they walked out of the room and headed for the kitchen. She grabbed two sodas from the fridge and handed him one. "Why don't you turn on the game and I'll heat up dinner?" she suggested.

Pulling an Orioles frosty mug from the freezer, he poured his soda into it and wandered back out to the living room, rummaging through the cushions on the sofa for the remote control.

Becca watched him run through the familiar routine. Her father came over almost every night for dinner. That was all going to change in a few weeks.

What was he going to do when she left?

Who would he eat with? Who would feed him?

Sliding the chicken into the microwave, she reminded herself that her father was in his late fifties. He could take care of himself.

Then, why did she feel so guilty?

She scooped leftover mashed potatoes into a bowl and stole another glance back out at the living room. Her father had found the remote and was settling onto the sofa, flipping through the channels for the baseball game. He was wearing the same thing he always wore, a plain white T-shirt and faded bleach-stained khakis with sneakers so beat-up they looked like something he'd accidentally dredged up in one of his fishing nets.

"How was your day?" she asked over the voice of the announcer calling the plays of the game.

"Same as yesterday."

The microwave beeped and she pulled the chicken out,

popping the mashed potatoes in and resetting the timer. *Same as yesterday* meant that whatever her father had pulled out of the Bay today wasn't coming anywhere close to what he needed to make ends meet.

It was still early in the season, but it seemed like every year the reports got worse. Retrieving the heated potatoes from the microwave, she filled their plates with food. She walked over to the sofa and set them down on the coffee table, just as her phone began to ring.

"This might be Tom," she said, digging the phone out of her pocket and checking the screen. Sure enough... "Hey," she said brightly, picking up the call.

"Hey," Tom said. "Are you still coming to D.C. tonight?"

"Tonight?" Her brows pinched together. "No. I'm staying here this weekend."

"You are?"

"Yes." She threw a quick glance at her father. "It's Easter..."

There was a pause on the other end of the line. "I completely forgot about that."

Becca covered the mouthpiece and smiled down at her father, pretending everything was fine. "I think I'll make a salad," she whispered as she headed back into the kitchen. As soon as she was out of earshot, she spoke back into the phone. "You forgot about Easter?"

"Things have been crazy here. A big case came in today. Everyone's been called back into the office."

He paused and Becca could hear him speaking to someone else in the office, another lawyer or an assistant maybe. Then she heard the sound of a door shutting. When he came back on the line, it was quieter in the background. "Sorry," he said. "It's a really big case. High profile client."

It was always a big case, Becca thought. And the firm always took precedence, no matter what. "You're not going to be tied up for the whole weekend, are you?"

"I don't know. It's possible."

"Annie and Della are throwing a big party at the café on Sunday," she protested.

"I know," he said, and his voice sounded weary. "Look, Becca, you know I need to do whatever it takes right now. There's a lot of competition to make partner this year. I'm doing this for us, remember?"

For us.

Becca knew how hard he worked. She knew he wanted to start a family as badly as she did. But, as he'd reminded her countless times, children were expensive. He wanted to make sure they were set up financially first.

How could she argue with that?

She heard more commotion in the background. "Do you want to call me back later? Something happened today and I'd really like to talk when you have time to—"

"Hang on, Becca. Hang on, just a second."

She heard Tom's office door open again. All the background noise from the hallway rushed back through the receiver. She held the phone away from her ear as he engaged in a lengthy discussion with whoever had barged in. When he finally came back on the line, the noise in the background was deafening.

"Why don't you come up here for the night," he said, trying to speak over the noise. "I might not be home until after midnight, but we can order take-out and stay up and watch those comedy shows you love."

It was a small sacrifice, Becca thought. He hated those shows and rarely agreed to watch them with her. But she always went to D.C. on the weekends. She couldn't remember the last time he'd agreed to spend the weekend on the island. Come to think of it, she couldn't remember the last time he'd even mentioned wanting to visit the island.

"I think I'll stay here tonight," Becca said.

"Okay," he said, not even bothering to put up a fight.

Becca looked out the window over the sink, at the view of the marshes shimmering in the fading sunlight. She knew she should offer to go to D.C., to spend the holiday with Tom since he couldn't get away. It wasn't his fault his job was so demanding.

But she really wanted to celebrate Easter on Heron Island. She wanted to watch the kids hunt for eggs on the docks of the marina. She wanted to go to brunch with the rest of the islanders at the café. She wanted to spend the day with her father.

"I'll call you later, okay?" Tom said. It sounded like more people were swarming around him in the background, trying to pull him away. "I've got to run, but I'll call you later."

She heard the beep, indicating that he'd already ended the call. "Yeah, okay," she said softly. Lowering the phone to her side, she looked back out the window, at a blue heron spreading its wings and gliding gracefully over the horizon.

"Becca?"

Becca's gaze shot to the doorway. She hadn't realized her father had gotten up from the sofa and had come into the kitchen.

"Are you sure everything's okay?" he asked quietly.

"Everything's fine." She forced a wobbly smile back on her face. She didn't like her father to see her like this...so vulnerable.

She was the strong one. She had always been the strong one.

She had been the one who had held what was left of their family together after her mother had died.

"Something came up at work for Tom." She walked over to the fridge to pull out a head of lettuce. "He won't be coming this weekend after all."

Her father continued to watch her for several long moments in silence. "He hasn't come down to the island in a while."

"I know." She carried the lettuce back over to the counter and reached for a cutting board. "He's been so busy with all these cases. The firm is working him like crazy."

Her father was quiet again for a long time. The only sound in the kitchen was the chop of the knife against the cutting board. "I guess it'll be easier for you both once you're living over there."

Becca nodded, swallowing the lump in her throat.

Her father walked over, laying a hand on her shoulder. "I'm going to miss you though."

"I know," she whispered. "Me, too."

"You promise you'll still come home on the weekends?"

She set the knife down, laying her hand over his. "I promise."

He smiled and she squeezed his hand reassuringly. But if Tom was working late every night and the only time they could spend together was on the weekends, and he always wanted to be in D.C., how was she ever going to keep that promise?

Driving away from the inn, Colin dialed his father's number. The sun was beginning to set and warm golden rays slanted through the branches of the white pines and dogwoods lining the marshes. An ebbing tide rubbed against the muddy shoreline, the salty scent drifting through the open windows of the truck as he waited for his father's voicemail to pick up.

"Hi, Dad," he said, after the recorded greeting. "It's me. I know you're tied up at the fundraiser for a couple more hours, but call me as soon as you get this. We have a situation."

He ended the call and slid the phone back in his pocket. Becca might think there were only a handful of people who knew about the possibility of the elementary school shutting down, but if he'd learned anything from working on his father's campaign over the past six months, it was that damaging news had a way of leaking at the worst possible moment.

The press would have a field day if they found out this school was in danger of closing, because Heron Island Elementary wasn't just *any* school. It was Taylor Malone's school—the sole survivor of the Mount Pleasant school shooting.

Colin's hand tightened around the steering wheel. Whenever he thought about the deranged teenager who had killed those seventeen innocent children in their second grade classroom in D.C. before turning the gun on himself last September, he felt a wave of white-hot rage.

Before leaving the SEALs, he had spent ten years fighting to keep the people of this country safe from terrorists who wanted to destroy them and everything they stood for. The thought that something like this would happen at home, by one of their own people, did not sit well.

It did not sit well at all.

Passing the small brick building flanked by playing fields, he eased off the gas pedal. Most of the classrooms were dark, cleared out for the holiday weekend, but he could see the colorful student artwork taped to the big glass windows and a sign hanging outside the library advertising a bake sale for the following week.

This school was where Taylor had come to start over. It was where she had come to escape the memories of her past. It was where she had finally managed to get control of the demons that still haunted her.

He knew a little something about demons.

While he didn't personally suffer from the psychological disorder that affected so many post-9/11 veterans, many of his friends struggled with PTSD. It was one of the reasons why he'd decided to open the veterans' center. Too many of his fellow former service members were slipping through the cracks, unable to cope with the transition to civilian life after having served multiple back-to-back deployments to Iraq and Afghanistan.

He was counting on the tranquility of this island to work its magic on the men and women who came to stay at the inn.

Driving through the village, Colin took in the splash of tulips sprouting in the gardens along Main Street. Crabapple and cherry trees bloomed in the tiny front yards of the ice cream parlor, bookstore, and antique shop. Pulling his truck to the curb across the street from the Wind Chime Café, he cut the engine and opened the driver's side door.

The beams of the front porch were covered in homemade wind chimes. They filled the air with a quirky combination of clinks, clangs, and rings as he stepped out of the truck. He waved to the pretty redhead sweeping the porch and made his way across the street.

"You're just in time," Annie Malone said. "Della's about to pull a cake out of the oven."

He ducked under a low hanging oak branch covered in bright green leaves. "What kind of cake?"

"White chocolate almond with vanilla bean icing."

"Sounds fancy."

"She's still testing out recipes for Becca's wedding."

Right, Colin thought. The wedding. It was hard to come into the village these days without being reminded of the upcoming celebration. There was a sign on the sidewalk outside the ice cream parlor advertising "I Do" sundaes, "Meant to Be" milk-shakes, and "Happily Ever After" waffle cones. The window display of Gladys' Flower Shop had turned into an explosion of white flowers. Even the Sail Winds Bookstore had replaced its usual collection of nautical themed hardbacks for stacks of classic love stories and books on how to plan the perfect wedding.

It wasn't every day that someone on the island got married. He understood why everyone was making such a big deal about it. There was a time, not too long ago, when he'd actually enjoyed weddings.

But after his own engagement had come to a grinding halt—and he'd had plenty of time to think about how easy it had been for his fiancée to give him his ring back and derail their future when he'd been laid up in bed for weeks recovering from surgery—he'd begun to view the entire institution as a joke.

What was the point in spending so much time and effort on one day to celebrate a union that probably wouldn't even last?

Hoping to get a moment's reprieve from the wedding fever this island had fallen under, he climbed the steps to the porch and peered through the open door of the café for a glimpse of whatever specials Will's aunt, Della Dozier, had whipped up that day. When he spotted the counter and dining tables covered in white bows, boxes of silver bells, and reams of ivory lace, he groaned. "This whole island has gone wedding crazy."

Annie Malone laughed. "Becca's insisting on doing everything herself. The least we could do was offer to help with the decorations." She gave him a friendly hug, then stepped back, smiling. "But we might have gotten a little carried away."

Colin shook his head at the dining room filled with craft supplies. "I ran into Becca at the inn this afternoon. It was the first time I've seen her in months."

Annie reached up to adjust the strings of a chime that had gotten tangled. "How did she seem to you?"

"She seemed okay." He watched her closely for signs that she might have already heard about the threat to the school. "Why?"

"She's been pretty overwhelmed lately," Annie said. "I know she's got a lot going on right now with the wedding and the move, but I think it's starting to take a toll. I'm worried about her."

Colin reached up, helping her untangle the strings that were too high for her to reach. "I'm sure she'll be fine. Moves are always stressful."

"True." Annie stepped back, picking up the broom to finish sweeping the porch. "She's been planning this wedding for so long. She probably just wants everything to be perfect."

He nodded, reassured that Annie's concerns about Becca had nothing to do with the school. "So," he said, leaning his shoulder against a whitewashed porch beam. "What's he like?"

"Who?"

"Becca's fiancé."

"Tom?" Annie glanced back up, surprised. "You've never met him?"

Colin shook his head.

Annie hesitated, then went back to sweeping. "I think I'll let you make your own judgment when you meet him."

"Why? You don't like him?"

Annie swept the small pile of dirt into the bed of rosemary bushes and boxwoods. "I've only met him a few times. He doesn't come down to the island much."

"But...?"

"I didn't *dislike* him," she said carefully. "But I didn't really like him that much either."

Colin frowned. He was surprised Annie hadn't mentioned her misgivings about Becca's fiancé before. He had gotten into the habit of stopping by the café whenever he came down to the island. Since Will was still stationed at the SEAL base in Virginia Beach and couldn't make it home every weekend, he had asked Colin to keep an eye on Annie.

Not that she ever needed anything. Annie was one of the most competent and independent women he'd ever met. But he'd like to think they had become good friends over the past few months. "What does Will think of him?"

Annie glanced out at the street, lowering her voice when she saw that a few of her neighbors were within earshot. "Will doesn't like him at all."

Colin's frown deepened. Will didn't like him either? "How many other people feel this way?"

"Colin!" The screen door swung open and Taylor Malone ran out of the house, holding up a brand new softball mitt. "Look!"

Colin bottled the rest of his unanswered questions about Becca, at least for now, and turned his attention on Taylor. "Where'd you get that?"

"Della gave it to me," Taylor said. "Mom said I could try out for the team at school next year."

Colin glanced back over at Annie. "They have a softball team at Heron Island Elementary?"

"It's a *very* small team," she said, smiling.

Colin took the glove from Taylor when she handed it to him. The leather was so shiny and stiff, it squeaked when he tried to bend it. "You're going to need to break this in first."

"I know." Her big green eyes looked up at him hopefully. "You want to play catch?"

He laughed. "Sure, but only until Della ices that cake."

"Deal." She took his hand, leading him down to the front yard.

Sometimes, it was hard to believe this was the same kid who he'd met six months ago. She had come so far from the shy, frightened girl she'd once been.

Reaching down, he pried the softball from the mouth of Taylor's yellow lab, Riley, who never left her side. Wiping the slobber off the ball on the hem of his T-shirt, he wondered how the transformation had taken place without him really noticing.

Was it possible that he'd spent *too much* time here?

Had he been so focused on looking after Taylor and Annie, that he hadn't realized some of Will's other friends might need help?

It was probably too late to do anything at this point, but it couldn't hurt to ask Becca a few questions when he spent the evening with her on Saturday.

Just to get a better picture of the situation.

Will and Annie would want to know if their friend was making a mistake.

FOUR

There was no reason to be so nervous, Becca thought, checking her reflection in the rear view mirror one last time before stepping out of her car in downtown Annapolis two nights later. She was only about to meet the most powerful man in her state, and it was only her co-workers' jobs, Taylor's future, and her entire community at stake.

Pressing a hand to her stomach, she willed her insides to settle. She'd been up past midnight scouring the Internet for articles on the impacts of school closures on rural communities. She'd read stories about towns that had shrunk in population by double-digit percentage points, local businesses that had shut down because families with young children no longer wanted to live there, property values that had dropped to record lows when locals had left in search of better opportunities.

Heron Island was one of the last few hidden gems on the Eastern Shore, but it wouldn't take long for a developer to swoop in and gobble up all the cheap land. The islanders had already fought off one developer last year. Would they be able to win that battle again if their community was in danger of falling apart?

She took several deep breaths, trying to focus on the delighted squeals of a group of children tossing bits of bread to the seagulls that wheeled and dipped over Spa Creek. She had practiced her pitch to the governor so many times over the past two days, she could recite it from memory now.

Everyone was depending on her.

She wasn't going to let them down.

Closing the door to her car with a determined click, she paid the parking meter and scanned the bustling City Dock for Colin. She hadn't expected so many tourists to be out yet. He had said to meet near the bronze statue of Alex Hadley, but maybe they should have picked a less crowded spot.

Her heart did another funny little stutter step when she spotted him.

He was standing about ten yards away, watching her with that cool-as-ice gaze. A blue button down shirt stretched across his broad shoulders. His hands were dipped into the pockets of a pair of dark gray pants, and the thick, wavy black hair that swept back from his rugged face looked like it was still damp from a recent shower.

She should have known it wouldn't take long to find him. He wasn't the kind of man you could easily miss in a crowd. At six-foot-four, he stood at least a head taller than everyone around him.

Crossing the street, she threaded her way through the groups of tourists to where he stood. "Hey." She attempted a breezy smile. "I hope you haven't been waiting long."

"Not long at all."

A group of women in their late-twenties walked by, gawking as they craned their necks to get a better look.

She didn't blame them.

"I'm surprised it's so busy here tonight." Becca took in the lines outside the seafood restaurants surrounding the harbor. "I didn't expect to see so many tourists out yet."

"It's mostly locals," Colin said. "The first warm Saturday of the year always draws everyone out of their homes."

That explained it, Becca thought as a balmy breeze brushed over her bare arms, carrying the faint scent of coffee and Old Bay Seasoning. She'd always loved Annapolis. It was the perfect sized city, not so big that it felt overwhelming, but big enough to soak in a bit of culture.

"How was the drive?" Colin asked.

"Good," she said, tipping forward slightly as a group of teenagers jostled her from behind.

Colin caught her by the elbow, steadying her.

The moment his work-roughened fingers grazed her bare skin, an unexpected flash of heat shot through her. She drew in a breath and tried to step back, but one of her heels caught between a crack in the bricks.

"I've got you," Colin said, his strong hand holding her in place. He held her gaze for several long beats, then glanced down at the offending heel. A slow smile spread across his lips. "Nice shoes."

Becca's insides twisted...for a different reason this time.

Tugging her heel free, she smoothed her hands down the front of her dress, trying to regain her composure. But when she glanced back up, and caught his heated gaze following the path of her hands, every muscle in her body contracted.

His eyes were so intense. So blue.

His gaze lifted back to her face, and she braced herself for another comment about the shoes.

Wearing them had definitely been a mistake.

But he didn't say anything about her shoes. He just stood there, close enough so she could smell the soap on his skin and something else—something strong and masculine and uniquely *Colin*—and continued to study her.

"Did you do something different to your hair?" he asked.

"What?" she stammered, pushing at the curtain of brown hair that fell to her shoulders.

"It looks different." He reached up, touching the ends. "Longer."

Her mouth went dry when his fingers grazed her collarbone. He was right. It was longer, probably because she'd spent an hour flat ironing it before she'd left the house tonight. She couldn't believe he'd noticed. Men never noticed things like that.

"I like it," he murmured.

A traitorous curl of attraction took root inside her. It started low in her belly, coiling and spiraling as it spread. She remembered something that Will had told her once, that Colin had been one of the best snipers on the SEAL teams before his career had been cut short. He would have to possess an incredible attention to detail to have earned that kind of reputation. And it probably wasn't something he could turn on and off at whim.

But she wasn't sure how she felt about that attention being focused on *her*.

Taking a step back, she gathered her hair into a hasty ponytail at the back of her neck and searched for something—anything—to talk about that would make him stop looking at her like that. "You have an apartment downtown, right?" she managed finally, forcing the words out.

He nodded.

"That must be nice." She gazed past him at the historic streets that spiraled out from the harbor, focusing on the colorful potted plants that graced many of the brick stoops to avoid meeting his eyes. "To be so close to everything."

"It is."

"Are you going to hold onto it so you have a place to stay when you come up to Annapolis?"

"I haven't decided yet." He continued to watch her for several more moments before finally nodding for her to walk with him toward the strip of restaurants along the north side of the harbor. "I'll be spending most of my time on the island so I don't know if it makes sense to keep it."

As soon as his attention was focused elsewhere, she released her hair and fell into step beside him. "You're renting the Murphy's old place, right? The one by the marina?"

"Temporarily." He steered her around a group of teenagers attempting a series of tricks on their skateboards. "I'm still looking for the right place to buy."

She looked up at him, surprised. "You're thinking of buying?"

He nodded, pausing at the edge of the curb, waiting for a few cars to pass.

"I didn't realize you were planning to stay that long."

Now it was his turn to look surprised. "What do you mean?"

"I thought you were just moving to the island to help Will get the business started."

"Why would you think that?"

"I don't know. I guess I thought the inn would be more of a stepping-stone for you—the first of many projects you'd start for veterans."

He seemed to ponder that as they started across the street.

"How long *are* you planning to stay?" she asked.

"For good."

Becca's brows shot up. "You want to move to the island for good?"

"Yes." He laughed, pausing again when they reached the opposite curb. "Why is that so shocking?"

"Because..."

"Because...*what*?"

"Because...people like you don't move to Heron Island."

"People like me?"

Becca watched the wind blow a lock of black hair into his eyes and she fought the urge to reach up and brush it aside. "We don't get a lot of people who are"—*young, single, attractive*—"unattached moving to Heron Island."

"Ryan's unattached."

That was true, Becca thought. Ryan Callahan, one of her best friends from childhood, had recently moved back to the island to open an environmental center. But Ryan was an anomaly. And he was *from* the island. That was different. "Ryan grew up on Heron Island. It's his home."

"Annie moved there and she was unattached."

Becca bit her lip. That was true, too. But Annie's circumstances had been so unique. She'd needed a place to escape to, a place for her daughter to heal. "Annie was trying to get away from something."

"So what are you saying?" Colin asked. "Unless you're attached, originally from there, or trying to get away from something, you can't move to Heron Island?"

"No. It's just...unusual."

"But not unheard of?"

"No, I guess not." She blew out a breath. "I didn't realize you liked it there so much."

"I love it there."

Becca's heart flooded with a rush of warmth. He loved it there? Enough to spend the rest of his life there?

"Is that why you're marrying a guy who lives in D.C.?" Colin asked. "Because there aren't enough single men to choose from on the island?"

"What?" Becca froze, stunned by the bluntness of his question. "No. I... Tom and I have been together forever."

"So it's comfort? Familiarity?"

"N-no," Becca stammered. "Of course not. We love each other."

"Do you want to move to D.C.?"

Becca stared at him. *Yes* was the obvious answer. *Yes* was the answer she gave to everyone else. But when she opened her mouth, the word caught in her throat and a bubble of panic welled up inside her.

There had to be a part of her, at least a small part, that was looking forward to moving to D.C. She *wanted* to live with Tom. She *wanted* to spend the rest of her life with him. She was in love with him. "It's going to be an adjustment," she admitted finally, lifting her chin, "but I think it'll be good for me."

"How?"

"I've never lived in a city," she said, falling back on one of the arguments Tom always made when she voiced her own fears. "Everyone should live in a city at least once in their life."

"Cities are overrated."

Frustrated, because he was echoing all her own thoughts, she turned and started walking toward the restaurant. She was getting married in three weeks. She was getting married to a man she had met in high school, who she had known almost her entire life. They were going to start a family. They were going to live happily ever after. That was the end of the discussion.

"What neighborhood does your fiancé live in?" Colin asked, his long strides catching up to her easily.

She noticed that he didn't use Tom's actual name. For some reason, that pissed her off. "He has an apartment in Woodley Park, but he wants to buy a house in Georgetown."

"He?"

"We," she corrected quickly, squeezing her eyes shut. "I meant, we."

Colin reached for the door handle when they got to the restaurant. "Georgetown's a pricey neighborhood."

Yes, Becca thought. It was very pricey. And it would mean that she would have to let go of her home on the island—a topic she and Tom had had several long discussions about recently.

Tom wanted a place where he could entertain clients and host dinner parties on the weekends, a place that would impress the other partners at his firm.

All she wanted was a place in the country to escape to.

The rent in Woodley Park was high, but nowhere near as high as Georgetown. If they kept the apartment Tom lived in now, they could afford to swing both his rent and her small mortgage payment on their joint incomes.

Colin held the door open for her, and she walked inside.

The scent of lemons and horseradish pulled her into a large dining room filled with at least two hundred people. Laughter and conversations swirled through the air and several waiters in white shirts and black pants circulated with trays of canapés and refreshments.

Several people glanced their way. A group of middle-aged men in khaki pants and sport coats nodded their greeting to Colin. An elderly man wearing a Vietnam Veteran ball cap lifted his beer in a silent salute. Two younger men in polo shirts peeled off from their groups in mid-conversation and headed their way.

Becca felt a sudden sucking sensation, like she was about to be swallowed whole. Resisting the urge to flee, she looked over at the bar, where a cluster of women in their mid-thirties stood with their heads bent together, each of them giving her a dirty look.

Three hours, she thought, squaring her shoulders. Three hours and she'd be back in her car, alone, where she'd have plenty of time to think about why she didn't have better answers to Colin's questions, why her body felt like it was on fire when he touched her, and why it had *never* felt that way when Tom touched her.

Until then, she needed to make sure it didn't happen again.

COLIN WATCHED Becca's whole body stiffen as she took in the scene before them. He didn't blame her. He'd grown up in this world. He should have been used to it by now.

He wasn't.

Part of the reason he'd joined the military was to get away from all this.

He would rather take a dull saw to his good leg than suffer through another evening filled with mind-numbing cocktail party chitchat. It wasn't that he didn't want to support his father. He liked his father. He respected his father.

In the past four years as governor, his father had done some good things for the state and a lot of good things for veterans, despite his own public objections to the wars. But no matter how decent the man behind the name on the ticket was, there was always a certain amount of pandering, posturing, and saying whatever the public needed to hear to get the vote.

In the end, everything in politics came down to winning.

When he spotted the two men heading toward them, heirs to the largest casino chain in Maryland, he moved closer to Becca. They thought that since their father had made a sizeable donation to the veterans' center they deserved something in return. He knew the names of every single person in this room, and what each one hoped to gain in return for their support. It was only a matter of time before more people spotted him and they were swarmed.

Feeling an unexpected surge of protectiveness, he placed his hand on the small of Becca's back. She flinched at the contact and immediately shifted two steps to the right. Interesting, he thought, letting his hand drop back to his side. So he wasn't the only one who felt something when he touched her.

It had caught him off guard when he'd grabbed her arm out

on the street earlier to keep her from falling. He'd liked the way her skin had felt in his hands—soft, warm, and feminine. He'd liked the way she'd smelled, like honeysuckle and vanilla. And he'd liked the way her pupils had dilated slightly, making her brown eyes appear darker and more mysterious.

What he did *not* like was the way she'd answered his questions about her fiancé.

After what Annie had told him two days ago, he'd begun to recall a few passing comments that some of the other islanders had made about Tom over the winter. Once he'd taken the time to think about it, he'd remembered that even Ryan Callahan had gone uncharacteristically quiet whenever Tom's name had been mentioned. Ryan was one of the most easygoing people Colin had ever met. If Ryan had a problem with Becca's fiancé, there had to be something wrong with the guy.

Which left him with one question: if none of her friends liked him, why was Becca marrying him?

"Colin." His stepmother swept through the crowd, her blond hair pulled back in a sophisticated knot, a pair of diamond studs winking at her ears. "I'm so glad you're here." She lifted up onto her toes, giving him a quick kiss on the cheek. "Your father's running late and there's a man at the bar who wants to talk to him about funding for the new medical center in Calvert County."

"I can talk to him. What's his name?"

"Don O'Brien."

He turned back to Becca. "Want to head up to the bar with me? Grab a drink before my father gets here?"

"Sure." She looked hesitantly at his stepmother.

Right, Colin thought, not everyone was used to meeting the First Lady of Maryland. "Becca, this is my stepmother, Natalie Foley. Natalie, this is Becca Haddaway."

Becca smiled shyly, offering her hand. "It's an honor to meet you, Mrs. Foley."

Natalie Foley was rarely caught off guard. After a lifetime of working the same political scene—first as the daughter of a judge, then as the communications director for a long standing Maryland senator, and now married to his father—she was always at least two steps ahead of every other person in the room when it came to who was who.

But Becca wasn't part of their usual circle of acquaintances.

The startled, and unexpectedly pleased, expression that crossed Natalie's face made Colin pause. He had brought Becca tonight so she could talk to his father about the school and so he could get a night off from his stepmother's relentless matchmaking attempts, but he hadn't considered how Natalie might react to her.

Even in three inch heels and a dress that hugged and flattered in all the right places, Becca still oozed girl next door sweetness. She wore very little makeup and almost no jewelry, except for the single gold charm that hung around her neck. She looked nothing like any of the women Colin had ever brought to one of his father's campaign events.

Natalie recovered quickly, taking Becca's hand, but there was no mistaking the spark of curiosity in her green eyes. "Please, call me Natalie."

"Becca's a teacher on the island," Colin explained. "She's hoping to talk to Dad about some of the challenges her district is going to face in the upcoming budget environment."

"Oh?" Natalie said, surprised. Most of the women he brought only had one goal—to be seen with him as much as possible. "I didn't realize..."

"I'd like to introduce them when he gets here," Colin said. "Would you tell him to come find us when he arrives?"

"Of course," Natalie said, looking back and forth between them. "But there's no need to rush off."

Actually, there was, Colin thought. It wouldn't take long for his stepmother to notice Becca's engagement ring and he was hoping to put her off at least until they sat down to dinner. As soon as Natalie realized Becca wasn't a potential match for him, she would start scanning the room to find someone else she could introduce him to. "Becca just got out of the car from a long drive. She could probably use something to drink."

Natalie simply lifted her hand and a waiter appeared out of nowhere carrying a tray filled with over a dozen glasses of white wine. She smiled as she plucked a glass off the tray and handed it to Becca. "Here you go, dear."

"Thanks," Becca said, smiling back at her. "I really enjoyed the speech you made at the charter school in Frederick last week, the one on bullying awareness and prevention."

Natalie paused, her wine glass halfway to her lips. "Were you there?"

"No." Becca shook her head. "I saw the clip on the news later that night. All of us, at least all the teachers I work with, are grateful that you're putting a spotlight on such an important subject. The more people who are aware of what's going on, the better our chances are of figuring out how to deal with it."

"I couldn't agree more." Natalie glanced back up at Colin. The spark of curiosity had bloomed into full-fledged admiration.

Colin stifled a groan.

None of the women he'd ever brought to a campaign event had bothered to ask his stepmother anything about her political initiatives. They were much more interested in complimenting her designer clothes and gossiping about mutual acquaintances.

He knew how seriously Natalie took her role as First Lady. Becca had just scored major points.

"Colin," Natalie suggested, "why don't you head up to the bar on your own? I'm happy to keep Becca company while you talk to Don." She smiled warmly at Becca, her expression a little too eager. "I'm sure we'll find all kinds of things to talk about."

"Natalie," Colin warned.

"What?" Natalie glanced back up at him innocently. "I just want to find out how the two of you met."

"How we met?" Becca asked, confused.

Colin sighed. So much for getting the night off. He should have known Natalie wouldn't waste any time pouncing on the mystery woman he'd brought. He might as well put a stop to the charade before his stepmother got her hopes up any higher. "Becca and I met last fall on my first trip down to Heron Island. I invited her tonight so she could talk to Dad about her school. We're friends, Natalie. That's all."

Natalie blinked. "Friends?"

"*Just* friends."

"Well," Natalie said, undeterred, "your father and I were friends for years before..."

Colin reached for Becca's left hand, lifting it up so his stepmother could see her engagement ring.

Natalie trailed off, staring down at the tear-shaped diamond. "You're...engaged."

Becca nodded, confusion clouding her eyes as she looked back and forth between them. "I'm getting married in a few weeks...at the inn where Colin's opening the veterans' center."

"Oh."

Natalie looked so crestfallen, Colin couldn't help feeling a prick of guilt. He knew his stepmother meant well. She might have only been married to his father for the past three years, but she'd been more of a mother to him than his own ever had.

Natalie was the one who had come to sit with him every day when he'd been recovering at Walter Reed last year. Natalie was the one who had cared for him when he'd been discharged from the hospital and he'd spent the first few weeks stumbling around the house on his new prosthesis, ready to take out his anger on anyone who came near him.

Natalie was the one who had driven him to his physical therapy appointments those first few months, bringing him ice packs and heating pads when she'd picked him up, never saying a word as he sat in miserable silence beside her, wallowing in his own self-pity. There were very few people who had seen him like that.

He didn't care to remember the person he'd been back then.

But she had never once treated him like a victim. She had never made him feel like there was anything wrong with him that he couldn't overcome. She had waited patiently for him to heal and then she'd sat him down and told him, in no uncertain terms, that it was time for him to find a nice woman to marry and settle down.

Natalie had never had any children of her own. All she wanted now was a few grandchildren to spoil and a daughter-in-law to pamper.

He knew it wasn't that much to ask.

But the thought of making that kind of commitment again, only to have it thrown back in his face...

He didn't know if he could take that kind of rejection a second time.

He leaned down, giving Natalie a quick kiss on the cheek. "I'm sorry to disappoint you."

"That's okay," Natalie said, her tone wistful as she waved him toward the bar. "Go do what you need to do. I'll introduce Becca around to some of our friends."

He started to turn, and it was only then that he realized he was still holding her hand.

Becca must have realized it at the same time, because he heard her sharp intake of breath as she jerked her hand free.

What the hell?

Her fingers darted up to the charm on her necklace, moving it back and forth on the chain.

The need to reach for her again, to feel her soft hand tucked back in his, whipped through him fast and hard. Shoving his hands in his pockets, he turned. A dozen questions fired off in his mind all at once, but he didn't have time to answer any of them because, three steps later, he came face-to-face with his father's campaign manager.

Glenn Davis, a short, wiry man in his mid-fifties, gestured toward a quiet corner of the room. "We need to talk."

"Now?"

Glenn nodded.

Reigning in his irritation because his father's campaign manager often thought the world was coming to an end when it wasn't, Colin followed him through the groups of laughing, chattering people to the edge of the room. "What is it?"

"There's been a complication."

Tell me about it, Colin thought as another waiter carrying a tray of drinks appeared by his side. He snagged a pint of stout off the tray and took a long swallow as his gaze strayed back to where Becca was talking with a group of his stepmother's friends.

"Is that her?" Glenn followed his eyes across the room. "The teacher who wants to talk to Nick about her school tonight?"

Colin nodded, noticing for the first time the way the stretchy material of Becca's pale yellow dress crossed over her small breasts. A simple knot off to one side of her slender waist held the thin fabric together. All it would take was one gentle tug to release it and reveal what was hidden underneath.

He took another long sip of the beer.

Shit. This just went way past complicated.

Beside him, Glenn scanned the faces of the few people still within earshot and lowered his voice. "I spoke with the principal at your friend's school about an hour ago. I told her that the governor was aware of the situation and might be willing to make a few calls on their behalf if she could provide us with the names and numbers of the board members."

Colin nodded, his gaze dropping to Becca's smooth, toned legs. How had he never noticed her legs before?

Was this the first time he'd ever seen them bare?

Pulling out his smartphone, Glenn thumbed through a few screens. "She just sent the list of names, including the consultant the board recently hired to help them with the analysis." He clicked on the message and turned the phone around, showing the screen to Colin. "This is who they hired."

Colin read the name and all thoughts of Becca's legs vanished. "Tell me this is a joke."

"I wish it was," Glenn said grimly.

There was only one person in this state who wouldn't be swayed, even the slightest bit, by a phone call from him or the governor—Lydia Vanzant.

His father's ex-wife.

His mother.

"When was the last time you talked to her?" Glenn asked.

"It's been years."

"That's what I thought." Glenn shook his head, slipping his smartphone back into his pocket. "Look, Colin, I know you're not going to like this, but we need to steer clear of the issue with the school. We can't afford the bad press it'll stir up. Not now, not with Lydia's name attached to it."

"You can't be serious."

"I'm dead serious," Glenn said. "We wanted to help your friend, but our hands are tied now."

"What about Taylor?" Colin asked.

"We'll lose a few points in the polls when the news breaks, but if we get out in front of it, make a formal statement before the press gets hold of it, we can control the message. We need to stay detached from it. We can't afford to get involved in another public fight with Lydia. The divorce scandal almost cost us the election last time. We can't afford to dredge it back up again."

"This is bullshit," Colin said.

"Your father pays me a lot of money to deal with his bullshit," Glenn said. "I know what I'm doing. Leave it alone."

No way, Colin thought, shaking his head. There was no way he was going to leave it alone. He searched the room for Becca again. She was still standing beside his stepmother, laughing now at something someone had said.

He swore he could hear it, a soft, bell-like sound drifting over the rest of the noise in the crowded room. There was something so sweet, so innocent, in her smile. He felt that same sudden, overwhelming need to protect her again, just like he had when they'd first walked into the room. He lifted the pint, taking another long swallow.

"Leave it alone, Colin," Glenn warned.

Colin lowered the glass, looking back at his father's campaign manager. "No."

FIVE

*H*ow was last night?" Shelley asked Becca the next day as they walked down Main Street to the Wind Chime Café where Annie and Della were hosting an Easter brunch for the islanders.

"It was interesting," Becca said, stepping off the sidewalk to let a group of children dash by in search of hidden eggs. Their peals of laughter rang out, filling the air.

She wished she could feel so lighthearted.

Her conversation with Nick Foley had gone well enough. He had listened patiently to her stories about Taylor and had assured her that he would do everything in his power to keep the school open. But she had seen him exchange several tense looks across the table with Colin during dinner. And Colin had spent most of the hour before dinner huddled in a corner with his father's campaign manager.

When she'd confronted Colin about it at the end of the night, he'd admitted that they'd run into a slight complication, but he wouldn't give her any details—only that they might need a few more days to work on the situation with the school.

Motioning for Shelley to slow down so their neighbors walking ahead of them wouldn't overhear, Becca lowered her voice. "Colin wants us to keep the news to ourselves for a few more days."

Shelley nodded. "I got a similar email from Glenn Davis last night. He wants me to postpone the announcement to the teachers until Friday."

Becca paused under the boughs of a flowering dogwood tree. Sunlight slanted through the branches, dappling the sidewalk. "What did you tell him?"

"I said I needed some time to think about it," Shelley replied. "I don't like the idea of this news getting out without me being able to break it to the rest of the staff first. And, frankly, now that I know who the board hired as their consultant, I'm not sure the governor *can* help us."

"Who did they hire?"

"Lydia Vanzant."

"Nick Foley's ex-wife?"

Shelley nodded.

Becca felt a wave of uneasiness. Lydia Vanzant wasn't just the former wife of their governor. She was also one of the most respected figures in the field of education. She had served as the chief administrator in the Baltimore County School District for three decades before being elected Chancellor of the Prince George's County Public Schools. She had successfully transformed two of the worst school districts in their state into two of the best.

Not everyone agreed with her tactics, but her track record was indisputable. In every school district where she'd served, test scores had gone up, attrition rates had fallen, and graduation rates had reached nearly one hundred percent.

Unfortunately, her hardline reform strategies included a strong push for consolidation.

"Can our district even afford to hire her?" Becca asked. "Her consultant rates must be through the roof."

"No," Shelley murmured. "Which is why I think this might be personal."

Becca felt a sinking feeling form in her gut. "Are Lydia and the governor even on speaking terms?"

"I don't know," Shelley admitted as they started to walk again. "It was a really nasty divorce. They both said some terrible things about each other, and the papers printed every detail they could get their hands on. It almost cost Nick Foley his first election."

No wonder Colin had said they'd needed more time, Becca thought. But why had he kept the news about Lydia from her? If his mother was the complication they'd run into, he must have known she would find out eventually.

The café came into view, with its pale blue siding and dark purple shutters. Wind chimes hung from the beams of the porch, sparkling in the sunlight and filling the air with their soft tinkling songs. The small front yard was already packed with islanders and an egg dyeing station had been set up under the oak tree for the kids.

"I feel uncomfortable keeping this from Annie," Becca said. "From everyone."

"Me, too," Shelley said. "They deserve to know."

"What should we do?"

Shelley took a deep breath. "Glenn assured me that they would have everything under control by the end of the week. I would hate to upset everyone on the island unnecessarily. I haven't made my final decision yet, but I'm leaning toward keeping quiet."

Becca nodded. She understood where Shelley was coming from, but it didn't make her feel any better. Scanning the yard for her favorite student, she spotted Taylor under the oak tree, dipping a hard boiled egg into a bowl of blue food coloring. Taylor's best friend, Jess Casper, was beside her, adding stickers to her own yellow egg. They were both wearing flower crowns and their mouths were rimmed in chocolate.

Taylor glanced up and grinned. "Look, Miss Haddaway!" She held up her egg. "It's the same color as a robin's egg."

Becca's heart softened. When Taylor had first moved to the island, it had been hard for her to make friends. She'd spent most of her free time chasing birds and butterflies through the hundreds of acres of undeveloped marshlands west of the village. She had become fascinated with the wildlife, memorizing the different species by name and coming up with clever little ways to identify each of them by their markings or their calls.

Sometimes it was hard to believe that the carefree child in front of her now was the same frightened little girl who had survived that terrible shooting in D.C. last fall, but Becca knew that appearances could be deceiving. Taylor still suffered setbacks. At least once every couple of weeks something would happen to trigger a memory from that day.

It would take years for Taylor to work through the lingering effects of that trauma.

She had come a long way in a very short amount of time, but how much of that progress would be lost if she had to switch schools again so soon? Would she be able to cope in a class triple the size of what she was used to—one with kids who wouldn't understand why she still jumped whenever an engine backfired or hid in the closet during a thunderstorm?

Becca watched Taylor place her blue egg into a wire rack on the table so it could dry. "I want to set up my own meeting with Lydia," she said firmly. "I know you didn't think it would make any difference for me to speak with the board on my own about Taylor. But I need to do this. I need to try."

Shelley laid a comforting hand on Becca's shoulder. "We're

going to do everything we can, Becca. But I think we should both be prepared for the fact that we might not win this battle. Our chances were never very good. Now, I think they might be even worse." She squeezed her shoulder. "Let's just try to enjoy the day, okay?" She scanned the crowd. "Is Tom meeting us here?"

Becca shook her head. "He couldn't make it."

"Why not?"

"A big case came in on Thursday. He had to work through the weekend."

Shelley was quiet for a few beats. "He's been working a lot of weekends lately."

"I know. It won't be like this forever."

Shelley's hand dropped away from her shoulder. "If you say so."

Becca felt a tightening in her chest as they turned up the path to the café. She spotted a group of her friends chatting in a circle beside the porch. A few feet away, her father was standing with a cluster of watermen. Their deep voices rumbled through the yard, blending with the cheerful jumble of conversations going on all around them.

She knew every single person here. She knew each of their parents, their children, their spouses. She knew where they worked, what kinds of cars they drove, what they planted in their gardens each year. She knew who was struggling to make ends meet and whose lives hadn't turned out quite the way they'd hoped.

But she also knew that every single person here loved this island as much as she did. They loved the sense of peace that came from living in a place surrounded on all sides by water. They loved spending their weekends out on the Bay with a fishing rod in their hands. They loved the slow pace of life in the village and the way the sky lit up with colors each night as the sun sank into the horizon.

Colin's question from the night before floated back: '*Are you marrying a guy who lives in D.C. because there aren't enough single men to choose from on the island?*'

Stepping over a crack where shoots of flowering thyme were breaking through the cement, she wrapped her arms tighter around the plastic container of deviled eggs she was carrying. She had been up until 3AM last night, unable to sleep, trying desperately to remember if there had ever been a time when Tom had made her feel the way Colin had when he'd touched her.

It was normal for the spark to wear off at some point in any relationship. She had been with Tom for fifteen years—since her sophomore year in high school. Of course she didn't still feel fireworks when he touched her now.

But she must have felt something in the beginning.

She must have.

A knot formed in her throat and she forced it back. Or... maybe they had just skipped that step. What mattered was that they had something to hold onto *after* the spark died, right?

She and Tom had a history. A past.

When everything in her life had fallen apart, Tom had been there to pick up the pieces.

She would never forget that.

Even if they'd been moving in different directions lately, they still had that past. They still had that memory of the people they had been before—the people they had been to each other.

Everyone changed. She and Tom were just going through a strange cycle right now...one where they weren't changing in sync. But they would get back on track again. They would.

It was only a matter of time.

Resolved, she climbed the steps to the porch where Della and Annie were laying out dishes of food on a long row of folding tables.

Della turned. Her curly, gray-blond hair was sticking up in a million directions. An apron dusted with flour was tied around her ample waist. She smiled as she took the container from Becca's hands and opened the top, peering inside.

"I got a little carried away," Becca said, feeling the need to explain herself when Della lifted a brow at the number of eggs inside.

"You didn't have to bring anything," Annie said, smoothing a pink cloth over the table by the window. "We have plenty of food."

"I know," Becca said, "but I always make deviled eggs on Easter."

"Of course you do, honey," Della said gently, setting the container down between a roasted vegetable quiche and a coconut cake. "But everyone would have understood if you didn't have time to make them this year. Don't you have enough to do with the wedding and the move?"

Becca felt a prick of annoyance. She *always* made deviled eggs on Easter, just like her mother had before her, and her grandmother had before her—from their family recipe with Old Bay Seasoning instead of paprika.

It was tradition.

She wished everyone would quit pushing her away and telling her that she didn't have time to do the things she loved anymore.

"Where's your fiancé?" a familiar voice slurred in her ear.

Becca stiffened when Jimmy's arm came around her and his sour, whiskey-scented breath brushed against her cheek. Disgusted, she pushed him away. "It's not even noon and you're already drunk."

He smiled, his arm tightening around her waist. "You need to lighten up, sweetheart."

"And you need to leave," she said coldly. "You have no business being here, around all these children, when you've been drinking."

"Can't." He grabbed a sugar cookie off one of the trays on the table. "Courtney got called into work at the hotel. I'm watching Luke."

Becca scanned the yard for Luke. She found him sitting on the curb beside Jimmy's truck, his back resting against one of the wheels. His head was bent over a notebook as he focused on a sketch he was working on. Becca felt another wave of frustration. He should be dyeing hard boiled eggs with Taylor or hunting for plastic ones with the rest of the kids down at the marina, not sitting by himself, drawing. "I'll watch Luke. You need to go home."

He reached up, touching her cheek. "I like the view better from here."

"That's enough," Ryan Callahan said, a warning in his voice as he strode out of the café. Taking Jimmy's elbow, he steered him toward the steps. "Becca's right. It's time for you to go home."

Jimmy jerked his arm free and Ryan pushed him, hard, toward the stairs. Jimmy stumbled, hiccupped, then burst out laughing as he looped his arm around Ryan's shoulders. "How about a game of pool at Rusty's?"

"Sure," Ryan murmured. "Right after I shove you off the pier to sober you up."

Joe Dozier, Della's husband, peeled off from the group of watermen and followed Ryan to lend a hand. The rest of the islanders watched them go with a mixture of pity and disapproval on their faces. All except for one man—Becca's father—who was staring down into his soda, his head bent in shame, unable to even look at the spectacle Jimmy was making of himself.

Because that had been him once.

"How about a cup of coffee?" Annie suggested lightly from behind her. "I just powered up the espresso machine."

Becca shook her head. She didn't need a cup of coffee. What she needed was for Jimmy to quit drinking and take care of Luke, for Tom to stop bailing on her, and for the board to drop their threat to close the school.

She looked back at Luke, who was standing now, unsure of what to do as he watched Jimmy walk away. Becca pushed off the railing, starting toward the steps.

Shelley stopped her. "I'll go," she said. "I'll tell Luke to come up to the porch and have something to eat with us."

Becca nodded, still so angry she could hardly speak. Spotting her best friend, Grace Callahan at the other end of the porch, Becca strode over to her. "We need to talk," she said, motioning for her friend to follow her around the side of the wraparound porch so the rest of the islanders couldn't hear them.

"What's up?" Grace asked.

Becca paused under a beam covered in wind chimes made of tinted sea glass. "What do you know about Lydia Vanzant?"

"Nick Foley's ex-wife?"

Becca nodded. She didn't care if Shelley thought their chances of saving the school were almost nonexistent. There was no way she was going to let a woman with an axe to grind against her ex-husband use them in some petty game of revenge.

Grace Callahan was one of the top political reporters for *The Washington Tribune*, the largest newspaper in D.C. If anyone could dig up information on the governor's former spouse, it would be Grace.

"Not that much," Grace said. "I mean, I know she had a hell of a reputation as a public school administrator, but you probably know more about that than I do. Other than that, I haven't read anything about her in years—at least not since the divorce. Why? What's going on?"

"I'm not sure yet."

A child's laughter drifted in from the yard, and they both

turned, watching Della adjust Taylor's flower crown so it wouldn't slip into her eyes while she filled her plate with food.

"Would you let me know if you hear anything, or see her name mentioned anywhere?" Becca asked.

"Sure," Grace said. "Is there anything in particular you want me to keep an eye out for?"

"No," Becca said as sunlight filtered through the glass, casting a kaleidoscope of colors over the side of the café. "But feel free to dig as deep as you want."

SIX

*C*olin drove through Severna Park, the affluent suburb north of Annapolis where he'd lived as a child. Waterfront estates sat back on sprawling lawns, surrounded by manicured gardens and hundred-year-old shade trees. Long paved driveways were filled with expensive cars, most likely belonging to family members who'd gathered together for the Easter holiday. In a few of the yards, children chased each other around, laughing and scouring the ground for eggs.

When he felt the familiar tug of longing for a family of his own, he clamped down on it. It had been over a year since he'd let his mind wander down that path. Holidays had always had a way of busting big fat holes through his defenses.

He'd spent most of the day alone, declining his father's invitation to join him and Natalie at church that morning. He'd never been particularly religious and he had no desire to be part of the obligatory photo op at the charity event afterwards. Holidays, in his family, had always been more about how to gain a political edge over an opponent than anything else.

Besides, he thought as he closed in on the last driveway at the end of the street and caught a glimpse of his childhood home—a three-story brick mansion with white columns and a sweeping view of the Severn River—he knew better than to show any signs of weakness around his mother.

He turned into his old driveway, passing under ten evenly spaced, perfectly pruned maple trees. Rolling to a stop beside the brick walkway, he cut the engine and stepped out of the truck. A curtain moved in one of the downstairs windows as he walked up to the door and knocked.

He waited, listening to the sound of her footsteps getting closer.

When the door swung open, his mother took one look at him and her expression turned stone cold. "You're not welcome here."

"It's not a social call."

She tried to close the door in his face, but he'd been expecting it, and stopped the heavy mahogany panel with his palm.

"What do you want?" she asked coldly.

"To talk."

"I have nothing to say to you."

"Then you can listen." He pushed the door open the rest of the way and walked past her into the house. "Because I have a few things to say to you."

His childhood home looked exactly the same—the cold gray interior, the white leather furniture, the polished marble floors and glass tables. The windows were shut, the air set to sixty-eight degrees, just as it had always been, even though the weather outside was perfect and everyone else had their windows open to let in the fresh air.

Two steps into the living room, he froze when he saw the pictures.

Of Hayden.

Everywhere.

Jesus.

Hayden blowing out the candles on his third birthday cake. Hayden learning how to ride a bicycle. Hayden winning first prize at the school science fair. Hayden posing with his prom date on the front steps. Hayden graduating from high school.

There were no pictures of Hayden in his uniform, after he'd joined the Navy at eighteen. And there were no pictures of Colin, not even in the background of any of the shots.

Colin looked back at his mother.

She regarded him coolly, her arms crossed over her chest. "Do the pictures make you uncomfortable?"

"No," he lied.

"They should."

Every muscle in his body clenched, walling off the grief. He tried not to think too much about Hayden. He'd never thought too much about the scrawny kid who had followed him everywhere, like a shadow, when they were growing up. By the time his brother had finally earned his respect, and a tentative bond had begun to form between them, it had been too late.

Five years had passed. Five years, three months, and seventeen days since Hayden's P-3C Orion had been shot down in Iraq.

His mother had cut him out of her life that day, the final resounding click in a door that had begun to swing shut a long time before that. It was hard to believe that this woman, this stranger, had ever loved him. But she had. At least for the first eight years of his life.

Until Hayden had come along.

Her miracle child. The child she had given up hope of having so many years before. The child who, if he had come along earlier, would have been all his parents had needed.

Instead, they'd resorted to adoption. And they'd gotten Colin. Because power couples like Nick Foley and Lydia Vanzant needed at least one child to soften their image, to gain the respect of other hardworking mothers and fathers, to tap into those deep-rooted family values that lived in the hearts of so many U.S. voters.

The memories reached up through the floorboards, cold fingers of loneliness and bitter resentments. He tried to force them back, pushing them into the dark corner all SEALs saved for thoughts that no longer served them. He hadn't come here to relive that time in his life, to remember how alone and unwanted he had once felt. It had been here, in this house, when he'd learned—for the first time, but certainly not the last—how easily he could be cast aside.

He had tried everything to win his mother's love back after Hayden came along: getting straight A's at school, excelling at every sport, joining all the clubs she encouraged him to, eventually getting accepted at the same Ivy League college she'd attended herself. But it had all been in vain.

The day Hayden had been born, he had ceased to exist in his mother's eyes.

Turning his back on the woman who still stood in the doorway, he spotted the laptop sitting on the writing desk beneath the wide window overlooking the backyard. A single spreadsheet covered in numbers was open on the screen and the words, "Consolidation," "Renovation," and "Demolition" stood out in bold block letters at the top of the columns—words that could only have to do with one thing.

"I know you're still angry with me, but if you need someone to attack, take it out on me," Colin said. "Don't take it out on Dad."

"He asked for this."

Colin turned. "How?"

"You think I don't still have friends in his office? You think I don't know about his decision to move funds allocated for education into a jobs program for veterans?"

Colin cursed under his breath. "I know you didn't agree with the war, and you're entitled to that opinion. But spending money on going to war and taking care of the men and women who served in it when they come home are two very different things. You can't be against helping the people who fought for your freedom."

"They should never have been over there in the first place."

Colin struggled to control his temper. "The people who went overseas volunteered to go. They *wanted* to go. You can't punish them for that. If Hayden was here, if *he* was the one standing here, asking you to support his friends when they came back home, you would be the one in Dad's office right now, fighting to move funds from every other program in this state to help veterans."

Grief and anger flashed through Lydia's eyes. "But Hayden's not here, is he? He'll never be standing here. Because of you."

Colin took a step toward her. "Hayden's death was not my fault."

"You knew he would follow in your footsteps," Lydia accused. "He idolized you."

"Hayden was eighteen when he enlisted." Colin's fingers curled into fists at his sides. "He was capable of making his own decisions."

"You encouraged him."

He hadn't, Colin thought. He had tried to talk him out of it. But what was the point in arguing about it now? Hayden was gone and nothing either of them could say or do would ever bring him back.

"Sometimes," Colin said, meeting his mother's gaze across the room. "I think you wish I'd died instead of Hayden."

"You're right," she said, opening the door. "I do."

≈

CURLED up on the sofa in her living room, Becca stared at the blank sheet of paper in her lap. It shouldn't be this hard, she thought. All she needed were a few sentences, a few simple phrases that captured her feelings. She didn't want to be overly gushy or use fancy flowery prose. Not when she had to say the words out loud, in front of over a hundred and fifty people.

She shuddered. How had she let this wedding get so big?

All she'd ever wanted was something simple, quiet, just family and a few close friends. She would have been perfectly happy to wake up on a pretty weekend morning, put on her mother's wedding dress, walk across the street to Magnolia Harbor, have one of the boat captains marry her and Tom, and head over to the café for a celebratory lunch.

But once the planning had started, and Tom had begun adding people, the guest list had taken on a life of its own. At this rate, close to half of Tom's law firm would be showing up.

Maybe that was why she was having so much trouble writing her vows.

It wasn't a fear of public speaking. She'd gotten over her shyness of talking in front of large groups of people a long time ago. But she was used to talking to students, parents, and other teachers. She was used to talking about the curriculum, teaching methods, and plans for the next school year.

She was *not* used to talking about her feelings. She had never been very good at talking about her feelings, even with her closest friends, let alone in front of a crowd of people, many of whom she didn't even know.

But it had been her idea that she and Tom write their own vows. It seemed so much more personal to say what was in your own heart rather than recite the canned script everyone else used.

Pressing the tip of her pen back to the paper, she scrawled, "Tom, I love you. I've loved you since we were sixteen. I can't wait to spend the rest of my life with you, to give you children, to grow old with you. I can't wait for our lives together to finally begin."

That was it, right?

That was all she had to say.

Simple. Honest. True.

A tug of uneasiness nagged at her as she reread the words. Something still felt off. Something...she couldn't put her finger on.

A knock on her door had her pushing the notebook aside. "Come in," she called, relieved by the interruption. It was probably her father, wanting to borrow some laundry detergent or coffee for the morning. Or maybe one of her students. She had told Luke to come over if he ever needed anything.

When whoever it was didn't just walk in, as most of her friends and neighbors would without a second thought, she stood and crossed the room to the door, opening it. The last thing she expected was to find the man who'd been invading her every thought for the past few days filling her doorway.

"Colin," she said, surprised. "Hi." Glancing down at the over-sized flannel shirt she was wearing over a thin tank top and cut off shorts, she quickly wrapped the plaid material around her midsection. "I wasn't expecting company."

"I should have called first." His voice was low and deep. It rumbled through the quiet neighborhood streets.

"No. It's fine. You didn't need to call. My door is always open." She stepped back, motioning for him to come in.

He walked inside, his gaze sweeping around her cluttered living room filled with wedding projects and packing boxes. Becca closed the door behind him, feeling suddenly self-conscious. Colin had never been to her house before. She imagined what it must look like through his eyes: the student artwork hanging on the walls, the antique knickknacks on the book-shelves, the hand-me-down furniture and mismatched lamps, the woven rugs covering worn wooden floorboards that squeaked when you stepped on them.

To her, everything about this house was cozy, comforting, familiar.

But she and Colin had come from very different backgrounds.

"I'm sorry about the mess." Gathering up an armful of magazines from the seat of the leather chair across from the sofa, she gestured for him to sit.

He walked over to the chair, resting his hands on the back, but he didn't sit.

Becca paused, noticing his tense expression for the first time. "Is everything all right?"

"No."

Her brows drew together at the hard edge in his voice. The sun had set and dusk was settling over the island. Even with a few of the table lamps burning, the lighting was dim, making his features appear harder, his eyes an even deeper shade of blue.

She waited, watching him as the silence stretched on. She had never seen him like this before. He was usually so calm, so lighthearted, so quick to fill the silence with a question or a casually flirtatious comment. She could sense the restless energy rippling off him now, the anger simmering beneath the surface.

"I'm afraid I have some bad news," he said finally.

Becca picked up the notebook she'd been using to work on her vows, quietly closing it and setting it on the table between them.

Colin's hands tightened around the back of the chair. "The complication with the school I mentioned the other day might be a bigger problem than we thought."

"It is...Lydia?" Becca asked.

He gazed back at her, obviously surprised that she knew.

"Shelley told me," Becca explained. "She thinks your mother's offering her services as a consultant to get back at your father."

"She's right."

Becca's heart sank. She had been hoping all day that Shelley had been wrong, or at least, if she hadn't been, that Colin would be able to appeal to his mother on their behalf. The fact that he was here, in her house, bearing bad news, meant that he must not think he had any sway over her. "Are you close with your mother?"

"No."

Maybe that was why he was so upset, Becca thought. "When was the last time you saw her?"

"A few hours ago."

"I thought you said you weren't close."

"We're not." His gaze drifted over to the window. "I went to her house this afternoon for the first time...in a long time. I thought I might be able to reason with her."

"It didn't go well?" Becca ventured.

He shook his head.

She wished he would sit down. She wished he would tell her what was wrong. She couldn't stand to see him like this. "Why aren't you and your mother close?"

He looked away, saying nothing.

Unable to stop herself, she walked out from behind the coffee table and placed a hand on his arm, pulling him toward the chair. "Colin, please sit down. Talk to me."

He didn't move, but he did look at her. Becca's breath caught when she saw the raw emotions in his eyes—grief, anger, pain. She could feel the warmth of his skin pulsing beneath her palm, a sharp contrast to those cool blue eyes and that calm exterior she had never seen a single crack in until now. The muscles in his arm flexed under her fingers, hard knots of tension, coiled, ready to spring.

Colin looked down, at where her fingers still rested on his arm, then back at her face. A new emotion swam into his eyes, a darker emotion, and his gaze flickered briefly down to her mouth.

Becca dropped her hand away from his arm, taking a step back. "I-I think I'll make some tea. Or...coffee. Would you prefer coffee? Or something else? I don't have any beer in the house, but I might have some sodas in the fridge..."

"Coffee's fine."

Coffee, Becca thought, walking quickly into the kitchen. Coffee would be good. She pulled the beans out of the freezer and padded across the floor in her bare feet to the coffee maker. She needed something to do with her hands, something to keep herself from touching him again.

Colin followed her into the kitchen. She was aware of him watching her as she ground the beans, filled the carafe with water, and fiddled with the buttons on the machine to adjust the settings. She tried not to notice the way her skin heated as his eyes tracked her across the kitchen.

Pressing the start button on the coffee maker, she turned to face him. "Is your father rethinking his offer to help us?"

Colin nodded. "He's concerned that it will distract from the other issues in the campaign."

Becca thought back to what Shelley had said earlier that day: *I think we should both be prepared for the fact that we might not win this battle. Our chances were never very good. Now, I think they might be even worse.*

"If your father isn't going to make those calls to the board members, then there's no reason Shelley should postpone her announcement until Friday."

"I agree."

Becca looked down at her feet. The date of the first public hearing could be announced as early as next week. The teachers deserved to know before that. Annie and Will deserved to know before that. If they were going to take this on as a community, they needed to start talking about it now.

"When do you think Shelley will tell the teachers?" Colin asked.

"She'll probably want to try to talk to Lydia first. I doubt it'll do anything, but she'll want to try. I would imagine by the end of the day on Tuesday, at the latest."

"When do you think she'll tell Annie?"

"We'll tell her together, when she comes to pick up Taylor from school on Tuesday."

"I'll call Will so he won't be blindsided, so they'll both know at the same time."

"Thanks," Becca said, wishing it hadn't come to this. She hated to think how Annie was going to react, how Taylor was going to react when they found out. She had wanted so badly to shield them from this.

The aroma of fresh brewed coffee floated into the air, but it did little to comfort her. She felt exhausted all of a sudden. She needed time to think, to process this new development. She didn't want him to see her like this, when she hadn't had a chance to collect her thoughts yet. But when she glanced back up and noticed the dark circles under his eyes and the faint lines of exhaustion around his mouth, she didn't have the heart to ask him to leave. She could tell there was something still bothering him, that there was a lot more on his mind than just the school. "If you ever want to talk, Colin. About anything. I'm here."

He held her gaze across the room, his big masculine frame leaning against her counter, making the kitchen seem small and impossibly cramped. A dark shadow of stubble covered his jaw and his wide shoulders blocked her view out the window of the marshes. "The offer goes both ways."

Becca opened her mouth, closed it. She didn't need to talk

about anything. There was nothing bothering her. At least, nothing she would share with him.

She thought back to the notebook, the vows—how hard it had been to write them.

Unconsciously, she reached up, fingering the charm dangling from the end of her necklace. "The mugs are in the cupboard behind you."

He turned, pulling two out.

She crossed the room, taking them from him, and he reached up, catching the charm at the end of her necklace in his hand.

"What is this?" he murmured.

She paused, her heart skipping a beat. "It's...nothing."

He gazed down at the worn gold pendant. "It's not nothing. You touch it whenever you're nervous."

"It's just a necklace."

"It's the only piece of jewelry you ever wear."

Becca tried to step back, but he kept his grip firm on the delicate chain. She could smell him, the dark heady scent of him mingling with the salt marshes. She could feel the warmth of his body, only inches from hers. The corners of his mouth were tilted down, those full kissable lips so close she could simply push up on her toes and reach them with her own.

What would he taste like? What would his mouth feel like moving over hers? What would it feel like to have his arms come around her, to feel her body pressed against that solid wall of muscle? It took all of her willpower not to reach up, run her hands over those broad shoulders and let her fingers tangle into that thick black hair.

"Becca," he said softly, his voice like ripples of water, right before a storm. "What is this?"

She swallowed as his gaze stayed focused on the charm that was so worn down even she could barely make out the shape anymore. "It's a dove."

"A peace dove?"

"A mourning dove."

His eyes lifted, meeting hers. "Who are you mourning?"

"No one," she said quickly, prying his fingers off the charm and stepping back. Her legs shook as she crossed the tiled floor back to the coffee maker. She set the mugs on the counter, pouring coffee into each of them, sloshing some over the side of hers.

He needed to leave now. It wasn't safe for her to be here with him, just the two of them. She didn't trust herself around him.

It wasn't just attraction anymore. He was starting to see through her, to ask too many questions, in ways no one else ever had for a very long time.

She set the carafe back on the heating pad with a clatter, picking up one of the mugs and holding it out to him.

He took it slowly from her hand. A rush of warmth shot up her arm when their fingers brushed.

He drank slowly from the cup, turning to face her refrigerator, taking in the collage of pictures and postcards held up with magnets. He slipped one free, showed it to her. "Is this your father?"

She nodded.

It was a picture of her father, Ryan, and Joe standing outside a duck blind a few years ago. The three men were dressed in camouflage hunting gear, their shotguns leaning against a wooden shed covered in cornhusks. Two Labrador retrievers sat at their feet.

"Does your fiancé like to hunt?" Colin asked.

"No." She noticed he still wouldn't use Tom's name.

He put the picture back, chose another. This one was of her, Grace, and Ryan out on Ryan's boat last fall. Becca was holding a giant rockfish, laughing at something Grace had said. "Did your fiancé take this?"

"No." She lifted her mug to her mouth, swallowing a sip of scalding coffee. Will had taken that one when he'd come home to visit last fall.

"Does he like to fish?"

"No."

He put the picture back on the fridge. "I hear you're pretty good at it."

"I am," she said. She was very good at fishing. She had grown up on the Bay. She had spent her weekends on her father's boat with a rod in her hands from the time she was five years old. She was the daughter of a waterman. It ran in her blood.

"Is this him?" Colin pointed to a picture of Tom sitting on her porch with a glass of wine in his hand.

She nodded.

He said nothing, studying the man in the picture.

Becca wrapped both hands around her mug.

He dropped the picture and turned, walking back out to the living room. He took in the student artwork taped to her walls. "Your students must really like you."

"They do."

He took another sip of coffee, like he hadn't noticed the sharp tone in her voice, like he had all the time in the world. "Do you want kids one day?"

"Of course." Then, before she could stop herself, she asked, "Do you?"

He nodded. "At least three."

She blinked. "Three?"

"I've always wanted a big family." He wandered over to the stairwell, ran his hand over the banister. "How long have you lived in this house?"

The questions kept coming, one right after the other. He wasn't even giving her time to come up for air. "I bought it after grad school, when I moved back to the island."

"How many bedrooms does it have?"

"Three."

"It would be a nice house for a family."

Yes, Becca thought, squeezing her mug. That was exactly what she'd thought, too, when she'd bought it. If it had been up to her, she and Tom would have been living here together, married with at least two children by now.

But life didn't always work out the way you'd hoped.

Colin drained the last of his coffee, setting the mug down on the table. "I should go."

Becca let out a breath. His moods shifted so fast, it was impossible to keep up. "Are you staying on the island tonight?"

"No." He shook his head. "I'm driving back to Annapolis."

Becca walked slowly out of the kitchen, opening the front door for him. He hadn't driven all the way out to the island just to tell her the news about the school in person, had he? Surely, they could have had that conversation over the phone...

Colin walked out onto the porch, taking in the comfortable furniture, the wicker porch swing with the bright yellow and red cushions, the plastic containers of pansies and violas she'd purchased impulsively from the grocery store last week but hadn't had time to plant.

"Colin," she said, when he started down the steps. She couldn't let him leave like this. She needed to say something— anything—to get back on even footing. "I was going through the final guest list for the wedding earlier, and I realized that I still haven't gotten your RSVP. You got my invitation, right?"

Colin paused on the second to last step. "I must have forgotten to mail it back."

"But you're coming, right?"

"Sure," he said after a moment's hesitation. "I'll be there."

"Should I put you down for two?"

He glanced back at her. It was dark now and the faint porch light cast shadows over his rugged face. "Two what?"

"Two people. You're bringing someone, right?"

His gaze shifted away again. "Yeah," he said, walking down the last step. "I'm bringing someone."

Becca stood in the doorway, watching him walk down the sidewalk to his truck. When he got in, and the engine revved, she watched him pull away until he turned onto Main Street, and his truck disappeared around the corner. She stood there for a long time, staring out at the darkness, until she felt the strangest sensation, like pieces of metal brushing against her wrist.

She glanced down, and felt the familiar tug of regret when she saw that her wrist was bare. She had lost her mother's charm bracelet years ago. She'd been helping her father move his boat back into the marina after he'd gotten some work done on it, and it had fallen into the water.

She'd gone in after it, searching for hours to recover the bracelet that her mother had worn every day until she'd died, and that Becca had worn every day since. But she hadn't been able to find it, and it had never washed up on the shore as she'd hoped it would in the days and weeks that had followed.

Looking back out at the dark street, she reached up, wrapping her fingers around the single mourning dove—the one charm that had fallen off a few weeks before she'd lost the bracelet, the one piece of her mother she still had left.

She turned, but just before she shut the door, she could swear she could hear it, just the faintest sound of the charms clinking together over the wind.

SEVEN

*H*e hadn't forgotten to mail back the RSVP, Colin thought as he walked from his apartment in downtown Annapolis to his father's office the next morning. Becca's wedding invitation had been sitting in a drawer in his desk for months now. When he'd first opened it, his initial reaction had been to find a reason to be out of town that weekend. The thought of sitting through a wedding, any wedding, had stirred up too many memories of everything he'd lost.

Now, he didn't want to go for an entirely different reason.

He was starting to feel something for Becca, something that went way beyond physical attraction, and he was pretty sure those feelings weren't one sided. He'd seen the look in her eyes when they'd been in her kitchen, when he'd caught her necklace in his hand and she'd been close enough for him to bend down and seal his lips over hers. He had known, without a doubt, that she'd wanted him to kiss her. And he would have, if it hadn't been for the flash of pain that had cut through those eyes when he'd asked her who she was mourning.

He didn't know what that was all about. But he would find out.

The woman had layers, a lot more than he'd realized, and every time he peeled one back, he wanted to know more.

Closing in on the Maryland State House from one of the side streets that spiraled out through the historic downtown, he watched the crunch of morning rush hour traffic inch around State Circle. He wanted to spend some time with Becca, to get to know her, to see where this—whatever this was—might go. But her wedding was less than three weeks away. And despite the fact that her fiancé was so obviously wrong for her, something was holding her to him. There was a connection there, a strong one, and he needed to know what it was.

A good operator always had all the facts before he made a move.

Slipping his phone out of his pocket, he punched in the number for the Wind Chime Café on Heron Island. He had a feeling he knew exactly who might be able to help him.

A familiar female voice answered after a few rings. "Wind Chime Café, this is Della."

"Hi, Della. It's Colin."

"Hi, Colin," Della said over the noise in the background— muffled voices, the clatter of coffee cups, the hiss of an espresso machine. "Do you want to talk to Annie?"

Colin paused at a crosswalk with several other pedestrians, waiting for the traffic light to change. He had briefly considered asking Annie about Becca. The two women had become good friends since Annie had moved to the island last fall. But Annie didn't have history there. She might not know much about Becca and Tom's past.

Della, on the other hand, was from Heron Island. She had been around the whole time Becca and Tom were growing up. "Actually, I want to talk to you."

"Well," Della said, adding a teasing note of importance into her voice. The kitchen door opened and closed with a distinctive squeak and the background noise from the dining room dimmed. "To what do I owe this honor?"

"I called to see if you have plans for dinner on Wednesday night."

"I don't think so. Why?"

"I'd like to take you out."

"I'm flattered, Colin, but I've been happily married for over thirty-five years."

Colin smiled, and some of the tension he'd been holding onto since his conversation with his mother the day before eased. "I know you've been wanting to try that new Italian restaurant that opened in St. Michaels a few weeks ago—the one across the street from the jewelry store. Name a time and I'll meet you there."

She let out a whistle. "That's a fancy restaurant."

"With an excellent chef, from what I hear. Maybe we can steal a few ideas for the café."

"Why do I get the feeling you're trying to butter me up for something?"

"I can't imagine what you mean," Colin said innocently.

Della laughed. "If you need a favor, hon, you can just ask. You don't need to take me out to dinner first. Why don't you drop by the café around closing time on Wednesday and we'll talk then?"

"I'd rather take you out somewhere in St. Michaels." The traffic light changed and he started across the street. "Some-where...not on the island."

There was a brief pause on the other end of the line. "Because you don't want anybody listening in?"

"Something like that."

"I see," Della said slowly and Colin heard the squeak of the oven door opening in the background, then the clatter of metal on wood as she set a tray of something that would probably make his mouth water on the counter. "I don't suppose this has anything to do with why your truck was parked outside Becca's house for over an hour last night?"

Colin faltered, almost missing the step up to the curb on the other side of the street. Della had noticed his truck outside Becca's house last night?

He hadn't thought twice about dropping by, but he'd forgotten that neighbors tended to be curious in small towns. And Heron Island was about as small as it got.

Becca had grown up on the island. She had friends there, family there—people who were watching out for her.

There were probably others who'd noticed his truck outside her house last night and wondered what he'd been doing there.

"Let's just say I have a few questions," he said.

"I'll do my best to answer them," Della said. "How about six o'clock?"

"I'll see you then," Colin said, and hung up.

The last thing he wanted was for Becca's friends and neighbors to start asking questions, to scare her off before he'd had a chance to figure out his next step. If he was even going to think about moving in on another man's territory this late in the game, he needed a plan, a solid one, one that wouldn't backfire.

Because if it did backfire, and somehow Becca got hurt in the process, every single person on that island would turn against him.

He was already going to be on thin ice with the islanders when they found out about the threat to the school. He wanted to put down roots on Heron Island. He wanted to build a life there. But no one was going to accept the man responsible for closing down their children's school.

He needed to find a way to save it to prove to Becca, and the rest of the islanders, that he was one of them.

It had been a year since he'd even considered getting close to a woman again for something more than just sex. But being in Becca's house last night—seeing those student drawings on her walls, listening to her talk about the school, hearing the passion in her voice for a place that meant so much to her, watching her work so hard to save it even though she was leaving at the end of the year and her own job wasn't even at stake—had hit him hard.

He'd spent a lot of time over the past year thinking about what kind of woman he didn't want to be with anymore, but he hadn't given much thought to what kind of woman he did want.

Until now.

He was starting to think he knew exactly who he wanted.

He'd lain awake most of last night, thinking of ways he could help Becca save the school. Sometime around 2 AM, an idea had finally taken root. It was risky, and his father's campaign manager was going to hate it, but it might be the only way.

Lifting his phone, he dialed a new number.

"*Washington Tribune*." The receptionist answered after the first ring. "How may I direct your call?"

"Grace Callahan," he said, walking onto the gated grounds of the State House. He had gotten to know Grace pretty well over the winter. While he'd never been a big fan of reporters, he liked her. He trusted her. And he knew she would do anything to protect her island, her community, and most of all Becca—who she'd been best friends with forever.

"This is Grace," she said as she picked up the line.

"Hey, Grace. It's Colin Foley."

"Hey," she said, her tone shifting from professional to friendly. "What's up?"

Flashing his badge to the security guard, Colin strode into the historic brick building that housed his father's offices. "I have a story idea I want to run by you."

"Whoa," Grace said, pausing in the middle of the living room at the inn that night when she saw the gaping hole in the wall beside the fireplace. "What happened here?"

"They found a crack in the foundation," Becca said, walking out of the farmhouse-style kitchen and handing her friend a glass of red wine from the bottle she'd brought over. "Jimmy's crew started working on it today. They had to tear out a section of the drywall to fix it."

Grace's eyes swung back to meet hers, widening. "Will it be done in time for the wedding?"

"It'll be done in time," Becca said firmly. "I had a long chat with Jimmy this afternoon."

Grace's expression darkened. "Did he apologize for his behavior on Sunday?"

Becca shook her head. "I don't think he even remembered being at the café."

"Unbelievable." Grace shrugged out of her black suit jacket and dropped it on the sofa. The white tank top and pencil skirt she wore underneath were rumpled from the long drive from D.C.

"What happened after Ryan walked him home?" Becca asked.

"Nothing," Grace said, scooping her long blond hair into a ponytail and snapping a rubber band around it to secure it in place. "Jimmy passed out on the couch almost as soon as they got there. Ryan said his house was a mess—empty bottles all over the place, dishes in the sink, overflowing trash cans. He and Joe stayed for a while to clean up, but Jimmy probably didn't even notice when he woke up."

"It's getting worse," Becca murmured, thinking about how quiet Luke had been in school again today. He had given her another drawing—a dog this time—and said he was going to ask his mom if they could get one soon. Becca already knew what the answer to that question was going to be. Courtney was barely managing to keep it together as it was. There was no way she was going to agree to take on a pet right now, which meant it would just be one more disappointment to add to Luke's growing list.

"Ryan said he didn't like the way Jimmy talked to you on the porch," Grace said, taking a sip of her wine.

Becca remembered the way her skin had crawled at the stench of whiskey on his breath, at the slurred voice so close to her ear. "I don't think he would do anything stupid, if that's what you mean."

"I don't think he would either, but he seems fixated on you right now for some reason. I know you have a lot of other things on your mind, but be careful, okay?"

"I'll be careful," Becca said.

It was all she had to say. The two women had been best friends since kindergarten. They had grown up on this island together. They had both lost their mothers at a young age. Both of their fathers were watermen and spent long stretches of time out on the water every day, which meant they hadn't always had a parent around to watch out for them. They had learned to watch each other's backs a long time ago.

Becca motioned for Grace to follow her over to the wide chopping block counter where Will's grandmother had spent her days cooking Chesapeake Bay-style fare for the inn's guests, but which was now covered in dozens of glass jars, boxes of tea lights, and piles of pre-cut lavender and lace ribbon.

"Is Annie here?" Grace asked.

"No," Becca said. "She called a little while ago and said she wasn't going to be able to make it."

Walking around to the other side of the counter, Becca didn't add that she'd actually been relieved when Annie had cancelled.

It meant that she wouldn't have to spend the next couple of hours pretending everything was fine to her face.

She had asked Shelley if they could tell Annie today, but Shelley had wanted to wait. She had wanted to give Lydia at least twenty-four hours to get back to her and she hadn't wanted Annie finding out, and possibly letting the news slip, before she'd had a chance to tell the rest of the teachers.

Becca understood where she was coming from, but she hated keeping secrets from her friends. She was tempted to tell Grace tonight—she knew her friend wouldn't tell anyone if she asked her not to—but it didn't seem fair to tell Grace when she hadn't told Annie.

Walking up to the counter, Grace gazed appreciatively at the gleaming remodeled kitchen. "This place looks amazing."

"I know," Becca said. "I can't believe how much Annie accomplished in such a short amount of time."

Grace pulled out one of the stools—the same stools Becca and Grace had spent hours on as kids when they'd come over to play with Will and had inevitably ended up staying for dinner. Each stool had been lovingly reupholstered and restored to mint condition, as had every other piece of furniture in this house.

Annie had done most of the work on the interior herself—repainting the rooms, replacing the curtains and a few of the rugs, adding a few new pieces of furniture here and there, and swapping out the broken appliances in the kitchen for modern energy efficient ones, while somehow managing to maintain all the original style and feel of the historic farmhouse that had been in Will's family for generations.

She'd even rehung all the Dozier's family pictures on the walls, right where they'd been before, re-matted and reframed to fit the new updated look. The effect was warm, welcoming, and made you feel like you were part of the family, even if you were only staying for one night.

At least, that's the way it made *her* feel, Becca thought. She could only hope the small group of guests Tom had chosen to stay at the inn on their wedding night would feel the same way.

Grace reached for a strip of white lace, wrapping it around one of the glass jars. "Are these for the aisle or the centerpieces?"

"Aisle," Becca answered, opening a box of tea lights and dropping one in each of the jars. She had moved most of the wedding supplies over to the inn this afternoon after Grace and Annie had offered to help with a few unfinished projects and discuss some last minute ideas for the food, flowers, and decorations.

"Is Gladys still doing the centerpieces?"

"Yes," Becca said, the metal casings of the tea lights making a clinking sound against the glass as they hit the bottom of each jar. "I stopped by her house after work and she said she put in the order for the flowers this morning."

"What about the vases?"

"Over there." Becca nodded to a stack of boxes in the corner filled with old milk bottles Gladys had been collecting all winter to display the simple arrangements of white peonies, Baby's Breath and English lavender. "Though I'm not sure how Tom's going to feel about using them. Did I tell you he's pushing for white tablecloths and assigned seating now?"

"Seriously?"

Becca nodded, reaching for another box of tea lights. "He's worried that the picnic tables and buffet dinner won't be classy enough for his co-workers."

Grace rolled her eyes. "The next thing you know, he's going to want to hire a team of waiters carrying silver trays."

Becca just looked at her.

"He already asked for that?"

Becca laughed at the appalled expression on her friend's face. "Don't worry. I said, no. And I said, no, to the white tablecloths. But I compromised by agreeing to assigned seating."

"Assigned seating at picnic tables?"

"I know." Becca dropped the last tea light into a jar at the edge of the counter. "It sounds ridiculous, but Tom's worried that some of the partners at his firm will be seated with people they won't have anything in common with."

Grace set down the ribbon she'd been about to tie around the strip of lace. "Please tell me you're kidding."

"I wish I was."

"This is your *wedding*, Becca, not an event to impress the partners at Tom's law firm."

Becca glanced up.

Grace opened her mouth, then closed it. "Sorry." She held up a hand. "I forgot."

"It's okay." Becca looked back down. Grace had never been a big fan of Tom's, but she had promised to try and keep things civil, at least until after the wedding. Becca secretly hated the fact that her best friend couldn't stand her future husband. Grace and Tom were two of the most important people in the world to her, and the fact that they couldn't get along upset her a lot more than she let on.

Pulling her smartphone out of her pocket, Grace scrolled through a few screens. "What do you want to do about place cards?" she asked, shifting the conversation back to wedding planning and away from Tom. "I bet we could find some online…"

"Already taken care of." Becca lifted the canvas bag off the stool beside her and passed it across the counter to Grace.

Grace took the bag and peered inside at over a hundred and fifty pieces of folded cardstock with the names of each guest written in large awkwardly shaped letters—letters that had clearly been written by children.

"It seemed like a good day to have the kids practice their penmanship," Becca said with a straight face.

Grace smiled. "I love it." She was about to hand the bag back when one of the cards caught her eye and she pulled it out, holding it up for Becca to see. The name, Colin Foley, was written in silver bubble letters on white cardstock. "Colin finally RSVP'd?"

Becca nodded. Reaching for a piece of lace, she wrapped it around one of the jars. "A couple of days ago."

Grace tapped the card lightly against the counter. "I had an interesting call from Colin today."

Becca pushed a pin into the ends of the lace to seal the piece together around the jar. "Oh, yeah?" she asked, trying to keep her voice casual. "What did he want?"

Grace turned the card over, laying it flat against the wood. "He wants me to write an article."

Becca reached for another strip of lace, feeling a pinch of uneasiness. "About what?"

"About the elementary school."

Becca's eyes met Grace's across the counter.

"I can't believe you didn't tell me," Grace said quietly.

"I'm so sorry," Becca said, setting the lace down. "I wanted to. Colin asked me not to say anything until he and his father had a chance to figure something out. I thought we had everything under control."

"Don't worry," Grace said. "I'm not angry with you. I just thought you would have told me. I know how much that school means to you."

Becca looked down, running her thumb over the edge of the lace. "I haven't told Annie yet, either."

"Well, she's going to find out soon enough. Colin wants me to break the story tomorrow, right after Shelley makes her announcement to the teachers. I went up to Annapolis today to interview the governor. It's going to be a major piece, Becca. But

I'm going to need an interview or a quote, at the least, from Annie to make it work."

Becca's heart sank. There was no way Annie would agree to that. "She hasn't given a single interview since the shooting."

"I know," Grace said. "And I respect that. But it's been over six months. Maybe she'll be willing to do it if I'm the reporter asking the questions and it's to save her daughter's school."

It was true, Becca thought. If Grace broke the news in *The Washington Tribune*, one of the most widely read papers in the country, the story could go viral. A quote from Annie could potentially convince the board to drop the threat. But was it fair of them to ask this of her?

In the weeks following the shooting, reporters had hounded both Annie and Taylor in D.C. Part of the reason they'd moved to Heron Island was to get away from all that. "If we open this door, more reporters will come to the island. Every newspaper and TV station will be calling the café, wanting a quote from Annie, wanting to interview Taylor."

"That's going to happen anyway," Grace said. "As soon as this story breaks, Annie and Taylor will be swarmed. The only question is, who's going to get to them first?"

EIGHT

*a*nnie, wait," Becca said, pushing out the double doors of the elementary school after her friend the next day.

Annie shook her head and kept walking. "I need to find Taylor."

"Taylor's with Della. She's fine. That's why we asked you to come alone. So you could have some time to process this."

"I don't need time to *process* this." Annie's boots clicked over the pavement as she made her way across the parking lot to the sidewalk leading back to the café. "I need to talk to my daughter."

Becca followed her past several small groups of islanders huddled together, all talking about the same thing. Now that Shelley had made her announcement to the teachers, word would spread fast across the island. A few of their neighbors stopped talking when Annie walked by, their expressions filled with concern.

"It's not over yet," Becca said, when she finally caught up with her. "The decision hasn't been made." She placed a hand on Annie's arm. "We're going to fight this."

Annie paused at the edge of the sidewalk. She looked down

at Becca's hand, then back up at her face. "Why aren't you as upset as I am?"

"What?"

"Shelley said all the teachers found out today."

"Yes, but—"

"When did you find out?"

Becca lowered her hand back to her side. "Thursday."

"Thursday?" Annie echoed. "You've known since *Thursday*, and you didn't tell me?"

It sounded awful when she put it that way, Becca thought. She watched her friend turn and walk away. She knew Annie needed time, that she probably wanted to be alone right now. But she didn't want her to think, even for a second, that this school meant any less to her than it did to everyone else on the island. Just because she was leaving didn't mean she wasn't going to do everything in her power to save it.

She started after her, picking up her pace until she'd closed in on her friend again a block away from the café. "The only reason I didn't tell you sooner was because we were trying to find a way to convince the board to reconsider their decision. We didn't want to upset everyone before we knew for sure. Colin was certain that—"

Annie stopped walking, turning slowly to face Becca again. "Colin?"

Becca nodded. "He's been trying to help us. His father—"

"*Colin* knew about this and he didn't tell me either?"

Becca trailed off when she saw the hurt expression on Annie's face. Her friend felt like she'd been betrayed, not by one, but *two* of her closest friends. And it was about to get a lot worse, Becca thought as she spotted Grace sitting on the steps of the café. Annie's participation would be crucial for the story's success, but she had a feeling Annie wasn't going to be feeling too warm and fuzzy about helping any of them right now.

Grace pushed slowly to her feet, her eyes filled with sympa-thy. "Hey, Annie."

"You know, too?" Annie asked.

Grace nodded.

Annie brushed past her, climbing the steps to the door. "Am I the last person on this island to find out?"

"I know you're upset," Grace said, "but I need to talk to you."

"About what?" Annie snapped, already reaching for the door.

"About what's happening. I don't like this any more than you do, but we need to act fast if we're going to fight this." Grace walked up the steps so they were eye-to-eye on the porch. "If we break this story before anyone else does, we might be able enlist the public's sympathy. If we can get enough people behind us, it might be enough to convince the board to drop the threat."

Annie stiffened. "You're writing about it?"

"Yes," Grace said.

"I guess I should have expected that," she said bitterly.

"It's the only way." Grace walked up the steps. "I know you don't want the press. I know you haven't given a single interview since the shooting last year and I respect that, but think how powerful it'll be if you speak out now, for the first time. If the public hears from you—about how important this school is for Taylor."

"No," Annie said, her voice flat.

"The rest of the story is already written. It's ready to go to press. All I need is a quote from you."

"No." Annie shook her head. "We moved here to get away from that. I won't subject Taylor to reporters again. I won't have them coming here, to this island, to our home."

"It's too late for that," Grace said. "This story is going to break whether you like it or not. Reporters are going to come here. They are going to ask you questions. They are going to ask Taylor questions. You can either speak now, as one of us, or you can let them wear you down until you say something you don't mean to say."

"They won't wear me down."

"They *will* wear you down. I can guarantee that. And when you do finally say something in the heat of the moment, they'll run with it, twisting your words in a hundred different directions on a dozen different news sources. All I need is one quote, Annie. We can get through this together. I know what I'm doing. I'm on your side. You need to let me do this."

Annie opened the door. "The only thing I need to do right now is talk to my daughter.

"Annie—"

"Find another way." She walked inside, slamming the door in Grace's face.

"I'm going to run the article," Grace said an hour later as she and Becca sat at a picnic table on the deck outside Rusty's, nursing a couple of beers. "With or without a quote from Annie."

"I know," Becca said, looking out at the water. A cold front was moving in, and dark clouds were already starting to gather along the horizon. White caps chopped over the surface of the Bay, and the few remaining fishing boats would be driven in soon by the rain.

"I'll wait another hour, in case she changes her mind," Grace said, "but I have to file the story soon before anyone else finds out about it. My editor's already sent three emails asking for it."

Becca nodded, wrapping the sides of her sweater tighter around her midsection to ward off the chill. She could hear the voices of her friends and neighbors inside the bar. Almost every islander had come into Rusty's after work to find out what was happening.

Everyone except Annie.

"I feel terrible," Becca said. "I should have told Annie as soon as I found out. I should never have kept this from her."

"She'll understand," Grace said. "Just give her some time. She's still getting used to the news. Everyone is."

Becca knew Grace was right, but it still didn't make her feel any better. She would never forget the look on Annie's face when she'd found out that two of her closest friends had hidden the news from her.

"By the way," Grace said. "I looked into Lydia Vanzant's public activities over the past several years, and I haven't found anything that would discredit her professionally. Her record is squeaky clean."

Becca picked at the label on the beverage she'd hardly touched at all over the past hour, slowly peeling it off the bottle. She thought about how upset Colin had been when he'd come to her house on Sunday. She still didn't know what had happened between him and his mother, but whatever it was, it had hurt him a lot. "Did you see Colin when you went to Annapolis yesterday?"

Grace nodded.

"How did he seem to you?"

Grace took a sip of her beer. "Fine. Why?"

"Did he say anything to you about meeting with his mother over the weekend?"

Grace shook her head. "No. Nothing."

Becca looked back out at the water. "He went to her house on Easter to talk about the school and it didn't go well. He wouldn't tell me what happened, but he said they're not close and he seemed really upset afterwards. I thought he might have mentioned something to you about it."

Grace shook her head again. "Where did you run into him on Easter? I didn't see him at the café."

"He came over that night."

"To your house?"

Becca nodded.

Grace looked at her curiously. "I didn't realize you two were that close."

"We're not," Becca said quickly. "I mean, we weren't, until recently. We've spent a lot of time together over the past week trying to figure out what to do about the school. That's why he stopped by—to talk about the school."

Grace leaned back, studying her. "Fair enough," she said finally, a mischievous smile spreading across her face. "I guess I wouldn't mind if Colin decided to stop by my house to talk about the school either."

Becca paused, her beer bottle halfway to her lips. "What?"

"Come on, Becca" Grace said, laughing. "That man is seriously hot. I don't care if you *are* engaged, you'd have to be blind not to notice."

"Well, sure," Becca said, taking a long sip of her beer to quench the sudden dryness in her throat. "He's...hot."

"He's gorgeous," Grace said. "I'd ask him out myself if he didn't turn every conversation we had into some question about you."

Becca almost choked on her beer.

Grace laughed again and handed her a napkin. "I think he has a crush on you."

"That's ridiculous," Becca scoffed. She grabbed the napkin from Grace and wiped off the bottle, refusing to meet her friend's eyes. The last thing she wanted was for Grace to know how she felt about Colin. If her friend thought there was even a chance she might be interested in someone else, she'd do everything in her power to convince her to call off the wedding.

An alarm dinged on Grace's phone and her friend checked the screen for whatever message had popped up. It probably had something to do with work, because she snapped up the device and typed out a hurried message before setting it back down and turning her attention back to Becca.

"That was my editor," she said, and Becca breathed a sigh of relief at the change in subject. "She wants me to cover some event at the Smithsonian on Saturday. Do you think we can push the practice run at the salon back a few hours?"

Becca blinked. The practice run at the salon? "Is that *this* Saturday?"

Grace nodded. "We'll be two weeks away from the wedding on Saturday."

Two weeks, Becca thought, fighting back the urge to panic. How had it snuck up on her so fast? She'd been so focused on the school, she'd hardly even had time to think about it. She still needed to sew the ring bearer pillow, pick out a suit for her father, rearrange the seating chart again—because Tom had added another two guests to the list this morning—and finish writing her vows.

She looked down at her hands, which were filled with tiny pieces of paper from the napkin she hadn't even realized she'd been shredding. She shoved the pieces into the pockets of her sweater, trying to get a grip. "It's just a hair appointment. You don't have to be there."

"I'm your Maid of Honor," Grace reminded her. "I'm supposed to be there for everything. Besides, what if she tries to give you one of those slicked back up-do's that make it look like your hair is shellacked to your head? I need to be there to intervene."

Becca curled her fingers around the pieces of paper in her pockets. How could Grace act so lighthearted at a time like this? "It feels wrong to spend an entire evening in a hair salon when so many of our friends are worried about losing their jobs."

"What are you talking about? It's not wrong. This is your

wedding, Becca. You've been looking forward to this day for years. No matter what else is happening on the island, we're all going to be there for you. We're all going to drink too much champagne and eat too much cake and dance until the generator runs out of gas. I'm as upset about the thought of the school closing as you are, but life goes on. If anything, your wedding will probably be a welcome distraction for a lot of people—a way for them to forget their troubles for a night."

Becca nodded, gazing down at a thin crack in the wooden table. Deep down, she knew Grace was right. But for some reason, it didn't feel right. It didn't feel right at all.

"Becca," Grace said gently. "We both know that I haven't always been a huge fan of Tom. I've always been honest with you about how I felt about him, but I promised to put aside my own feelings after you got engaged—for the wedding and for our friendship. But I need to ask...is everything all right with you two?"

"It's fine."

"Are you sure? Because—"

"I'm sure."

The boats in the marina rocked against the pilings, a restless creak of rubber on wood. Grace waited several beats, then asked, "Have you told Tom about the school?"

Becca nodded.

"What did he say?"

Becca slowly withdrew her hands from her pockets, opening her palms on the table and letting the wind catch the pieces of paper, swirling them up into the air. "He said it didn't matter because I was leaving anyway."

By the time Becca left Rusty's, it was dark and the first splattering of raindrops were beginning to fall. A few people had offered her a ride home, but she'd declined, wanting to take some time alone to think about what Grace had said out on the deck—that life went on.

It was true, she thought. Even if they couldn't save the school, it wouldn't be the end of the world. Her friends would lose their jobs, but they would find new ones eventually. Taylor and the rest of the kids would have to go to a different school, but kids were resilient. They would find a way to adjust.

The wind shook white petals from the branches of the wild pear trees lining the sidewalk. The flowers rained down around her shoulders, some getting stuck in her clothes before falling to the ground.

The online version of Grace's story had posted two hours ago without a quote from Annie, which meant they'd lost their one big chance of drawing on the public's sympathy. Most of the spin over the next few days would focus on the debate between the governor and his ex-wife, rather than the issue of Taylor and the islanders losing their school.

Brushing her fingers lightly over her bare wrist, where her mother's charm bracelet had been for so many years, she wished she could hear it. Just for a moment, she wished she could hear it again and feel that same sense of comfort she'd felt when she'd worn it every day.

Sometimes, when she was at work, teaching in the same classroom where her mother had taught, she swore she could feel her presence, as if she were still there, watching over her.

There were so few pieces of her mother she had left to hold on to, what would happen if the school closed and the county decided to tear down the building? Would she lose that connection, too?

Turning onto her street, she looked up at the dark clouds blotting the stars from the sky. Grace had said she should focus on

the wedding, on giving her friends and neighbors a reason to celebrate and forget their troubles for a night.

But what about her troubles?

What if, instead of being a welcome distraction from everything that was happening, the wedding was one of the reasons
why she couldn't sleep anymore?

What if she was starting to have second thoughts?

Stepping over a puddle, she walked slowly up the path to her
house. This was supposed to be the fun part. This was supposed
to be the part when she and her friends gossiped and drank too
much wine while they tested out hairstyles and makeup and
finalized the plans for the happiest day of her life.

She should be spending all her free time daydreaming of
kissing Tom under an arch of wildflowers in front of all their
friends and family after they both said, 'I do'. Instead, all she
could think about was how badly she'd wanted to kiss a different
man the night before—a man who was not her fiancé.

And she knew, without a doubt, there was something very
wrong with that.

She climbed the steps to her porch, not even noticing the dark
figure sitting on her swing. The metal hinges squeaked and she
jumped, almost dropping her keys when she saw the man push
slowly to his feet.

She stared, blinking rainwater out of her lashes as his face
registered in the darkness. "Tom?"

He walked over to her. "You're all wet," he said, running an
affectionate hand over her hair.

"What are you doing here?" she asked, baffled. He hadn't
come down to the island in months. It was so strange to see him
here. It was...almost as if he didn't belong.

"I came to apologize," he said quietly. He was still dressed in
his suit, his tie loosened at the collar, his shirt wrinkled from a
long day at work. There were circles under his eyes and lines of

exhaustion framing his mouth. "I'm sorry I've been so busy. I know today was hard for you. I wanted to be here. I'm sorry if I was abrupt on the phone the other day. I know what I said came out wrong. I know how much that school means to you."

His blue-green eyes were so earnest and genuine, she felt herself softening. He leaned down and she tilted her face up, as she had so many times before, and met his lips with hers. It was so easy, so familiar, so normal.

And she felt...absolutely nothing.

He eased back, taking her hand and leading her over to the porch swing. When they were sitting, he shrugged out of his jacket and wrapped it around her shoulders to keep her warm. "I saw Grace's article. Tell me everything I don't already know."

Becca let out a breath. It was so unexpected to see him here, to see him acting like this—so attentive, so caring—the way he had acted so many years before, back when they were teenagers and everything in their lives had fallen apart. He had been her rock then, and she had been desperate to get that person back for so long.

She had been so worried that the old Tom had disappeared completely. But maybe he was still in there. Maybe they were just going through a rough patch, like she'd hoped. Settling back into the curve of his arm, she told him everything.

He listened, asking a few questions, but mostly he just listened like he had so many times when they were younger. When she finished, he pulled her close, wrapping both arms around her, and they sat there for a long time, listening to the sound of the rain.

It felt safe. Secure. Comfortable.

Exactly the way it should feel.

She thought about the way Colin made her feel whenever he was around—nervous, jumpy, edgy, confused. Yes, she was attracted to him. But, as Grace had mentioned earlier at

Rusty's, who wasn't? It was just lust, she told herself. Nothing more.

"I have something for you," Tom said finally.

She looked up at him.

"I was going to wait until the night of the wedding to give it to you, but I thought you could use a pick-me-up today." He pulled a small turquoise jewelry box out of his pocket and handed it to her.

Becca took the box, surprised. He had never given her jewelry before.

"Open it," he urged.

Prying the top open, she stared down at the Tiffany's charm bracelet lying in a bed of white silk.

"I know it'll never replace your mother's," he said, lifting the bracelet out of the box and fastening it around her wrist. "But I wanted you to have it."

Touched, Becca looked down at the gleaming silver heart dangling from the shiny chain. There was nothing to be afraid of. No matter what happened, they would find a way to come through it together. They had weathered hard times before. They could do it again.

Besides, you didn't second-guess a fifteen-year relationship just because you didn't want to leave your home.

Home was wherever the heart was, right?

She laid her head on his shoulder, trying not to notice that the new weight on her wrist felt foreign, unwelcome. She stared down at the heavy silver heart dangling from the thick shiny links. Slowly, very slowly, she lifted her arm and shook her wrist, as she had so many times before when she'd still worn her mother's bracelet, when she'd needed to hear the sound of the delicate, lightweight charms to bring her comfort.

She thought for a second, fleetingly, that she could hear it, as she had the night before when Colin had been at her house—the faint tinkling sound drifting over the flower-scented wind. But it vanished as quickly as it had come. And, then, all she could hear was the hollow clink of silver on silver, the steady beat of the rain against the roof, and the sound of the wind tearing petals off the wild pear trees.

NINE

*W*ill Dozier woke to the sound of dripping. For a brief moment, he thought he was back in his house on the military base in Virginia Beach and one of the faucets was leaking again. Then he heard the wind chimes singing outside and felt the woman in his arms stir, and he smiled.

Pulling her close, he listened to the pitter-patter of rainwater falling from the leaves of the trees around the café. He wasn't thrilled with the circumstances that had brought him back to the island on such short notice, but as soon as Annie had called him yesterday and told him what was happening, he'd arranged to take a few days off.

If any reporters decided to come to the island to try to talk to Annie or Taylor, they would have to answer to him first.

Wrapping his arms tighter around his fiancée, he wished he didn't have to drive back to Virginia Beach on Friday. He wished he could stay through the weekend, to be here for Annie if she needed him. But he still had a few weeks of work left before he could move home for good, before he could wake up beside this woman every morning for the rest of his life.

When the phone on his nightstand buzzed, he reluctantly rolled away from her and reached for it. There was a text message on the screen from Ryan Callahan, his best friend from childhood.

I'm outside. You better get down here.

Slipping out of bed, he pulled on a pair of jeans and dragged a T-shirt over his head. When one of the wooden floorboards creaked under his weight, Annie opened her eyes.

"What's wrong?" she asked, sitting up immediately.

"Nothing." He leaned down and pressed a kiss to the top of her head. "Stay here. I'll be right back."

"What time is it?"

"Almost five."

She pushed the covers back, exposing a pair of long, lean legs. She'd worn one of his old flannel shirts to bed and the plaid material fell halfway down her slim thighs when she stood. He paused for a moment, watching her gather her thick red hair into a low ponytail, and felt a fierce swell of protectiveness toward this woman who had given him back the one thing he'd thought he'd lost forever—a family.

As long as she and Taylor were his, no one was going to hurt them ever again.

He reached for the doorknob. "Stay upstairs until I come back."

A brief flicker of understanding registered in her green eyes. "Someone's down there."

He nodded, half expecting her to say she was coming down with him. Annie had been a single mother for a long time before he'd come into her life. She was used to taking care of things, of protecting Taylor on her own. It would be a shift for both of them when he moved back to the island. They were going to have to make some adjustments in their new lives together—adjustments and compromises. But she needed to let him do this. She needed to let him step into this role from now on.

It was what he did. It was what he'd spent his whole life doing—protecting people.

She crossed the room to where he stood and touched her lips lightly to his. "I'll check on Taylor."

Relieved, he opened the door, letting her walk through it first. She slipped quietly into Taylor's bedroom and he crossed the small, second story apartment to the stairs. It was still dark out and Main Street should have been empty except for a few watermen heading down to the docks for the day. When he got to the bottom of the steps, he spotted Ryan's silver Chevy parked in front of the café.

His friend was standing in the yard, talking to a woman with a stiff helmet of blond hair and a black suit that looked glaringly formal compared to his friend's sweatshirt, Carhartts, and faded ball cap. Across the street, a man was unloading a giant camera bag from the back of a white Channel Six news van.

The string of silver chimes hanging from the knob rang softly as Will opened the door and stepped out onto the porch.

The camera flashed through the darkness, blinding him. He waited for his vision to come back into focus, looking straight at the source, into the lens, not moving for several long beats until the man across the street slowly lowered the device.

A second man stepped out of a small blue sedan parked under the oak tree. He was wearing jeans and a button down shirt so wrinkled it looked like he might have slept in his car overnight. He carried a small tape recorder and a notebook in one hand—a newspaper reporter, most likely.

Ryan's chocolate lab, Zoey, let out a low growl when he stepped onto the lawn.

The man glared at the animal. "What's wrong with your dog?"

"She doesn't like you," Ryan said.

"Well, hang onto her," he snapped. "I came for breakfast, not to get attacked by some redneck's dog."

Zoey growled again.

"The café doesn't open for another hour," Will said, his voice measured and calm, despite the anger building inside him.

The reporter flashed him a smile. "I think I'll sit on the steps until it opens. I heard this place has the best sweet rolls in Maryland. Don't want to miss the first batch out of the oven."

Will stepped into his path.

The reporter's smile faded. "Look, man. I don't know who the hell you are, but this is a public restaurant and I have just as much of a right to be here as you do."

Will's hand shot out, grabbing the recording device from the man's hand before he had a chance to blink. Will snapped it in half, letting the pieces fall onto the lawn.

Before the man had a chance to say anything, the blonde jogged across the lawn, stepping between them. "Sir, excuse me. Hi." She smiled, batting her eyelashes up at him. "I'm Miranda. I'm with Channel Six News out of Baltimore. My producer is willing to pay a very competitive rate for an exclusive interview with Annie and Taylor."

She laid her hand on Will's arm, giving it a flirtatious squeeze in case he hadn't gotten the message. "If you'd just come back over to the van and let me discuss the terms, I think you'd be more than satisfied with the arrangement."

Will looked down at where her fingers rested on his arm.

The blond helmet quivered as she quickly pulled her hand back.

The other reporter grabbed what was left of his recording

device off the grass, narrowing his eyes at Will. "You'll be getting a bill for this."

Will barely looked at him. "I wouldn't hold your breath waiting for a check."

The man walked away and Will looked back at the woman. He didn't smile. He didn't say anything. He just continued to stare at her overly made up face until she huffed out a breath and stepped back.

Frustrated that he hadn't fallen for her feminine charms, she tugged on the hem of her blazer, pulling the top down a half an inch to expose what, under different circumstances, he might have considered an impressive display of cleavage.

"Is that how you get your stories?" Will asked, his gaze flicking down, then back up with complete disinterest. "Because, if it is, that's just sad."

Her smile vanished, her face flushing bright red. She started to turn, but her heel wobbled over a loose patch of dirt and she stumbled. "Gary," she said to her cameraman, as she tromped back across the yard. "I think we should go."

The man stepped out from behind his camera, which he'd set up on a tripod aimed toward the front door of the café. "Our producer really wants this clip."

Another car drove up the street from the opposite direction and pulled up to the curb outside the café. Della stepped out of the driver's seat, her arms loaded with containers of fresh baked pastries. She took one look at the gathering of people in the yard and her eyes widened. "What's going on here?"

The cameraman snapped her picture and Della staggered back, blinking against the bright flash.

Ryan walked over to her, taking the baked goods from her arms and holding her elbow to steady her until her vision came back.

Will crossed the yard slowly to where the cameraman stood.

He held out his hand. The cameraman started to protest, but when he looked up and caught the expression in Will's eyes, he simply handed his camera over.

Will unfastened the back, taking out the memory card and the battery, and pocketed them both. "Do you want to keep this camera?" he asked quietly, the threat unmistakable in his voice.

"It's against the law to assault a reporter," the man said, but his voice shook and he took a step back.

"I said," Will repeated slowly, "do you want to keep this camera?"

"Yes," the man squeaked.

"Then I suggest, you leave."

The man snatched the camera back and grabbed his tripod, dashing back across the street to where the female reporter was already waiting in the van. Within seconds, his door had slammed and they were driving away.

Della walked over to Will, her expression livid. Rubbing her eyes to get the spots out of her vision from the blinding flash, she blinked a few more times, then took the container of scones back from Ryan. "When did this start?"

"A few minutes ago." Ryan ran his hand over Zoey's sleek brown head when the dog walked over and nudged his leg with her nose. Looking out at the street as another flash of headlights came over the bridge, he shook his head. "Here comes another one."

Will reached into his aunt's container, taking an almond scone for himself and handing one to Ryan. "I hope you didn't have any plans today." Breaking off a corner of the pastry, he fed a bite to the dog. "I have a feeling we're going to be doing this for a while."

∽

SPRAYING up water from the still slick roads, Colin steered his truck around a fallen branch and took in the long stretches of corn and soybean fields through the windshield. Farmhouses and oak trees dotted the flat, rural landscape, and early morning sunlight filtered through the rows of crops, glistening green from last night's rain.

He was only a few miles away from Heron Island, but the two hour drive from Annapolis had done nothing to calm him down. As soon as Grace had told him last night that she was running the article without a quote from Annie, he knew his plan had backfired.

He had tried calling the café all evening, but Annie had refused to answer, and he didn't blame her. The press was having a field day at the notion of another public battle between Nick Foley and his ex-wife, and the real story—the one about Taylor and the other children potentially losing their school—had gotten buried in the frenzy.

He would have driven down the night before, as soon as the article had released online, but Will had already been on his way home by then. As soon as Colin had called his friend and filled him in on the news, Will had dropped everything and headed back to the island to be with his fiancée and future step-daughter, not only to make sure that they were okay, but to run interference if any reporters came to the café.

Will had been pissed at Colin, understandably, for not telling him right away. Colin knew now that that had been a mistake. He had wanted to take care of the situation, to fix it before anyone else found out. He hadn't wanted the islanders to know that he was responsible for those budget cuts, that he was the one who was responsible for shutting down their school.

Now that everyone knew the role he'd played, he wasn't sure where he stood anymore. His whole life he had felt like an outsider. He had never fit into his father's political world. He had been an afterthought to his mother as soon as she'd given birth to a child of her own blood. Even on the SEAL teams, when he'd finally found the family he'd never had before, he had unintentionally gravitated toward a specialty that had set him apart, that had isolated him behind the scope of a sniper rifle.

It shouldn't have surprised him that that was where he'd felt most natural—alone, separated, detached. Even if it hadn't been what he'd wanted. Even if all he'd ever wanted was to belong, to be accepted, to be recognized—not for some political role he could fill, not for his skill with a firearm, not for the way he'd looked in his uniform—but for who he was.

He had hoped, maybe foolishly, that Heron Island could be that place for him. But what if the islanders didn't see him the same way he saw them? What if they still saw him as an outsider?

What if they would always see him that way?

A thin grove of white pines blocked the sun, casting long shadows over the road. When he came out on the other side of the trees, the land narrowed and wetlands wove in and out of the freshly planted fields. A flash of bright orange caught the corner of his eye, and he glanced out the passenger side window, spotting a figure walking along the edge of the water. His first thought was that it was probably one of the farmers checking his crops, but when he took a closer look, he saw that it was a child wearing a backpack.

Glancing in the rear view mirror to see if there was a yellow bus lumbering down the long road to pick him up, he realized that he hadn't seen another vehicle on the road for several miles. It seemed odd that the kid was walking toward St. Michaels instead of Heron Island. If his family lived all the way out here, wouldn't he go to school on the island? And shouldn't he be heading that way fairly soon?

Slowing the truck, Colin scanned the fields for a home that could belong to the kid's family, but the only farmhouse he could see was on the opposite side of the road. Trusting his gut instinct that there was something wrong with this picture, he veered onto a dirt road reserved for tractors and farm equipment. His truck rumbled over the deep grooves and ruts filled with rainwater. Mud sprayed up from the back tires and sunlight streamed through the rain soaked leaves of the sycamores bordering the fields.

When he was a few hundred feet away, the kid stopped abruptly and turned, meeting his eyes through the windshield. Colin got a good look at his face for the first time. The kid couldn't be more than seven or eight years old. He was wearing a fleece jacket that was a few sizes too big. His ripped jeans were splattered with mud and his blue eyes seemed vaguely familiar.

Colin rolled to a stop. "Hey," he said, leaning his arm out the window and keeping his tone light and friendly. "You need a ride somewhere?"

The kid shook his head.

Colin cut the engine and opened the door, stepping out of the truck. As far as this kid was concerned, he was probably no more than a stranger. He understood why he might be wary of getting in the car with him, but he wasn't going to let him wander off alone into the wilderness on a school day. If his parents hadn't realized he was missing yet, they would probably be worried sick when they did. "Where are you going?"

The kid started walking again. "Nowhere."

Colin closed the door and started after him. "What's your name?"

The kid said nothing. He simply adjusted the straps of his pack and continued to tromp through the muddy field toward the next line of trees where he would be able to disappear from sight for a while.

"My name's Colin Foley."

"I know who you are," the kid shot back.

Interesting, Colin thought, taking in the shaggy brown hair and the bright orange backpack that was crammed so tight that whatever was inside was straining the tattered seams. If this kid knew who he was, then he was probably from the island. "Where do you live?"

The kid jerked a thumb over his shoulder, pointing back toward the island.

Colin kept his steps light and soft, maintaining a comfortable, nonthreatening distance between them. "Shouldn't you be going to school soon?"

"I'm not going."

"Why not?"

The kid shrugged. "The school's closing anyway. What's the point?"

Colin let that sink in. "It might not close," he said after a few moments. "And even if it does, you'll still have to go to school somewhere, even if it's in a different town."

"Whatever."

Colin continued to follow him through the rows of soybeans. "What grade are you in?"

"Second."

Second, Colin thought. That meant he was in Becca's class. Looking down at the kid's shoes, he saw that they were soaking wet. The laces were untied, dragging behind him, tangled in mud-caked knots. From the look of things, he'd probably been walking for a few hours. How could have gotten so far from the island without anyone coming after him yet?

It wasn't like he'd been that hard to spot from the road.

"Don't you think your friends are going to wonder where you are when you don't show up at school today?" Colin asked.

The kid shrugged, picking up his pace.

"What about your parents?" Colin asked. "Don't you think they might be worried about you?"

"No."

"No?"

The kid shook his head.

"I doubt that," Colin murmured.

"Really?" The kid spun around, facing him for the first time since they'd left the dirt road. "I bet no one's even noticed I'm gone."

Colin stopped walking. If that was true, then they had a much bigger problem. "Why would you think that?"

The kid squeezed his hands into fists at his sides. "I know it."

Colin studied the kid's face again. There was definitely something familiar about his features, but he still couldn't place him. "Look," he said, switching tactics. "Maybe you're right, but how about I give your mother a quick call anyway, just to let her know you're safe?"

The kid shook his head. "My mom's at work."

"That's okay," Colin said, pulling out his phone. "Where does she work? I can look up the number."

"She can't take calls at work."

Colin paused. That seemed unlikely. "Does she have a cell phone?"

"She never remembers to charge it."

"Okay," Colin said slowly, "what about your dad?"

"My dad's dead."

Colin lowered the phone back to his side, the words hanging between them. He'd lost enough friends to know there was nothing anyone could say to make the grief feel better, so he just stood there, watching as the kid swiped at a tear.

A bluebird trilled from the branches of a flowering dogwood at the edge of the field as he tried to remember who had died recently on the island. When he recalled that Jimmy Faulkner's brother had lost a short and sudden battle to pancreatic cancer over the winter, he took a closer look at the kid. Yeah, that was why he looked so familiar. He must have seen him hanging around the inn from time to time when Jimmy was working. "Are you Luke Faulkner?"

The kid nodded.

"Is Jimmy Faulkner your uncle?"

He nodded again.

"I know Jimmy pretty well," Colin said. "I could give him a call. Maybe he could take the day off and you guys could hang out for a while."

Luke looked down, shaking his head.

"Why not?"

Luke jammed the toe of his sneaker into a row of soybeans. "He and my mom had a big fight last night."

"About what?"

Luke lifted a shoulder, like he didn't really care, but Colin knew he cared. He cared a lot—enough to run away because of whatever had been said during that fight. "There's this thing at school on Friday."

"What kind of thing?"

"We're supposed to bring a parent with us." Luke glanced up, then back down, embarrassed. "You know, like to spend the day with us."

"Your mom can't go?" Colin guessed.

Luke shook his head. "She has to work, so she asked Uncle Jimmy if he could go with me."

"What did he say?"

"He said, no."

Colin reached out, laying a hand on Luke's shoulder. "Hey," he said gently, "don't worry. We'll find someone to go with you."

Luke's gaze flickered back up. "Who?"

"I don't know yet, but trust me. We'll find someone." Colin squeezed his shoulder, frowning again when he felt how bony it was. Eyeing the bulging pack hanging off Luke's back, he nodded toward it. "Do you have any food in there?"

"I have a jar of peanut butter."

"Did you eat anything before you left the house this morning?"

Luke looked back down at his feet, lowering his voice. "I usually eat breakfast at school."

"What time do they serve breakfast?"

"Seven forty-five," Luke said, his voice barely above a whisper.

Colin checked his watch. "It's almost eight o'clock. If we leave now, we might still be able to catch it."

Luke looked back up at him hopefully.

"Come on," Colin said. He kept his tone upbeat to mask the anger building inside him. "I stopped at a fast food restaurant on drive over. I might have a leftover hash brown in the car. It's probably cold, but—"

"I like hash browns."

Colin nodded toward where his truck was parked, and Luke followed him back across the field. They climbed into the cabin and Colin handed him the bag with the cold hash brown. By the time they got back to the main road, Luke had already wolfed it down. They drove in silence as Colin thought about the conversation he was going to have with Jimmy soon. It wasn't long before he could feel the kid's eyes on him.

He glanced over and Luke looked away quickly.

Gazing back at the road, Colin waited a few beats, then glanced back. The kid was staring at him again.

"What's up?" Colin asked.

Luke's gaze dropped to where he was fiddling with the fast food bag. "Is it true?"

"Is what true?"

The paper crunched and crinkled. "That you lost your leg."

Ah, Colin thought. The missing leg. Of course. Adults were usually too polite to ask, but most kids hadn't learned to mask their curiosity behind manners and propriety yet. The first time he'd seen a kid staring at his prosthesis with confusion and maybe even a little bit of fear, it had caught him off guard.

He was numb to it now. He'd gotten used to the way kids looked at him when he was wearing shorts. He respected their honesty. It was actually kind of refreshing that they didn't try to avoid it. He wished more people would ask him about it, would talk about it, would just get it out there in the open instead of sneaking glances when he wasn't looking.

"You want to see it?" Colin asked.

Luke nodded hesitantly.

Colin hiked up the bottom portion of his jeans, revealing the long metal pole that connected his prosthetic foot to the socket where his stump rested just below his left knee.

"Whoa," Luke said, his eyes widening.

Colin let the hem fall back down.

"Did that happen...in Afghanistan?" Luke asked, his voice filled with awe.

Colin nodded.

"How?"

"A grenade."

Luke lifted his gaze back to Colin's face. "Did it hurt?"

"It hurt like hell. I mean..." Colin cleared his throat, shifting in his seat. "It hurt *a lot*."

"Do you have to wear it all the time?"

"I take it off at night, and sometimes when I'm at home alone. I can get around pretty well on crutches." He slowed as they neared the drawbridge, waiting for a charter boat to pass through the channel and the light to turn green. "I have a different prosthesis for running. It's made of lightweight carbon fiber instead of steel."

"You can run...without a real leg?"

Colin nodded.

"How far?"

"I'm training for a marathon. I'm up to about fifteen miles now."

"Fifteen *miles*?" Luke stared up at him in awe. It was the same way kids used to stare at him when he was in his uniform, or when they found out he was a SEAL—back when he was whole. It had been a long time since a kid had looked up to him like that, like he was someone to be admired and respected.

"Can I see it?"

"What?" Colin asked.

"Your running leg?"

"I don't have it with me, but I can show you another time."

"That would be cool."

Cool? Colin looked back over at Luke, who was sitting up straight now, gazing out the windshield with an oddly pleased look on his face, almost like he was proud to be in the passenger seat, like he wasn't afraid or ashamed of anything anymore.

The light turned green and the truck rumbled over the wooden planks of the drawbridge, past The Tackle Box where a few islanders were gathered outside, chatting and filling up their cars with gas. He didn't see Jimmy anywhere. And no one looked particularly concerned, as they would have if they'd known a child was missing.

"I'm going to drop you off at school, and then swing by your uncle's house for some dry clothes," Colin said. "I'll bring them by later, okay?"

"Okay," Luke said.

Colin would have preferred to take the kid back to Jimmy's first, but he didn't want him to overhear their conversation. He was going to have a nice long chat with Luke's uncle, and he didn't want the kid around in case things got ugly, which they probably would.

They drove through the village, past the Wind Chime Café and the quaint cluster of homes, and pulled into the parking lot of the school. There were a few parents dropping their kids off, but it was still early so the lot was fairly empty. Turning off the engine, his gaze lingered for a moment on an unfamiliar black Acura idling in front of the entrance. It was an expensive model, far nicer than most of the cars the islanders drove, and seemed out of place.

Figuring it must belong to someone's out of town relative, he opened the door. Luke hopped out on the other side and they were about to start across the lot to the school when both front doors of the Acura opened and a man and a woman stepped out. Colin paused when he spotted Becca.

Her back was to him, but he caught a glimpse of her profile when she turned and smiled at the man walking around the front of the car to say goodbye. He was dressed in a business suit and his polished shoes clicked over the pavement with each step. He was of average height and build with short brown hair and light eyes. It took a moment for it to register that it was the same man in the picture on her refrigerator—her fiancé.

Colin watched as Tom leaned down and Becca tilted her face up to meet his, so naturally it was obvious she'd been doing it all her life. The kiss was brief, chaste even, but the sight of it had his heart twisting painfully in his chest.

"Keegan!" Luke shouted, shouldering his backpack when he spotted one of his friends. "Wait up."

Colin tore his gaze from the pair at the entrance, looking back down at Luke.

"Thanks, Mr. Foley," Luke said, already jogging across the lot to meet up with his friend. "I'll see you later."

Colin said nothing, not even noticing when someone new

walked up beside him. He felt a soft hand touch his arm and he glanced down with a start. Della Dozier's blue eyes met his.

"Della." He cleared his throat. "Hey."

"Hey, Colin." She gave his arm a gentle squeeze. "You know that conversation you wanted to have over dinner tonight?"

He nodded.

"I think we should have it now."

TEN

"H ere." Della pried the top off a metal tin and held it out to Colin. "I baked these for the teachers to make them feel better, but I think you might need them more."

"Thanks," Colin said dryly, but it didn't stop him from selecting a large lemon bar from the tin and biting into it. The rich, buttery crust was almost enough to make him forget what he'd just seen outside the school—almost.

Before walking over to sit on one of the benches at the marina across the street, they had gone into the front office to talk to Shelley about Luke. The principal had arranged for the receptionist to retrieve a set of dry clothes from his mother's house, and promised they would find a stand in for Friday if Jimmy couldn't be bothered to show up.

Colin was fairly certain Jimmy would show up after he'd finished with him later, but that could wait until he'd heard what Della had to say.

A seagull cawed, circling overhead, most likely lured by the crumbs from the lemon bar that kept breaking off and falling onto the dock.

Della set the tin down on the bench between them. The scent of butter and sugar mingled with the salty air. "You know that no one on the island blames you about what's happening with the school."

He wasn't so sure about that.

"Becca told us how you tried to save it," Della said. "It's not your fault that your mother's still carrying a grudge against your father. It's unfortunate that we had to get caught in the crossfire, but this fight isn't over yet."

Colin looked out at the water. Most of the slips that the watermen rented were empty, but a few sailboats bobbed in the sheltered harbor. He could just make out the faint outline of a charter boat in the distance, probably filled with wealthy Western Shore businessmen hoping to land a record setting striped bass during trophy season. The quiet simplicity of it reminded him why he had decided to move here, why he had wanted to open the veterans' center here, why he had fallen in love with this place from the moment he'd set foot on it.

"Was that the first time you'd seen Tom?" Della asked.

Colin nodded, as a heron tiptoed out of the marshes, its long curved neck undulating with each silent step through the shallow water.

"He's not the one for her," Della said quietly.

Colin watched the blue heron pause, go impossibly still, then plunge its beak into the water and come back out with a wriggling perch. Silver scales flashed in the sunlight before the heron tilted back its elegant head and swallowed the fish whole. "How do you know?"

"He won't make her happy," Della said. "He never has."

Colin looked back over at the woman on the bench beside him. Della didn't like Tom either? If this many people close to Becca didn't think he was right for her, why were they all letting her go through with it? "If he doesn't make her happy, then why are they still together?"

A cloud of sadness passed over Della's eyes. "Because something happened a long time ago that Becca hasn't been able to let go of yet."

"What?"

Setting the top back on the tin, Della took a deep breath. "It has to do with their mothers."

Colin frowned. "Their mothers?"

Della nodded. "Becca's mother and Tom's mother were best friends. They grew up on the island together. They both taught at the elementary school. They both married their high school sweethearts. They both had their first child the same year.

"When Becca and Tom were little, their mothers used to joke all the time about them getting married. They used to dress them up and make them have pretend weddings and take lots of pictures. We all thought it was cute and harmless, and it probably was, at the time.

"As the kids got older, they grew apart. They hung out with different crowds at school. Tom was more interested in sports and partying. Becca preferred to spend most of her time sailing and fishing with Grace and Ryan. By the time they were both sixteen, Tom had made it clear to everyone that he couldn't wait to leave the island as soon as he could find a decent scholarship to a college as far away as possible. Becca would have been perfectly happy to stay here forever. And that might have been the end of any further connection between them, if it hadn't been for the night both of their mothers were killed, together, in the same car accident."

The lemon bar in Colin's stomach turned into a hard, heavy brick. He imagined Becca as a teenager, receiving that news, her whole world turned upside down in the blink of an eye. He knew what it felt like to lose people, to wonder why it had happened to them, and not you.

He thought back to the night in her kitchen, when he'd reached for the charm on her necklace, the flash of pain in her eyes when he'd asked her who she was mourning. It was all starting to make sense now—why she had become a teacher, why the school meant so much to her, why she was marrying a guy she'd met in high school, why that single charm was the only piece of jewelry she ever wore.

It was all because of her mother. A way to hold onto her memory, a way to never let her go.

"After the accident," Della went on, "things were...messy for Becca at home. Her father fell apart and she had to hold things together for both of them. We all tried to help, but she wouldn't accept it. She refused to talk about what happened to her mother. The only person she would talk to was Tom."

Jesus, Colin thought, rubbing a hand over his face. No wonder she couldn't let go of him.

"They have a bond," Della said, "something that forged them together a long time ago under terrible circumstances. They've both seen each other at their worst, at their weakest. That's when they fell in love. But they've both grown a lot since then. They've both changed, especially Tom."

Colin thought about the bonds that had formed between himself and his friends who'd lost teammates at war. He knew how strong those bonds could be, how important they could be as a way to deal with the anger, the grief, the pain. That was part of the reason he'd wanted to start the veterans' center—to bring people together again who'd been torn apart, to forge those same connections back home.

Colin looked back out at the water. "Maybe you're wrong. Maybe they do belong together."

"No," Della said firmly. "Becca belongs here—on Heron Island."

He wasn't so sure about that anymore, Colin thought. Now that he knew what was holding her to Tom, he understood why none of her friends had tried to intervene. Maybe it would be best if he backed off, if he simply let her go.

"Colin." Della's blue eyes lifted, meeting his. "I'm going to say the same thing I said to Annie about Will six months ago. Becca belongs here. All she needs is a reason to stay."

ALL SHE NEEDS IS *a reason to stay?*

Walking away from Magnolia Harbor, Colin thought about what Della had said. Yes, he was interested in Becca. Yes, he wanted to explore where things might go between them. But he wasn't about to break up a fifteen-year relationship between two people who'd obviously been through a lot together, just so he could see where things might go.

Della had said that Tom had never made Becca happy, but who really knew what went on in any relationship besides the two people who were in it? So what if none of Becca's friends liked Tom? It was her life. She was smart enough to make her own decisions. And she'd been planning to marry this guy for years.

Turning on to the street where Jimmy Faulkner lived, he jammed his hands into his pockets. He had let himself get caught up in his feelings for Becca because she was the first woman he had thought about wanting something serious with since his fiancée. He had actually been stupid enough to start thinking about things like marriage and family and children, things he hadn't allowed himself to think about in a long time.

He should have known better. It was safer to stay single, to keep his relationships light and simple and meaningless. As long as he felt nothing for the women he went out with, he wouldn't ever have to risk another rejection.

Walking up the path to Jimmy's gray shingled bungalow, he stepped over a broken clay pot that had probably once held a plant, but was filled now with moldy soil and water. Even if Becca did call off the wedding, and they dated for a while, she might eventually realize, like his fiancée had, that he wasn't enough for her. That she didn't want to spend the rest of her life with a man who wasn't whole.

It was time to let her go and refocus on the mission at hand. He would have a quick chat with Jimmy about Luke, check in with the crew at the inn to make sure they were on track to finish in two weeks, stop by the café and apologize to Annie, then head back to Annapolis to help his father with the speech for the announcement about the jobs program tomorrow.

He climbed the steps to the door and knocked. When no one answered, he noted that the shades were still drawn in all the windows. He tried the handle. It turned easily and he let himself in.

"Jimmy?" he called, stepping into the dark living room.

The stench of whiskey and cigarette smoke greeted him, along with a disgruntled groan from the man passed out on the couch in front of the television. Jimmy didn't even bother to get up. He continued to lie there, his baseball cap pulled down low over his eyes, blocking out the rest of the world.

Colin stood in the doorway, taking in the cigarette butts and ashes scattered over the floor, the dirty dishes crusted with food piled on every flat surface, the empty bottles of bourbon over-flowing from the trashcan.

"Get up," he said, his voice low and filled with warning.

"Go away," Jimmy mumbled through the brim of his cap.

"Get up," Colin repeated, slower this time.

Jimmy ignored him, shifting a little on the cushions to get more comfortable.

Colin crossed the room, reached down, and hauled the contractor up to his feet. "I said, *get up.*"

Jimmy blinked up at him, bleary eyed and barely coherent. "What the hell, man?"

Colin shoved him, hard, against the wall. A frame fell and glass broke, shattering to the floor.

"Fuck, man!" Jimmy shuffled his bare feet to avoid stepping on the glass. "What's your problem?"

Colin took a step closer, towering over him. "What's *my* problem?"

A brief flicker of fear flashed through the contractor's blood-shot eyes and Jimmy lifted his hands in a sign of surrender. "I checked in with the crew at the inn over an hour ago. Everyone's there. Everything's on track."

"I didn't come here to talk about the inn." Colin reached around him and jerked the blinds open, flooding the room with sunlight.

Jimmy squeezed his eyes shut, a pained expression crossing his face before he opened them again, squinting up at Colin. "What did you come here to talk about?"

"Your nephew."

"Luke?" he asked, confused. He glanced around the room, as if he were looking for him, as if he might still be here.

"I found him walking along the road toward St. Michaels a half an hour ago," Colin told him.

Jimmy blinked. "What?"

"He was running away."

"That's ridiculous," Jimmy scoffed.

"He was right," Colin said, shaking his head at the man in front of him in disgust. "He said you wouldn't even notice."

"Christ," Jimmy said, scrubbing a hand over his puffy face. "I can't keep tabs on the kid all the time."

"He's your nephew. It's your responsibility to keep tabs on him when his mother's at work."

Jimmy narrowed his eyes. "How is this any of your business?"

Colin's hand shot out, grabbing the front of Jimmy's shirt. "It became my business as soon as I found him walking along the side of the road this morning." He pushed the contractor back against the wall, holding him there. "Don't you even want to know why he was running away?"

Jimmy said nothing.

"He overheard the fight last night, the one when you told his mother you wouldn't go to school with him on Friday."

"I'm not his father," Jimmy spat, struggling to get free.

"Maybe not," Colin said, continuing to hold him in place. "But you're the closest thing he's got right now."

"It's just a stupid school thing."

"You're going."

"I'm—"

Colin's hand twisted tighter into his shirt. "You're going," he repeated, and there was no mistaking the threat behind the words this time. "Do you understand me?"

That brief flicker of fear returned and Jimmy nodded, slightly.

"Good." Colin released his grip and lowered his arm back to his side.

"Jimmy?" a female voice said from the doorway.

Colin turned, taking in the wisp of a woman with dirty blond hair in her late thirties. Her blue eyes widened when she saw the glass on the floor.

"What's going on?" she asked.

"Nothing, sis," Jimmy said, stepping over the glass and digging through the blankets on the sofa for his cigarettes.

Sis, Colin thought, turning to face the woman in the door. Jimmy didn't have a sister, so this must be his sister-in-law, his brother's widow—Luke's mother.

"I just came from the school," she said. Her face was pale, her expression frazzled. She was wearing a bleach-stained T-shirt, loose fitting gray sweatpants tied with a string around her thin hips, and a pair of battered sneakers. She held a bucket filled with cleaning supplies in one hand. "Shelley said Luke ran away this morning."

Jimmy lit a cigarette and exhaled a long stream of smoke. "He's fine now." Without another word, he walked across the room and into the bathroom, shutting the door behind him.

Courtney stared at Colin from across the room. "Shelley said you found him."

Colin nodded.

"Thank you," she said.

"You're welcome."

She stepped into the house timidly, like she was a little afraid of him. She set down the bucket of cleaning supplies and started gathering up the empty bottles on the counters, dumping them into the already full trashcan.

He picked up the ashtray overflowing with butts on the coffee table and carried it over to the kitchen. She took it from his hand, stiffly. "Thank you," she said. "I'll take it from here. You've done enough."

His hand dropped back to his side, but he didn't leave. He stood by the door, watching her quick, efficient movements as she picked up bottles, carried dishes over to the sink, and folded the musty blankets on the sofa, like she'd done it a hundred times before.

"You're not helping," he said quietly.

Her gaze flickered up, then dropped back to the floor, where she was scooping up fallen ashes.

"You're not helping by cleaning up after him, by protecting him. You're enabling him."

"We're doing the best we can," she said tightly.

Colin watched her carry the dustpan of ashes over to the trash, then twist the bag up, lifting it out of the plastic bin, as if it weighed nothing. She wasn't a stranger to hard work, Colin realized. And she was too proud to ask for help. She probably thought if they kept moving forward, putting one foot in front of the other, they'd both make it through to the other side of their grief eventually.

He used to think that grief could be buried in hard work, that it didn't really have to be dealt with, that it didn't have to be faced head on.

He knew better now.

"How long has this been going on?" Colin asked.

She set the bag by the door, walking back into the kitchen to start on the dishes in the sink. "It's no big deal. He's been drinking a little more than normal since his brother passed away. It won't last forever."

"It's a big deal if he's numbing his grief in an entire bottle of whiskey every night."

She turned on the water, squeezing in a bit of soap. The dishes clinked together as she stacked them, one by one, into the sink. "We all deal with grief in different ways."

"Yeah," Colin said bitterly, thinking about all the former service men and women who were back in this country now, struggling to process what they'd seen during back-to-back deployments in two of the longest wars in U.S. history—many of them turning to alcohol when they couldn't find the support they needed in their communities.

"You're right," he said, turning to let himself out. "We all deal with grief in different ways. And this is the worst way."

ELEVEN

*B*ecca kept a close eye on Luke throughout the rest of the day. He didn't appear to be in any distress. If anything, he seemed oddly pleased with himself, which worried her. She didn't want him to think that running away was a good way to get attention. She knew he needed attention...desperately. But what if he had gotten hurt? Or lost?

Or picked up by a stranger who had no business giving a child a ride?

Standing at the window of her classroom while her students read the assignment she'd passed out a few minutes ago, she wondered for the hundredth time that day what would have happened if Colin hadn't spotted him from the road. How far would he have gotten? How long would it have taken them to find him?

Outside, the wind pushed at the swings on the playground, the metal chains creaking as they swayed back and forth. She wished Colin had come to her when he'd dropped Luke off at school that morning. She wished he had told her what had happened instead of going to Shelley.

Why hadn't he come to her?

It didn't make any sense.

The last time she'd seen him had been at her house two days ago. He'd been so intense, so interested in *her*. And now...what? He was avoiding her?

Wrapping her arms around her midsection, she tried to soothe the hollow, aching emptiness that had begun to grow inside her, as she'd lain awake last night next to Tom, unable to sleep. She needed time to think, to process, to try and make sense of everything that was happening.

But she didn't have time. She was supposed to be getting married in two and a half weeks. She was supposed to be delirious with happiness and excitement. Instead, she was beginning to wonder if she was about to make the biggest mistake of her life.

How had everything gotten so complicated?

Reaching out, she adjusted the cotton ball dangling from the tail of a construction paper bunny one of her second graders had made during their Easter party the week before. Sunlight slanted in the window, reflecting off the silver heart dangling from the charm bracelet around her wrist.

She wanted to like it. She wanted so badly to like the bracelet Tom had given her, the bracelet he'd been saving for their wedding night. But every time she looked at it, all she could think about was how heavy it felt, how big and thick the chain was around her small wrist, and how she wished more than anything that she could have her mother's bracelet back.

"Miss Haddaway?"

"Yes?" Becca turned away from the window, grateful for the distraction.

Audrey Morris pointed to a word on the handout in front of her. "What's this word?"

Becca walked over and knelt beside Audrey's desk. She glanced down at the word, 'escape' and lowered her voice so she wouldn't disturb the other fifteen students who were still reading. "Can you sound out the syllables for me?"

Audrey bit her lip, shaking her head.

"Okay," Becca said, covering the letters, 'es,' with her thumb so Audrey could only see the word 'cape'. "How about just the second syllable?"

"Cape," Audrey whispered, her eyes lighting up. "Like what Superman wears."

"That's right," Becca said, smiling and moving her thumb to reveal the rest of the word again. "Now, put the two together."

"Es-cape," Audrey said, slowly sounding out each syllable.

"Exactly." Becca nodded. "It means to get away or break free from something that's trapping you."

Audrey furrowed her brow, looking back down at the story. "Why would the kitty want to escape?"

That, Becca thought, was one of the questions she was planning to address with the class once everyone had finished reading the story. She had chosen this assignment specifically for Luke, hoping he might draw some lessons from it. Looking around the room, she saw that most of the kids were almost done writing down their answers to the questions on their worksheets. "Is everybody finished?"

When they all nodded and chorused, "yes," she pushed to her feet.

"Jennifer." Becca walked to the front of the room and called on an outgoing blonde in the front row. "What's this story about?"

"It's about a kitty that runs away from home," Jennifer answered confidently.

Becca nodded. "Why does the kitty run away?"

"Because its owner, Emily, left the door open by mistake."

Becca lifted her gaze to where a red-haired boy sat in the back. "Travis, what happened when Emily realized her cat was missing?"

Travis set down the pencil he'd been doodling with. "She tried to find it."

"Did it take a long time?"

Travis nodded.

"How long?"

"All day."

Becca walked down one of the rows, pausing beside the desk of a black-haired girl who sat by the wall of cubbies. "Where did she finally find it?"

"In a tree," Jill Showalter answered.

"Then what happened?"

"She had to call a fireman to come and rescue it."

"That's right." Becca looked back out at the rest of the class. "She had to call a fireman to bring a ladder and climb up the tree and carry the cat back down." Her gaze lingered on Luke, who was sketching a tree into the margin of the assignment. She felt a pinch of frustration, and briefly considered telling him to pay attention, then reconsidered. "So," she said, clasping her hands behind her back, "who can tell me what the moral of this story is?"

Travis raised his hand.

"Yes, Travis?"

"If your cat runs away, you should call a fireman."

Becca smiled and a few of the girls giggled. "I think there's a little more to it than that."

"You shouldn't leave your door open," another student guessed.

"That's closer," Becca said encouragingly, waiting for another hand to go up.

Taylor finally raised her hand.

"Yes, Taylor?"

"You should take care of your animals or they'll run away," she said.

Becca nodded. Yes, that was definitely part of the lesson she'd been hoping to impart on her students today. The other part was that running away could be dangerous and it could cause a lot of worry and stress for everyone who cared about you.

When Luke raised his hand, Becca glanced up, surprised. Maybe he had been paying attention. "Yes?" she said, as she walked back up to the front of the room and tried to appear casual, like she hadn't been waiting specifically to hear what he had to say. "What do you think the moral of the story is, Luke?"

Luke's plastic chair creaked as he shifted in his seat. "If no one takes care of you, you should run away and someone brave will rescue you."

Becca stopped walking, and fifteen pairs of eyes followed hers, swinging back around to stare at Luke.

Instead of shrinking in his seat, trying to disappear like he usually did whenever he had to answer a question in class, he sat up straight, looked her right in the eye, and beamed.

Tom Jacobson could feel a migraine coming on. Digging through his briefcase for a bottle of aspirin, he wondered how much longer he was going to have to wait for the client his partner had asked him to stay late to meet. He'd been called into the office in Baltimore that morning to work on a fraud case. It was close to 10PM now, and he still needed to stop by the D.C. office before he went home to pick up some files for court tomorrow.

He rubbed a hand over his eyes, which were starting to throb from spending the past three hours crosschecking one of the prosecution's key witnesses' phone records with her testimony from the week before. It was bullshit work that could have been done by any paralegal, but the staff had gone home hours ago, and he couldn't afford to make any more mistakes in front of the partners.

He'd lost a few cases recently. Easy cases. Cases he should have won. And he'd heard rumors that the firm was thinking of downsizing—cutting back on some of the practice areas they'd built up to diversify after the recession. As one of three fourth-year associates specializing in financial law and vying for partner this year, there was a good chance that he would be laid off if he didn't make the cut. Bailey, Stromwell, and Goldwater didn't waste time cultivating mediocre talent. They only wanted the best.

The phone in his pocket vibrated, and he pulled it out, blinking against the stars edging his peripheral vision as he checked the name on the screen. When he saw that it was Becca, he hit ignore. He didn't have the energy to deal with her right now.

The only reason he'd driven all the way out to the island to see her the night before was because he'd felt like he'd needed to do something to get things back on track between them. A few of his co-workers had mentioned recently that it looked better for a man to be married—to be settled down with a wife and a couple of kids—when it came time for the partners to make their final decision about which associates would become permanent members of the family at the firm.

He was only a couple of weeks away from checking that marriage box, but Becca had been so distant lately, he'd wanted to make sure she wasn't having second thoughts. He'd stopped by Tiffany's on the way out of the city to find a piece of jewelry to soften her up. He'd hardly been able to believe his luck when he'd seen the charm bracelet in the display case. Telling her that he'd been saving it for their wedding night had been the icing on the cake. Becca was far too sweet, far too trusting, to realize it had been a lie.

He wasn't sure what her problem was lately. She was usually so supportive, so understanding. But over the past few months, she'd been making comments about how she wished he didn't have to work such long hours, how she wished he could find time to drive out to the island on the weekends. He thought she knew what he'd signed up for, what they'd *both* signed up for. Yes, he was busy. Yes, he worked long hours. But that's what he had to do to work his way up in the firm. And he needed her by his side—attending the events they were invited to in the city, socializing with the right people, getting to know the part-ners' wives. Every decision they made, including how they spent their time on the weekends, reflected on his commitment to the firm.

He hadn't told her that his job was in danger. He knew she would try to talk him into working at one of the smaller firms on the Eastern Shore, so she wouldn't have to move so far away from her father. He couldn't let her think that was an option. She needed to let the island go so they could begin their lives together. Their future was in D.C.

When the elevator dinged—*finally*—he chomped down a few more aspirin and rose, making his way out to the reception area. He'd never personally met the woman who was coming in tonight, but the firm considered her one of their most valuable clients. If he could make her happy, it might make up for some of the other mistakes he'd made recently.

"Ms. Vanzant," he said, offering the woman his most charming smile and holding out his hand. "I'm Tom Jacobson. I understand you have a few questions about the paperwork for setting up your new LLC."

Lydia Vanzant took his hand, but she didn't return his smile. "Where's Richard?"

"Richard had to step out at the last minute for a family emergency." Actually, that was a lie. Richard Goldwater, one of their three name partners and original founders, had been systematically offloading his clients as his campaign had picked up steam. Six months ago, he had shocked everyone at the firm by throwing his hat into the race for governor.

No one had thought the defense attorney would stand a chance in the primaries, but his platform had gained momentum with help from an enthusiastic base of supporters and a campaign manager who had a reputation for transforming even the most unlikely candidates into frontrunners. Richard currently held a double-digit lead in the polls and there was no doubt in anyone's mind that he would soon be the chosen candidate for the party that would challenge Nick Foley in the general elections later this year.

"I'll reschedule," Lydia said coolly, turning to leave.

"Wait," Tom said, knowing it was his job to smooth out the ruffled feathers of any client who would have preferred to meet with a partner, especially one as important at Lydia Vanzant. "I work closely with Richard on all of his cases. He asked me to personally see that you were taken care of tonight. Can I get you a glass of water? Some tea?"

She looked back at him, sizing him up. "How old are you?"

"Thirty-two."

"You don't look thirty-two."

He smiled again, trying to put her at ease. "I have a young face."

Her light green eyes narrowed as they swept over his tailored suit, silk tie, and Italian leather shoes. "Where did you go to school?"

"Georgetown."

"Law school or undergrad?"

"Both."

She continued to study him. "How long have you been working here?"

"Four years. Richard recruited me right out of law school. He and my father are good friends." That wasn't exactly true either. Richard Goldwater had hired Tom's father to take him and his friends out fishing on his charter boat a few times over the years. Richard barely gave Tom the time of day. He probably got a good laugh out of the fact that he was employing the son of a fisherman.

A few more black spots swam into his vision, but the connection seemed to impress Lydia and she turned all the way back to face him now. "Are you from the area?" she asked.

"I grew up on the Eastern Shore."

"Where?"

"Heron Island."

Lydia paused, just for a beat. "Heron Island?"

He nodded.

"I take it you've been following the news?"

"Yes," he said. "And I'm on your side about the decision to close the school."

She regarded him with new interest. "You are?"

He nodded again. As far as he was concerned, the best thing that could happen was for the elementary school to shut down. Maybe, then, Becca could finally cut her ties to the island for good. He didn't know why she was holding on so hard to the past. He couldn't wait to escape the island when they'd been growing up. There was no way he could go back there now. *I would be like taking a giant step backwards, like admitting defeat.*

"Enrollment has been down for years," Tom said. "Fewer young people are staying on the island to raise children. It doesn't make sense to keep it open when the funds could be used to support the larger schools in the county. The elementary schools in Easton and St. Michaels have enough trouble paying competitive teacher salaries and retaining experienced tutors and aids. With the extra money, they could invest in their current staff and add more special needs programs."

"My thoughts exactly," she said, surprised.

Tom shrugged, as if he'd just rattled those ideas off the top of his head, when in fact, he'd done his research before she'd come in tonight. Lydia had been quoted in tons of articles over the years about her reasons for consolidations. A simple Google search over lunch had brought up dozens of hits.

As soon as he'd read Grace's article the day before, and had seen how bad it had made Nick Foley look, he'd known that his connection to Becca and the island could give Richard Goldwater an advantage over the current governor. The only reason he'd asked Becca to tell him everything that hadn't made its way into the article was to see if there was anything that Richard might be able to use for his campaign against the governor.

"Do you still have family on the island?" Lydia asked curiously.

"My fiancée still lives there, but she's moving as soon as we get married."

"Do you drive back and forth a lot?"

"Not really."

"Why not?"

Aside from the fact that he had nothing in common with anyone who lived there anymore, he couldn't stand the sight of the two small white crosses lining the side of the road at the blind curve a mile past St. Michaels. They brought back to many memories—memories he would prefer to forget. Particularly this time of year, when there was a fresh bouquet of flowers lying on the ground beside the crosses each week, flowers that only one person still bothered to put there.

"I guess I prefer to leave the past in the past," Tom said. "And, to be honest, I don't have much free time to do anything anymore. Everyone at the firm is pulling long hours to make sure Richard's clients are in good hands so he has time to focus on the campaign."

"Are you going to vote for him?"

"I'm a D.C. resident, so I can't," Tom said. "But I would if I could. Not just because he's my boss, but because I'd rather see anyone in the statehouse besides Nick Foley."

Lydia angled her head. "You're not a fan of the current governor?"

Tom shook his head.

"In that case..." Lydia smiled and nodded toward a small conference room off the side of the reception area. "Shall we?"

"Of course." Tom gestured for her to walk ahead of him into the private room. He closed the door behind them, even though there were only a handful of lawyers left on the floor.

He'd met with a few clients at night before, ones who didn't want anyone to see them coming into the building during normal business hours. He hadn't spotted anything in Lydia's LLC contract that would warrant an after hours meeting, but she was probably trying to keep a low profile after all the press she'd gotten over the past couple days.

Tom gestured for her to sit as he set two copies of the agreement on the table. "Was there anything in particular you'd like to go over, or should we run through each section from the beginning?"

Reaching into her purse, she pulled out an envelope and slid it across the table to him. "I didn't come here to talk about the LLC."

Tom paused, looking down at the envelope. Slowly lowering himself to the chair across from her, he picked it up and pulled out what looked like a large stack of financial statements from an organization he'd never heard of before. "What's this?"

"Accounting records from the charity I used to run with my ex-husband." Lydia sat back, folding her hands in her lap. "In the late nineties, we opened a school for young children in an impoverished region of the Dominican Republic. We were both Peace Corps volunteers there when we were in our twenties. We wanted to do something to give back, once we'd both gotten established in our careers." A ghost of a smile flitted across her face, then vanished. "It was a long time ago."

He glanced back down, searching for the date of the most recent statement. It was from five years ago, when she and the governor had still been married, when Nick Foley had been running for his first term. He flipped through the pages, and saw that she'd highlighted five different contributions of $10,000 each that had come into their account that year, all from a direct wire transfer tied to an account in the Cayman Islands. "Who are these transfers from?"

"Henry Cooper."

Tom glanced up, his eyes widening. Henry Cooper was the owner of the largest casino chain in Maryland. Anyone who had paid attention to local politics over the past few years knew that Nick Foley had passed new legislation allowing casinos to open all over the state, promising that the millions of dollars of new tax revenue would go to roads, social programs, and schools. He didn't know if the governor had made good on that promise, but there was a casino open in almost every county now. "Are you suggesting that the governor accepted donations to his personal charity in exchange for kickbacks?"

"I'm suggesting that Richard might want to look into it."

Tom reached back into the envelope, to see if there was anything else inside. His fingers met the sharp edges of a photograph and he slid it out, staring down at a glossy picture of the waterfront inn on Heron Island where he was supposed to get married in two and a half weeks. "What's this?"

"The governor is announcing a new jobs program for veterans tomorrow," Lydia said. "I bet, if you look closely enough, you'll find some similarities to what went on before."

TWELVE

S tanding on the lawn of the Maryland State House the next day, waiting for his father to deliver his speech, Colin couldn't help feeling a rush of pride. It had been a long time since he'd felt any real pride in his work. He wished the announcement about the jobs program didn't have to come so close on the heels of the news about the school closing, but maybe it would help the public understand that those budget cuts hadn't been for nothing.

In politics, there were always sacrifices, and while he didn't want to sacrifice the island school, there was a reason those funds had been moved around—to help veterans. As angry as he'd been at finding Jimmy Faulkner passed out in a drunken haze the day before, it had helped shift everything back into focus. Alcoholism was something a huge number of veterans struggled with in this country.

Late at night, when Colin lay in bed remembering the faces of his fallen teammates, it was the friends he'd lost back home whose faces haunted him the most. Death at war, as awful as it was, he could wrap his head around. But the guys who died back home, the ones who went over the edge when they returned to their families, their hometowns, the country that had asked them to serve in the first place, those were the ones who kept him up at night.

They should have been treated like heroes, not left to suffer in silence.

He had joined the SEALs straight out of college because he'd been a senior at Columbia University in 2001. He'd seen the Twin Towers go down in New York. He'd seen the devastation, the horror, the fear reflected in the faces of his fellow Americans, and he'd wanted revenge.

He'd gotten it—four tours of it—in dry, sandy places SEALs rarely deployed to before the War on Terror. He'd worked along-side Marines and Army platoons in Fallujah and Ramadi, fast roped into the mountains of Afghanistan in helicopters flown by both Navy and Special Operations Aviation Regiment pilots, ran ops with coalition forces from several European countries. Before the end of his second tour in Iraq, he had already begun to earn the reputation of being one of the SEALs deadliest snipers.

But it wasn't the number of kills or an addiction to the adrenaline rush that had him re-upping his contract year after year. For the first time in his life, he'd felt like he'd belonged to something, like he'd been part of something bigger than himself. As a SEAL, he'd had a purpose, not only to gather intelligence and take out key targets, but also to protect his fellow teammates—teammates who had been more of a family to him than his own ever had.

As the wars in Iraq and Afghanistan had dragged on, and the people back home had begun to question their reasons for still being over there, for him, it had always come down to the same thing—the guys on his team. As long as they were still there, as long as they were still fighting, he wanted to be with them.

When he'd returned from his final deployment in Afghanistan, so badly wounded that he was no longer able to serve on the teams that had become his family, the hardest part hadn't been the months of physical recovery. It had been coming to terms with the fact that he couldn't go back there, that he couldn't use his skills and his weapons and his years of training to protect his brothers.

That he wasn't ever going to be in the fight anymore.

Without that mission, that purpose anymore, he had floundered for months trying to figure out what to do with his life. He'd spent a lot of time at Walter Reed, talking to fellow wounded warriors—men and women who were dealing with injuries a hell of a lot worse than his. And the more people he'd talked to, the more he'd begun to realize that there was another fight going on back home.

A fight that was just as important.

Over two million post-9/11 veterans were back home now, struggling to figure out how to transfer the skills and values they'd learned in the military into a largely civilian workforce. Many of them had enlisted right out of high school. Many of them had served several back-to-back deployments. For many of them, it was the only life they'd ever known.

Which was why, as he stood shoulder-to-shoulder with the people he'd worked tirelessly with over the past six months to launch this jobs program, he felt for the first time, in a very long time, that he was finally doing something meaningful with his life again. Scanning the faces of the people who'd gathered on the lawn for the announcement, he spotted his friend, Nate Murphy, on the other side of the wall of reporters.

The former Marine owned the company they'd contracted to build and maintain the electronic database that would match Maryland veterans with openings in the private and public sector. Nate caught his eye and peeled off from the group of people he was standing with beside the magnolia tree. Rounding the mass of reporters, he walked over to where Colin stood.

Nate grinned, holding out his hand. "Congratulations."

"Thanks, man," Colin said, shaking his hand. "Any activity on the site yet?"

Nate nodded. "Close to a hundred people have signed up and the governor hasn't even started his speech yet."

"How's the website holding up."

"Like a dream." Nate reached into his pocket, pulling out the phone Colin had lent him a little while ago. "My head IT guy loaded the app onto your phone and tested out all the features. Everything's fully functional. We set you up as an admin for the site so you can enroll people when you meet them. All you need is their name and email address. As soon as you hit save, the program will send them a temporary password so they can complete the application when they get home."

Colin took the phone, scrolled through a few of the features, and once he was satisfied that everything was working properly, he slipped it into his pocket.

"How's everything going with the veterans' center?" Nate asked.

"Good," Colin said. "We're still on track to open on Memorial Day. You're coming down for the event, right?"

"I wouldn't miss it."

In a few weeks, he and Will would start working hands on with some of the wounded warriors who were struggling the most with the transition back to civilian life. He was counting on this new state program to open up all kinds of doors for them. "I'll be sending people your way, so you better be ready to hire."

Nate smiled. "I'll be ready."

A few cameras flashed their way—reporters who wanted to capture the shot of two men with combat muscles and war wounds looking with satisfaction on something they had accomplished together. He almost didn't notice when Glenn Davis walked down the steps, wearing a grim expression on his face.

His father's campaign manager moved quickly through the crowd to where the press secretary stood, chatting with several reporters. He whispered something in her ear, and the smile on her face vanished.

When the phone in his pocket buzzed, Colin pulled it out, frowning down at the breaking news alert.

"Hey, man," Nate murmured from beside him, his own phone in his hand. "You seeing this?"

Colin nodded slowly, staring down at the headline: *"Richard Goldwater Accuses Governor Foley of Corruption."*

He clicked on the link, which led him to an article with a video clip of the frontrunner for the party that would be running against his father in the fall holding a press conference at his campaign headquarters on the other side of town. The clip had posted only moments ago, timed to air right before his father's announcement.

He scanned the transcript under the video, his eyes widening as he read the words: "I have proof in my hands that Nick Foley has been accepting contributions to charities in exchange for making deals with big businesses all over this state. Earlier this week, he signed a new piece of legislation loosening gambling laws in exchange for a $40,000 donation from the owner of Cooper's Casinos to his son's wounded warrior charity."

Colin tore his eyes from the screen and looked up at the man striding toward the podium. His father's white smile flashed for the cameras. His deep voice boomed over the lawn as he began to deliver the opening lines of a speech that Colin had helped write.

"Holy shit," Nate breathed as the governor's press secretary walked quickly up to the podium, whispering something in his ear as the mass of reporters began cutting him off, shouting his name, and firing off a hundred questions at once.

~

"Damn it," Becca murmured, as she tried calling Colin for the fifth time that day and his voicemail picked up again. She'd heard the news about Richard Goldwater's accusation on her lunch break and she'd been trying to reach him ever since. She didn't believe it. Not for a second.

She had met Colin's father. She had shaken his hand. She had looked him in the eye. He might be a professional politician, trained to say whatever his constituents wanted to hear to get elected, but he wasn't a liar. And he wasn't corrupt.

Richard Goldwater's accusation was nothing more than a political stunt to sabotage the jobs program and to hurt both Colin and his father. And she had a feeling she knew exactly who was behind it.

Shoving her phone back in her purse, she walked out of the empty classroom and down the deserted hallway. She knew how much that program, and the veterans' center, meant to Colin. She knew how hard he had been working on both all winter.

If she was right, and Lydia was behind this, then it wasn't just about the school anymore. The school was only the beginning of her plot to take down the governor. She wasn't going to let the fate of the island, and the future of the children who lived here, get wrapped up in some petty game of revenge. They had to find a way to stop her.

Pushing out the double doors, the wind whipped the hair back from her face. Pink petals snapped off from the branches of the dogwood trees, raining down on the few cars that were left in the parking lot. She ducked her head against the salty gusts and crossed the lot, slipping into the driver's seat of her Corolla.

She sent Annie a quick text message, asking for Colin's address, then tossed the phone onto the passenger seat and backed out of the spot. A small voice in the back of her head warned that going to him now might be a mistake, that showing up on his doorstep when he wouldn't even answer her calls probably wasn't a wise decision. But she needed to see him. She needed to talk to him. She needed to make sure he was okay.

Two hours later, she found a parking spot in his neighborhood, a few blocks from his apartment, and stepped out of the car. The scent of fried fish and hops blew through the streets, riding the heavy winds that pushed at the wooden signs hanging from the eaves of some of the restaurants. An inky blue dusk was settling over the harbor and gas lamps flickered outside a few of the historic homes, casting a warm glow over the old brick and cobblestone streets.

She read the numbers on the houses, searching for the address that Annie had texted back to her. When she found the three-story brick row house, she climbed the steps and knocked on the door to the first floor apartment. Nerves fluttered in her belly as she realized she hadn't given much thought to what she would say. She heard footsteps coming toward her, and she stepped back, quickly running a hand through her windblown hair.

The door opened and, despite having two hours to prepare, the sight of him caught her completely off guard. He was wearing a gray T-shirt and mesh running shorts. His rugged, strong boned face glistened with sweat. The thick black hair that swept back from his forehead was damp with it, and from the looks of the dark V staining the thin cotton material clinging to the hard muscles of his chest and shoulders, he'd just gotten back from a run.

But it wasn't the hard, athletic body in the doorway that had her heart skipping a beat. It was the gleaming contraption suspended from the lower half of his left leg. Her gaze flickered down—she couldn't help it—past the washboard abs, narrow hips, and big powerful thighs to where his stump rested in a padded socket secured to a slim, high tech piece of curved metal.

It was the first time she'd ever seen him in shorts. The first time she'd ever seen the prosthesis.

She'd known it was there. She'd heard the story of how he'd lost his leg, but she'd never seen the physical proof of that injury. She'd never considered the reality of what Colin had been through, the shock and trauma of the actual event, the months of rehab and therapy that would have come afterwards, the effect it must have had on him both physically and physiologically.

Ever since she'd met him, he'd seemed cool and confident and completely at ease with himself and his situation. But it couldn't have been easy at first. It had to have been difficult for him, at least when he'd first come back.

"What are you doing here, Becca?" Colin asked, snapping her out of her thoughts.

Her gaze lifted, surprised by the cold, unfriendly tone of his voice. A wall of defense shielded the emotions in his eyes and she realized, to her horror, that she had been staring—that she hadn't said a word since he'd opened the door.

She didn't want him to think she was judging him, that she thought any less of him because of what she'd just seen. If anything, seeing him like this—exposed, vulnerable, wounded— made her feel more toward him. Made her feel like she was finally starting to understand him.

"I wanted to make sure you were okay," she said.

"I'm fine."

He wasn't fine, she thought. Just like he hadn't been fine the other night when he'd come to her house. "I heard what Richard Goldwater said about your father today, what he said about the veterans' center. I know you're not fine. That had to have hurt you."

A muscle on the side of his neck ticked, a tiny betrayal of the emotions he was hiding underneath the stony expression. He had probably gone for a run to try to get some of the frustration out, to clear his head. And now, here she was, forcing him to face it again.

But she wasn't leaving until she knew he was okay.

They were friends now.

Friends...

The word seemed strange, even to her, like it couldn't possibly apply to them. But if they weren't friends, what were they?

She lifted her chin. Whatever they were, she wouldn't let a friend off the hook on a night like tonight. And she wasn't letting him off either. "I know it's not true. I know it's a set up. Lydia's behind it, isn't she?"

He didn't confirm it or deny it. He just stood there, looking down at her, his hand still on the doorknob, waiting for her to leave.

"I wish you would tell me what happened between you and your mother," Becca said. "I might be able to help you."

"I don't need your help," he said and the words cut through her like a knife. Because that's what she did. She helped people. She couldn't stand seeing someone in need and not offering some kind of assistance or support.

But not everyone wanted help, did they? Colin was probably the last person who would admit that he needed it. As a SEAL, he had been the one who provided the help, the one who carried out the missions that were too dangerous for everyone else. SEALs were the ones who got the job done when no one else could, not the ones who called for backup.

She thought about everything he had done in the past year—launching the jobs program, setting up the veterans' center, stepping in for Will whenever Annie needed a hand with Taylor, offering to help save the elementary school. And it didn't stop there. When he'd found an eight-year-old boy wandering alone down the side of the road two days ago, he hadn't called someone else to deal with it. He had picked him up, brought him back to school, and became that little boy's hero in the space of less than an hour.

Maybe that was why she was so drawn to him. Maybe that was why she couldn't seem to shake him from her thoughts, no matter how hard she tried. If it was just attraction, she could have pushed him out by now. But it was more than that. She admired him. She respected him. And the more time she spent with him, the harder he became to resist.

The voice in the back of her head, the one that had warned her not to come in the first place, told her that it was time to go. That she should turn around, walk back to her car, get in, and drive away from this man as fast as possible. But she couldn't leave. Not yet. Not until he told her what was going on.

If Lydia was behind this, then they were in this together. He was going to accept her help, whether he liked it or not, even if she had to use another tactic. If offering help wouldn't get him to open up, then she would have to push him, make him angry, force him to fight with her.

"I would have thought," she said, her gaze dropping briefly to the sweat staining his T-shirt, then back up to his face, "that after what happened today, you would be working on trying to find a way to discredit your mother, not taking time off for a run."

The stony expression remained intact, but she caught the flicker of anger deep in his eyes, a tiny crack in the veneer.

"But maybe none of this really matters to you," she challenged.

"What are you talking about?" he asked tightly.

"You never wanted to work on your father's campaign," Becca said, angling her head. "Maybe you knew all along that he was corrupt, and you're just pissed off now because the truth came out and screwed up your precious veterans' center."

Colin's eyes flashed. "That's bullshit and you know it."

"Is it? Or have you been working in politics for long enough now that you can't even tell the difference between a truth and a lie?"

He turned, stalking back into the apartment and over to a table by the fireplace where a large stack of papers was piled beside a laptop and a few empty coffee cups. He grabbed a handful of papers off the table and held them up. "Do you know what these are?"

She shook her head, following him inside.

"Résumés," he said, still struggling to keep his emotions in check as he turned back to face her. "I get at least twenty-five a week from vets who need jobs. And you know what I do? I try to help them. Because it's the least I can do." His fingers curled around the papers, crumpling them. "You know what pissed me off the most today?"

She shook her head again.

"It wasn't finding out that my father might be corrupt. It wasn't hearing from three different donors that they were pulling their funding for the veterans' center. It was when that son of a bitch, Goldwater, called it a charity." He threw the papers against the wall, scattering them. "It's not a fucking charity!"

He grabbed another stack of papers off the table. "None of these guys are asking for a handout. They *want* to work. They *want* to be useful. They were willing to go to war—to lay down their lives for their country—and now they don't even have a way to feed their families."

He squeezed the papers, the muscles in his forearm flexing. "We have vets living on the street now. We have vets who are so messed up with PTSD they can't even leave their homes to try and find a job. We have vets who are so badly wounded they would rather put a gun in their mouth and pull the trigger than try to find someone who might hire them and give them a chance."

He wasn't angry with her for barging in on him like this, Becca realized, her heart going out to him. He was angry because Goldwater's accusation had undercut the importance of the program his father had been planning to announce today. He was angry because he knew the system was broken and no matter how hard he tried to fix it, he would never be able to save every man and woman who carried those scars of war. And, mostly, he was angry because in comparing his veterans' center to a charity, Richard Goldwater had reduced him and every other wounded warrior out there to nothing more than a charity case.

"Colin," she said softly, walking toward him.

His jaw was still clenched. The muscles of his shoulders and chest were coiled so tight, it looked like he could snap again at any moment. But beneath the anger, she could see the pain in his eyes—the pain of what he had been through, and the desperate need to protect others like him from ever feeling that helplessness, that hopelessness, that despair.

"Don't," he said, his voice hoarse with emotion when she reached up and laid a hand on his arm.

She could hear the warning in his voice, feel the low thrumming of blood through his skin, warm beneath of palm. "What?" she asked gently.

He looked away. "I don't need your sympathy."

No, she thought. He didn't. No one who spent five minutes with this man would think he needed an ounce of sympathy from anyone. But she couldn't stand the fact that what had happened today had hurt him, that it had added to his pain in any way.

Colin had gone from being a member of one of the most elite and respected fighting forces in the military—deploying to war zones, carrying out missions in the most dangerous places in the world, and spending every other waking moment training.

Now, instead of doing what he was trained to do, what he *wanted* to do, he was going to cocktail parties and fundraisers, dousing political fires for his father, and spending his free time reading résumés to help his fellow former service members find jobs.

"Do you miss it?" she asked softly.

"What?" he asked, still not looking at her.

"Being a SEAL?"

"Every day."

He said it so fast, so automatically, her heart broke for him. Reaching up slowly, she laid a hand on his cheek. "I think what you're doing now is amazing."

He looked at her then, and the emotions in his eyes took her breath away.

She was crossing a dangerous line, Becca thought. Maybe, somewhere, deep down, she knew she had already crossed it simply by coming here tonight. The wind raced through the street, snapping branches off the maple trees, tearing petals off the azaleas. She knew she should pull her hand back, but she couldn't do it. She couldn't stop touching him. Recklessly, she pressed up on her toes and brushed her lips over his.

It was only supposed to be a fleeting offer of comfort, while she stole a brief, selfish pleasure...to know what he tasted like. But there was nothing fleeting or comfortable in the way his mouth met hers—in a kiss so possessive, so demanding, there was nothing she could do but surrender to it.

She heard the sound of papers falling as his arms came around her, as she melted into him. His fingers curled into the back of her shirt, molding her closer. She kissed him back desperately, hungrily, pushing her hands into his hair, letting her fingers tangle in those thick black locks as she'd wanted to so badly for days now. His hands were everywhere, touching every surface of her.

She had never been kissed like this before. She had never felt anything like this before.

She didn't want it to stop.

Her blood hummed, pumping faster. She could feel his desire, the hard length of him pressing against her. There were too many clothes, too much material between them. She needed to feel him—all of him.

As if he'd read her mind, his hands dipped beneath the hem of her shirt, cruising up the front of her stomach, heating her flesh. When his calloused palm closed over her breast, a small sound escaped from deep in her throat.

Where had this been all her life? Where had he been?

Across the street, a clay pot tumbled off a neighbor's porch and cracked as it hit the brick sidewalk. A group of children dashed by, laughing as they raced toward the harbor. Somewhere, in the back of her mind, a small piece of reality clicked back into the place.

"Wait," she whispered. "Stop."

His eyes lifted, locking on hers. They were wild and hungry, filled with a sexual desire so raw and powerful, it nearly brought her to her knees.

"I can't do this," she whispered.

"Becca," he breathed, still holding her. His voice was thick with need, with longing for her. "Don't go."

"I have to," she said, as guilt settled its gray wings around her shoulders. What had she done? What was she thinking? "This was a mistake," she said, quickly untangling herself from his arms. "I'm sorry. I should never have come."

THIRTEEN

The sense of peace that usually swept over Colin whenever he crossed the four-mile bridge over the Chesapeake Bay to Maryland's Eastern Shore didn't come this time. Restless, edgy, and still pissed as hell about everything that had happened the day before, he cranked up the speakers, trying to lose himself in the music, but he couldn't shake the slow burning frustration that grew with every mile closer he came to Heron Island...and Becca.

He'd considered going after her at least a dozen times the night before, but he'd forced himself to wait, to sleep on it. Because he hadn't known what he would say when he saw her again. The truth was, he didn't want to *say* anything. He wanted to kiss her again. He wanted his mouth on hers. He wanted his hands on her body. He wanted to strip her clothes off and bury himself inside her as many times as it took until she promised never to run away again.

He knew, without a doubt, that he could have her. That if he got her alone again they *would* finish what they'd started. But he wanted her to come to him. He wanted her to end things with her fiancé first.

He didn't want to be a mistake she made and regretted afterwards.

After what Della had told him, he knew that calling off the wedding to Tom was not going to be an easy decision for her. He knew there was a chance that even if she was coming to realize that marrying Tom was a mistake, she might still go through with it because of the link they shared in their pasts.

He needed to find a way to convince her to stop living in the past, to start seeing her future in terms of what she wanted now, not what she might have wanted when she was sixteen. He wasn't sure how he was going to do that yet, but he would figure something out.

In the meantime, he needed to decide what to do about the veterans' center. If Goldwater's accusation was true, and his father had been doling out political favors in exchange for donations, then he and Will needed to start reaching out to the rest of their investors today to assure them that they'd had no idea what was happening.

Which was going to make them both look like a couple of complete idiots.

Passing a combine backing up traffic in the two right-hand lanes on Route 50, he gunned the engine. The donation they'd accepted from the casino owner several months ago had funded a large chunk of the renovations to the inn. If they were going to even think about giving that money back to cut ties with whatever corruption his father may or may not be involved in, they needed to find another influx of cash immediately.

When the Bluetooth connected to his speakers signaled an incoming call, he glanced down at the name lighting up the screen. *Glenn.* He was surprised it had taken his father's campaign manager this long to call. He punched a button on the wheel to answer. "Yeah."

"Where are you?" Glenn asked. "The press conference is in half an hour."

"I'm on my way to Heron Island."

"What?" Glenn's tone shifted from harried to panicked. "Why?"

"I need to take care of some things."

"We need you *here*, Colin. Your father needs you here. It's going to look really bad if you're not standing beside him when he responds to Goldwater's claim."

"I don't care how it looks."

There was a long pause on the other end of the line. "Colin," Glenn said, lowering his voice. "I know you're angry, but it's not true. None of it's true. Your father needs your support today."

"I'm not in a very supportive mood."

Glenn started to say something else, but Colin ended the call before he could finish his sentence. He'd already told his father to count him out for all future campaign events until this blew over. He'd spent the last six months playing the role of the perfect military hero son and it had backfired.

All he wanted now was to focus on the veterans' center.

He cranked the music back up and tried not to think about how much it bothered him that he didn't know whether or not his father was telling the truth. He usually had a pretty good read on people, but his father had been trained to twist words and narratives to appeal to the public, to say whatever people wanted to hear to get elected.

What would stop him from using that same technique on his son?

It was times like these when he longed the most for his former life on the teams. Things were so much easier overseas. Missions were clear. Goals were solid and tangible. Objectives were stated in black and white—*identify the targets, take them out, get the hell out of there.*

Back home, everything operated in shades of gray. And just when you thought you had a solid grip on the palette, a new shade would appear, throwing everything off balance again.

The highway split and he veered right, heading south along the peninsula toward the small coastal towns of Talbot County. He was meeting Will at the inn in half an hour. They'd already spoken over the phone to strategize the best way to deal with the fallout from the announcement, but his friend was headed back to the base in Virginia Beach today and he wanted to talk to him face-to-face before he left.

Besides, now that he knew their contractor was an alcoholic, he had zero faith in his ability to get the job done on time. At least one of them needed to be there to supervise the workers and make sure the renovations were still on track, despite the fact that they didn't know where the money was going to come from to pay them now.

Thirty minutes later, oyster shells crunched under his tires as he passed the hedge of flowering blackberry bushes and pulled into the circular driveway in front of the inn. Several work trucks were parked in the lot reserved for guests, and he could hear the whir of a power saw and the crack of hammers echoing over the water. Rolling to a stop beside Will's SUV, he watched his friend walk out the front door of the house to greet him.

Colin cut the engine and stepped out of the truck, pausing for a minute to let the circulation come back into his leg. "Hey."

"Hey," Will said, closing the distance between them.

Neither man smiled as they shook hands. Will's short brown hair was mussed, a beard covered his jaw, and his brown eyes looked tired and wary.

Colin eyed the long gash on his friend's left forearm. "What happened there?"

"I got into an argument with a cameraman who wanted to get a shot of Taylor coming out of school yesterday."

Colin felt a new wave of frustration. "Did he get the shot?"

"No," Will said. "But he's threatening to press charges now."

"Why?"

"He might have accidentally hit his head against the side of his news van and broken his nose afterwards."

Colin's lips twitched. He couldn't help it. He knew Will wasn't very happy with him at the moment, not only because he'd kept the news about the school from him, but because he was the one who'd talked him into leaving the teams to come back home and open the veterans' center. He couldn't have it falling apart before it even got off the ground. "I'm sorry, man. About everything."

Will shook his head. "I had no idea dealing with reporters would be as bad as some of the terrorists we've dealt with."

"Yeah," Colin said, shutting his car door. He'd dealt with reporters all his life. He'd left that world purposefully, choosing a branch of the military that was as far from the limelight as possible. When he'd gone to the recruiting office in NYC after 9/11, the most attractive part of the SEALs had been that they were the shadow warriors, the ones who got the job done under the cover of night, the ones who shied from the attention. He felt terrible for exposing his friends to this world—the world he had wanted so badly to leave behind.

"I need to hit the road soon," Will said, checking his watch, "but I wanted to get another look at the place before I left. See how much progress they'd made patching up the foundation."

"How's it look?" Colin asked, as they walked back toward the front door of the old farmhouse.

"I don't know," Will admitted. "It's a bigger job than I expected. Are you sure we're making the right decision to rush things like this? Maybe we ought to back off, give Jimmy's crew some time to catch any other mistakes and fix them now, before we open. Besides, after everything that happened yesterday, maybe it would be best if we let things cool off for a few weeks, see how the dust settles."

It wasn't an unreasonable suggestion, Colin thought, following him inside, past the stairwell, and into the living room, where a gaping hole in the wall beside the fireplace now offered a view out to the backyard. Two men were laying concrete in a trench that had been dug in the ground to grant them access to the base of the structure. He nodded to the two men, who he recognized as members of Jimmy's original crew. They nodded back, before going back to work.

Colin had kept a pretty close eye on the renovations over the winter, but he knew it was possible that Jimmy could have overlooked something if he'd spent most of the past few months in a drunken haze. But then he thought about their investors, the ones who hadn't pulled out since hearing the news yesterday, and all the people who were planning to fly out for the big showy patriotic opening on Memorial Day—most of the guys from their former team in San Diego, the wives of the two teammates they'd lost in Afghanistan last year, dozens of men and women he'd met at Walter Reed. "No," Colin said firmly. "That's not an option."

Will studied his friend's face for several moments, then motioned for Colin to follow him out the back door, and down the porch steps to the dock, where they could talk without being heard by the rest of the construction workers. "What are we going to do about the donation from the casino owner?"

"We need to give it back," Colin said.

"You're sure that's the right move?" Will asked. "Maybe we should wait it out, do a little digging into the situation on our own. If the money's not dirty, we don't have to give it back."

"It doesn't matter," Colin said, shaking his head. "As long as the rumor is out there, it can hurt us. We need to distance ourselves from it, make it clear that whether or not it's true, it has nothing to do with us."

"Where are we going to get the funds to replace it?"

"I don't know yet."

Will dipped his hands in his pockets, pausing when they got to the edge of the pier. The tide was high, only inches below the planks at their feet. "Are you sure what that guy's saying about your father is even true?"

"No," Colin admitted.

"Have you talked to him since the press conference?"

Colin nodded. "He's denying it."

"Do you believe him?"

Colin looked out at the water, where a red-tailed hawk soared overhead, gliding gracefully toward the tilted lighthouse a few miles offshore. "I don't know. I saw the bank statements Goldwaters' campaign leaked. My father's name is on them. It doesn't look good."

The clang of hammers behind them mingled with the peaceful sound of the water lapping at the pilings. "Annie thinks we should ask the Hadleys for the money."

"The Hadleys?" Colin glanced back at Will, surprised. He hadn't even considered asking the Hadleys. Taylor's grandparents on her father's side had only found out about her existence last fall when their good for nothing son had tried to come back into Annie's life and had almost succeeded in splitting Will and Annie up for good.

The Hadleys owned one of the biggest hotel chains in the U.S. and, last fall, Lance Hadley, Taylor's grandfather, had had his sights set on buying Will's grandparents' inn. Will had almost sold it to him, before he'd realized that Lance was planning to tear down the house and turn the property into a resort as soon as the deed had been transferred into his company's name.

Will's decision to come home and start the veterans' center

had saved the inn from that fate. But Colin didn't like the idea of having the same man who'd once been interested in buying the inn for his own company suddenly becoming one of their top investors. What if Lance had a different idea for the place or wanted to have more control over the operations and tried to exercise that power as soon as he had a financial stake in it? "How do you feel about that?"

"I don't feel comfortable asking him for money," Will said.

He wouldn't either, Colin thought, if he were in Will's shoes. But if they couldn't find anyone else to offer it up, they might not have a choice. "How did he take the news about the school?"

"Not good," Will said. "He called each of the board members at home as soon as Annie told him what was happening and offered to fund the school himself to keep it open."

"What did they say?"

"They said the district would be happy to accept a donation, but private funds aren't allowed to pay for regular operating expenses—books, day to day upkeep, teacher and staff salaries."

Colin shook his head, feeling even more frustrated.

"Lance is pissed," Will went on. "We all are. But the board's arguing that if he wants to invest in his granddaughter's future, he should support the elementary school in St. Michaels, rather than pour funds into a school that's just going to shut down eventually anyway."

In the distance, a sailboat cut through the open Bay, its tall silver mast glittering in the sunlight. The winds from the night before had calmed down, and the sky was dotted with puffy white clouds. Under different circumstances, Colin would have been happy to hang out here all day, soaking up the view. Instead, all he could think about was how it was his fault that his friends were in this mess. "How's Taylor doing?"

"She's pretty shaken up," Will said. "Riley's gone to school with her every day this week. The dog won't leave her side, which means that even if she's pretending everything's fine, it's not." He checked his watch again. "I wish I didn't have to leave her. Or Annie. But I should hit the road soon. We've got a team deploying tonight and I need to be there to help them get ready."

That was why he looked so ragged, Colin thought. It wasn't just the news about the school and the veterans' center. It was that he had to leave Annie and Taylor in a time of need. Annie and Will weren't legally married yet, but anyone who saw the three of them together knew that they were already a family.

He felt a twinge of envy for that bond, that closeness. *I want that*, he thought, then clamped down on the feeling. He had more important things to worry about right now. Turning, he walked with Will back to where their cars were parked. "I'm going to keep making calls today, see if I can round up some more donors. I'll let you know as soon as I hear something."

Will nodded. "I'll call the rest of the people on the list you sent yesterday, make sure they know that there's nothing to worry about, that we're still planning to open by Memorial Day."

Colin looked at the gaping hole in the exterior of the inn, hoping he wasn't making a mistake by not considering Will's idea of pushing back the opening, of waiting to see how the dust settled. But he couldn't do it. He couldn't sacrifice everything they'd worked so hard for. It would be like admitting defeat.

"Ryan said he'd keep an eye on the café for the next few days," Will said, as they rounded the side of the house. "Could you keep an eye on the school? I think most of the reporters have gotten the message by now, but you never know."

"Of course," Colin said. He would be happy to give any reporters who came to capture the story about Taylor a similar welcome to the one Will had given the cameraman who was threatening to press charges now.

Will stopped outside the door to his black SUV, pausing for a moment to look back at the inn. He was quiet for several moments, as if deciding whether or not to say what was on his mind. "Look, man," he said finally, "I know things are crazy right now, but I've been talking to a lot of people about what we're doing. They want to get involved, maybe start something similar in their own hometowns when they get out. I've heard from at least a half a dozen former team guys in the area who are working with troubled vets at shooting ranges, and they want to do more. I've gotten a few calls lately, asking if I could sit down with them, talk them through some of the steps of opening a nonprofit. I told them they should talk to you, since you've done most of the legwork to get this place up and running."

"Sure," Colin said, wondering why Will seemed hesitant to tell him this. He'd talk to anyone who wanted to start a program for vets and wanted to know how to get started. "Tell them to give me a call."

The whir of a power drill cut through the silence, and Will continued to stand there, not reaching for the handle of the car door. "Do you remember a guy named Austin Turner?"

Colin nodded. Everyone knew Austin Turner. He was a legend in the special operations community. He'd been a SEAL for over twenty years, retiring as a Master Chief Petty Officer from Team Six, the exclusive counterterrorism unit out of Virginia Beach, about five years ago. He had moved to L.A. afterwards, and opened a private security company, and made a ton of money by offering his services to high-profile celebrities who needed protection.

"He recently purchased a ranch in Colorado," Will said. "He's thinking about doing something similar to what we're doing, but on a much larger scale."

"Oh, yeah?"

Will nodded. "He called the other day, said he'd heard about what we were doing, offered to fly me out there and pay me an insane amount of money to give him some tips on how to get started. I told him if he wanted to pay someone for start up advice, it should be you."

"I'm sure I can tell him whatever he wants to know over the phone," Colin said, though the idea of meeting a legend like Austin Turner was very appealing. "I doubt he needs my advice anyway."

"Actually," Will said, "after I told him about you and everything you'd been doing over the past six months, he wanted to know if you'd be willing to come out there for a while, help him set the place up, organize the funding. He wants someone on the ground to run things so he can keep working in L.A., and only has to check in from time to time. I said you were taken, but it's up to you, man. If Austin's program is a success, he wants to open more places like it, all over the country. That's a hell of an opportunity. You've done an amazing job here—raising money, hiring everyone, overseeing the renovations, organizing the programs, building our network for businesses willing to hire vets. But you don't need to be here to run this place once we get it off the ground. You've already done all the heavy lifting. I can take it from here, if you want."

I can take it from here? The words rang in Colin's ears.

"Assuming we can find the money to replace what we have to give back to Henry Cooper, and we can convince the rest of our early donors that we didn't know anything about your father's alleged agreement with him," Will continued, "we'll be good to go."

Another drill screamed to life, closer this time. It felt like it was inches from Colin's ears. *Good to go?* What was Will saying? That he didn't want to work with him anymore? That he wasn't needed here?

Holy shit, Colin thought as the realization dawned. Maybe Will thought he was a liability now. Maybe he was trying to get rid of him by offering an opportunity that was practically impossible to refuse. He kept his body perfectly still, his expression carefully neutral, as his mind jumped to a dozen different conclusions all at once.

Yes, it would be amazing to work with Austin Turner. Not only because he had a huge amount of respect for the guy—every SEAL did—but with Austin's access to celebrities, they could tap into a network of funding that would put his current network to shame, *and* that money wouldn't be tainted by politics. The idea of opening private centers like this all over the country would be a dream come true. He thought about all the veterans he could help, all the men and women who would get a second chance when they needed it most.

He thought about the pride he had felt standing with Nate Murphy and the rest of his team the day before, when they'd been waiting for his father to walk out of the State House and announce the jobs program they had created, how good it had felt knowing they'd done something to help the people who had fought beside them overseas. There was no question in his mind that that was what he wanted to spend the rest of his life doing.

But taking Austin's offer would mean leaving. Leaving the island, leaving this place where he wanted to put down roots, where he wanted to have a home and start a family one day. But what if that was just him being selfish? He thought about what Becca had said that first night in Annapolis, when she'd said she'd assumed the inn was just a stepping-stone for him, the first of many projects he would launch for veterans in the future. Maybe she was right. Maybe it was just a stepping-stone.

It wouldn't be the only thing she'd been right about lately. He hadn't given her an answer the night before, when she'd asked if his mother was behind Richard Goldwater sabotaging his father's announcement, but he knew, without a doubt, regardless of whether or not his father was guilty, that there was only one person who could have tipped the other party off to that information—his mother.

And if his mother was behind everything that had happened yesterday, it was possible she wasn't just coming after his father anymore; she was coming after him now, too. She might be targeting this island simply because he had decided to move here, to settle here, to build a life here. She had already gone after the elementary school. Now she was going after the veterans' center. What would she go after next?

If he took himself off this island, out of this partnership with Will, maybe she would stop coming after his friends. She would still try to go after his father, but she could find other ways to do it. And his father could handle himself.

Looking up as a bald eagle soared over the pines that bordered the marshes, he thought about Annie and Will and Taylor and Becca and everyone on this island who would be affected if these two businesses failed. Maybe it would be best for everyone if he left.

Taking a deep breath, he looked back at Will. "I need some time to think about it."

Will nodded, opening the door to his SUV. "I figured you'd say that." He climbed into the driver's seat, closed the door, and rolled down the window. Leaning his arm out, he added, "I imagine you'll be hearing from Austin pretty soon though, and heads up, he can be pretty convincing."

Colin nodded. He didn't doubt it. However, he didn't think he'd need much convincing at this point anyway.

Will started the engine and glanced down at his phone to check his messages before putting the SUV into gear. When he paused, frowning down at a message on the screen, Colin assumed it was another donor pulling their funding.

"Who is it?" he asked.

"It's Annie," Will said, typing a message back and slipping

his phone back into his pocket. "There's this thing at the school today—all the kids are supposed to bring a parent with them. Annie's there now with Taylor and I guess there's a kid in her class who's been having some trouble at home lately."

"Luke?" Colin asked.

"Yeah," Will said, surprised. "Right, the kid you picked up on the road the other day. I heard about that. Anyway, Jimmy was supposed to go in place of his mom, but no one can find him. She wants me to try and track him down before I head back to Virginia Beach." He checked the clock on the dashboard. "I can probably spare about fifteen minutes. You want to come?"

Colin was tempted. But he knew what Will would find if he was able to track down Jimmy in the next fifteen minutes. Their contractor would be in no shape to spend the day at school with a bunch of eight-year-olds. As much as he wanted to find Jimmy himself and knock some sense into him, he couldn't stand the thought of Luke being the only kid at school who didn't have anyone to spend the day with him.

He remembered the look on Luke's face when he'd found him running away the other day, when the kid had said no one would even notice he was gone. He remembered the promise he'd made, that he would find someone to fill Jimmy's shoes. When he'd dropped Luke off and told Shelley what had happened, she'd said they would arrange for a back up. But what if they'd forgotten, or the other person had fallen through?

"You go ahead," Colin said, already walking back to his own truck. "There's something else I need to do."

FOURTEEN

She was going to kill Jimmy Faulkner, Becca thought, slipping out of the classroom filled with parents and students and jogging down the hallway to greet her father as he made his way across the parking lot from the marina. "I'm so sorry," she said, holding the door open for him. "Courtney left a message on my phone last night promising that Jimmy was going to be here today."

"It's okay." Her father's deep voice reverberated off the lockers as the heavy glass doors swung shut behind them. "I thought I might hear from you so I stayed close to shore."

He was still dressed in his waterman's clothes. A salt-and-sun-bleached baseball cap shaded his brown eyes and scruffy gray beard. He wore a white T-shirt over faded khakis, and his beat-up sneakers left a trail of mud on the tiles as they walked back to the classroom. He smelled like the Bay and gasoline, and she'd never been more relieved to see him.

When she'd told him about Luke running away on Tuesday because he didn't have anyone to bring to the event at school this week, he'd offered to fill in at the last minute if no one else stepped up to the plate. She was incredibly grateful he was here, but she knew it wasn't easy for him to miss a day of work for this.

"How's he doing?" her father asked, lowering his voice when they neared the door to the classroom.

"He's upset," Becca said, pulling her phone out to see if she'd gotten a message back from Jimmy yet. Nothing. She shoved the phone back in her pocket, frustrated. "Luke's the only one who didn't have a parent show up today."

They paused in the doorway, looking across the crowded room at where Luke sat at a table in the back with a few other students and parents. The hood of his sweatshirt was flipped up over his face, hiding it from view. He was slumped down in his seat, sketching in his notebook and trying to make himself as invisible as possible. The sight of the empty chair beside him was enough to make her blood boil all over again.

"If I find him at Rusty's later—" Becca began.

"Hey," her father murmured, concern knitting his brow. "I know you're angry, but I think you should steer clear of Jimmy for a few days."

Becca frowned. "Why?"

"I don't think he's in a good place right now."

Of course he wasn't, Becca thought, but that didn't mean he shouldn't have to answer for his actions.

"Why don't you let me talk to him this afternoon?" her father suggested. "Maybe I can convince him to come to a meeting with me later this week."

A meeting. Becca held his gaze. He meant an AA meeting. Even after all this time, her father still went to a meeting once a week. Not just to remind himself why he'd stopped drinking, but to show the newer members that it was possible to stay sober for over fifteen years.

She appreciated the offer, but she highly doubted that attending an AA meeting was going to cure Jimmy's drinking habit. And as far as staying out of it...? She didn't care that her father was the second person to warn her to be careful around Jimmy. There was no way she was letting Jimmy off the hook for this.

But she didn't have time to argue with him about it right now.

From the growing level of voices and conversations inside the classroom, it sounded like everyone was close to finishing the activity she'd left them with. "Okay," she said, nodding briefly to her father. "I'll steer clear, but only for a few days."

"Good," he said, giving her shoulder a squeeze.

Taking a deep breath, Becca stepped into the room filled with parents who'd taken the time out from their busy schedules to attend a day of school with their children. She knew it was a struggle for many of them to take a day off work, but by making that sacrifice, they sent a clear message to their children—that education was something to be valued and taken seriously. Every study showed that students whose parents became actively engaged in their school lives were more likely to succeed.

Many of the children in this room, especially the boys, would consider following in their fathers' footsteps when they graduated high school, by trying to make a living off the Bay. There was nothing wrong with that, but she knew how hard it had been for her father to make ends meet over the years. She wanted to make sure that every child in this room had the building blocks to succeed in case that path became impossible in their lives. With a solid education, they would have something to fall back on. They would have the basic knowledge and skills necessary to thrive in whatever profession they chose.

"All right, everyone," she said, raising her voice over the noise when she got to the front of the room. "Who wants to share their story?"

A few hands went up.

"Yes, Christine," she said, smiling down at a shy redhead at one of the front tables. "Why don't you start by reading us the sentence you picked from the jar? And speak up so everyone can hear you."

Christine held up the strip of paper she'd pulled from the glass jar that Becca had filled with prompts that morning. "There once was a jellyfish who befriended a crab."

A few kids giggled as Christine began to read the story her group had created from the prompt. Out of the corner of her eye, Becca watched her father slip into the empty chair beside Luke. She didn't want to make a big deal about the fact that he was here. It was fairly common for her father to drop by the school. Since the marina was directly across the street, he came in once or twice a week to check in on her or to visit with Shelley in the front office. The children were used to seeing him around.

A few of the parents waved when they spotted him, but most were too engrossed in the activity to notice. Good, she thought. She didn't want them to focus on anything but the activity. She wanted the transition to be seamless, and not draw attention to Luke in any way.

As Christine wrapped up her story, Becca saw her father lean over and say a few words to Luke. Luke stopped drawing, his gaze darting around the room to see if anyone was watching. Once he realized they weren't, he nodded in response to whatever her father had said, and then went back to sketching in his notebook. Becca felt a wave of relief when she saw him shift ever so slightly in his chair to move closer to her father.

Looking back at Christine as she finished her story, she smiled and said, "Very nice, Christine. Thank you." Everyone clapped and Becca looked around the room at the other groups. "Who's next?"

Robby Porter stood up from the table by the window. "We drew our story with pictures, instead of wrote it."

Becca smiled and walked over to the other side of the room to give the new group her undivided attention. She wasn't surprised Robby had decided to tell his story with pictures instead of words. A series of tests from a specialist earlier that year had concluded that he was dyslexic. She had been working with him after school on some of the longer reading assignments and he was making great progress. The fact that he had the confidence to lead the storytelling exercise today through pictures made her realize that he was starting to accept that not everyone was going to learn the same way and there was nothing wrong with that.

Feeling herself begin to relax for the first time that morning, Becca leaned a hip against the edge of her desk, listening to Robby as he launched into his story. This was exactly the kind of learning environment she'd worked hard to cultivate and nurture in her classroom. She wanted every one of her students to know that it was okay to think outside the box. Every child was different. Every child had different strengths and weaknesses and would learn what worked best for them. She was lucky to have such a small group of children to work with so she could shift her teaching methods depending on the needs of each class, and not always be stuck to the same curriculum.

She had chosen this activity specifically to begin the day with because it was interactive, and it would show the parents how important creativity could be, even when done fast. Making up stories was something they could do at home with their children, to keep them engaged, to keep their imaginations running wild. Learning didn't have to be all about tedious homework assignments and getting the highest test score. It could be fun, too.

More laughter broke out throughout the room as Robby regaled the class with a story about a fish that could sprout wings and fly to the moon and back when the tide was high. The accompanying illustrations were equally ridiculous, and the laughter grew louder as some of the kids started passing them around the room. Bob Hargrove blushed when his daughter made fun of the stick figure he'd drawn of a person pointing up at the sky from the end of a dock. "Hey," he said defensively, "I never said art was my thing."

Becca stole another glance at Luke. He had stopped sketching in his own notebook and was grinning down at one of Robby's drawings of a fish with huge wings, laughing with her father at how primitive it was.

"Look, Miss Haddaway," Audrey Morris said from a few chairs away as she held up the drawing she'd done. "It's a seahorse."

"That's wonderful, Audrey," Becca said, smiling. Beside Audrey, her mother, Rachel Morris, beamed with pride. The unexpected pang of envy came fast and hard, before Becca could stop it. She would never be sitting in this classroom with one of her own kids, Becca realized suddenly. She would never be sitting in any of these rooms, surrounded by her friends and neighbors, people she'd known her whole life, drawing pictures and making up stories about the world she'd grown up in.

I don't want to leave. The truth she had been trying so hard to push away for the past several weeks rose up, lodging in the back of her throat. She swallowed, hard, forcing it back. "Okay, everyone," she called, raising her voice over the swell of conversations. She needed to regain control, not just of the class, but of herself. This wasn't the time or the place to fall apart. "We still have a lot to do today, so why don't we move onto the next—"

A tall figure stepped into the doorway and she froze, every muscle in her body contracting when Colin's blue-eyed gaze met hers. What was he doing here? Her heart rate kicked into overdrive. Her palms began to sweat. The voices in the room faded to a quiet murmur as everyone turned to see what she was looking at.

Colin held her gaze for another long beat before breaking contact and scanning the faces in the room. When he spotted

Luke at a table in the back, he stepped through the doorway, cutting a clear path toward the child. Every pair of female eyes followed him as he crossed the room. Several of the men sat up straighter, sucking in their beer guts when he passed.

He wasn't the kind of man who could slip into a room unnoticed. Becca's fingers curled around the chipped wood at the edge of her desk. She hadn't seen him or spoken to him since the night before, when she'd gone to his apartment, when she'd kissed him. The memories swam back—his lips, warm and firm and hungry on hers. His hands, strong and calloused, cruising over her hips, her waist, her breasts. His voice, desperate and pleading, asking her to stay.

She looked quickly over at Luke, worried he wouldn't want the attention. But Luke's eyes were focused like lasers on Colin and it didn't appear that he seemed at all concerned that everyone else had gone completely quiet.

"Hey, buddy," Colin said easily, as if it were just the two of them in the room and close to thirty people weren't hanging on his every word. "Your uncle had to stay at the inn and work on something for me. I told him I'd stop by and see how you were doing."

It was a lie, Becca thought. Why would he come here and lie for Jimmy? Why would he cover for him this way? As far as she knew, Colin hadn't had any contact with Luke before the other day when he'd picked him up on the side of the road. He barely knew him.

Luke blinked, but he didn't hunch his shoulders or shy away from the attention. "I'm fine."

Colin gestured to the drawing of the flying fish. "What are you working on?"

Luke quickly passed the paper to another person at the table. "That's not mine."

Snagging a chair from the back of the room, Colin pulled it

up to the table. Nodding to the rest of the parents in the group, he sat down.

Luke stared at him. "You're...staying?"

Colin nodded.

Luke's eyes widened. "For how long?"

"As long as you want me to."

Luke's mouth fell open, stayed that way for a few beats, then broke into a wide grin. "Cool," he breathed, pushing the hood of his sweatshirt back from his face and scooting his chair closer to the table.

Beside him, Colin leaned back in his seat, folded his hands in his lap, and looked back at Becca, as if it were perfectly normal for him to offer to spend the day in a classroom with a child he barely knew.

Becca was aware, in some far off corner of her mind, that it was time for her to say something, to take charge of the room again. But her tongue felt thick, her mouth dry. She didn't trust herself to speak. Not yet.

How was she going to handle having him here, in her classroom, for the rest of the day?

She could barely be in the same room with Colin for five minutes without wanting to touch him, without wanting to be near him, without feeling—every time he looked at her—like her entire body was on fire. Tearing her eyes from his, she looked up at the clock in the back of the room, silently counting the hours left in the day.

The second hand ticked. A teacher's voice from a neighboring classroom drifted down the hall. Her gaze swept over the walls covered in student artwork, the wooden counter in the back overflowing with craft supplies, the bookshelves filled with worn paperbacks and hand-me-down textbooks, the cubbies painted bright rainbow colors.

Just as she had when he'd first come to her house, she imag-

ined how this room might look through his eyes—how this classroom, her mother's old classroom, a place that meant almost as
much to her as her own home, would look to him. Nerves
jumped, low in her belly, as if this were the first class she'd ever
taught, the first time she'd ever stood up in front of a room full of
parents and students.

Why did she care so much about what he thought?

When someone quietly cleared her throat in the front row,
she glanced down, jolted from her thoughts. Annie looked back at
her, watching her with a strange expression on her face. It was
the first time Annie had really looked at her in days, not since the
news about the school had come out.

Becca swallowed, looking away. Many of her friends were
watching her strangely now. When one woman lifted an
eyebrow, Becca felt a flush of color creep up her cheeks. Turning,
as several more brows went up, she glanced back at the day's
schedule printed in neat handwriting on the chalkboard. "Let's
move on," she said quickly, grabbing a math workbook from the
pile of books on her desk. "Everybody open to page fifteen."

"What about the next story?" a child in the front row asked.

Right, Becca thought, her heart fluttering in her throat. The
next story. They still had two more to go. She set the book back
down, her hands shaking as she wiped her damp palms over the
front of her skirt. How was she going to pull this off if she
couldn't get a hold of herself?

"Erica," she said, forcing herself to get a grip as she called on
one of the girls at the table in the back by the door. Her voice
sounded funny, far off, like she was speaking through a tunnel.
"Why don't you read us your story?"

Erica began to read the story, and Becca stole a glance at her
father. He was watching her closely, a worried look on his face.
She attempted a smile to put him at ease, but it felt forced, even
to her. She rested her hands on the back of her chair, trying to

regain her composure, letting a full minute pass before risking a glance back over at Colin.

When she did, she saw that his body was relaxed, his expression perfectly calm, but he was gazing back at her with the same heat and intensity as he had the night before. And she knew, without a doubt, that he hadn't taken his eyes off her since the moment he'd sat down.

She tried, fleetingly, to imagine that it was Tom in that chair, that it was Tom who had dropped everything to be here for Luke today, that it was Tom who had cleared his schedule to spend the day at the school.

But she knew he would never do that.

He would never dream of taking off a day of work to hang out with a kid he barely knew. He hadn't even been willing to take Easter Sunday off to spend the day with her and her father.

Colin held her gaze, as if it were just the two of them in the room, as if it had always been just the two of them.

She heard the faintest sound of silver charms clinking together—a delicate, familiar song drifting over the wind—and her heart simply turned over in her chest.

FIFTEEN

"We have a problem," Jenna Price said, walking into Tom's office in Baltimore and shutting the door.

Looking up from his computer, Tom eyed the firm's youngest investigator. Barely a year out of college, she had already managed to make a name for herself by uncovering valuable information on a number of cases that had led to several crucial verdicts coming out in their favor. Every lawyer at the firm fought over her time, not just because she was good at what she did, but because she was nice too look at, too.

"What's up?" he asked, reluctantly lifting his gaze from the perky breasts straining against her tight sweater. He'd earned a right to look a few months ago when they'd celebrated one of her first big wins by downing a bottle of champagne in his office and then screwing each other's brains out in the elevator on the way down to the parking garage.

"I did some digging into the claims Lydia made against Governor Foley, like you asked." Jenna sauntered up to his desk and dropped a manila envelope on it. "Turns out, our client was bending the truth a bit."

Tom frowned, reaching for the envelope. "What do you mean?"

Lowering herself to a chair across from him, she crossed her legs. Her short skirt rode up several inches, exposing a pair of long, toned thighs. Tom tried to focus on emptying the contents of the envelope but his gaze strayed helplessly back to her legs.

He knew what those legs felt like locked around his waist, what those breasts felt like pressed into his palms, what sounds she made when she came. They'd had a few more slip ups recently—two weeks ago in the copy room on the eleventh floor, a week ago in the supply closet down the hall, and the night before on the conference table in the boardroom after everyone else had left.

Who could blame him?

He had needs—needs a woman like Becca could never fulfill. It was unfortunate that Jenna was falling in love with him. He knew she was secretly hoping he'd leave his fiancé for her. But Jenna wasn't the kind of woman a man like him married. She was the kind of woman he had sex with before going home to a wife like Becca.

Tom forced his gaze back to the contents of the envelope, flipping through what looked to be a new set of financial statements and a collection of photographs of a man and a woman on a beach wrapped up in each other's arms. The woman in the photographs was obviously Lydia, about ten years younger, but he didn't recognize the man. "Who's that?"

"Henry Cooper."

Tom's eyes widened as all thoughts of a midday tryst with Jenna vanished. "What?"

"They were having an affair."

"But..." Tom struggled to wrap his head around it. "That doesn't make any sense."

"Actually, it makes perfect sense." Jenna leaned back in her chair. "Lydia said Henry invested in her charity in exchange for political favors once her husband got elected, but she never said *who* made those promises."

Tom looked back down at the photos. It did make sense. In a twisted way, it made perfect sense. With Henry's investment, Lydia would get the money she needed for her school in the Dominican Republic and, once her husband became governor, the Maryland school system she had worked in all her life would get a brand new stream of tax revenue that would flow in from the casinos.

A sinking feeling formed in his gut as he realized what he'd done. He'd handed this information to his boss to use publicly, against his opponent, before fact checking it. Richard had asked him specifically if he'd verified it, and he'd said that he had. But the truth was, he'd only done a quick Google search to make sure the school in the Dominican Republic existed, and as soon as he'd seen that it had, he'd simply assumed the rest was true.

If Richard found out about this, he'd lose his job. He looked back up at Jenna, racking his brain for a way to cover his ass. "Even if Lydia was the one who made the promises, the governor's still liable. His name was on the statements when the donations came into the account. He had to have known what was going on."

"Not necessarily. I managed to track down one of the original teachers at the school. She said Nick Foley never came down to the island, never even visited the school. It was entirely Lydia's project. Besides," she said, nodding to the rest of the papers in his hands. "He signed the entire account over to Lydia before the divorce, a year before he even announced he was running for governor. Any political favors he might have granted when he got into office would have gone to people who'd supported his campaign—not to a person who'd supported a charity that belonged to his ex-wife."

Tom's heart pounded as he flipped through the papers, desperate to find something that would excuse what he'd done. "So, what are you saying? That none of what Lydia said was true? What about the other contribution, the one Henry made to the veterans' center?"

"It took me about five minutes on the phone with his secretary to find out that the reason Henry Cooper invested in Colin Foley's wounded warrior charity was because his older brother was a Vietnam vet who lost both legs in the war." She gave him a long, measuring look. "Three months after he came home, he killed himself because he didn't want to spend the rest of his life in a wheelchair."

Tom gaped at her, his head spinning. Why would Lydia bring this information to them if it would fall apart so easily in an investigation? Why would she risk ruining her own reputation when the truth was exposed? "She must have known that we'd look into the claims, that we'd find out about the affair, the promises, Henry's brother...?"

"I think she was counting on Richard running with it before that, which is why she waited to bring it to us until the night before the announcement—so there wouldn't be enough time to do a thorough investigation. Besides," she said, nodding back to the pictures, "Lydia and Henry were very discreet. Those pictures weren't easy to track down. It'll take Nick Foley's investigators weeks to find them, if they even find them at all. In the meantime, enough voters will turn against him, will question his integrity as a leader. Even when the truth comes out, it'll seem like he's making excuses. It'll make him look weak."

Tom stared at her. "You think she's been sitting on this information all this time, just waiting to use it against her ex-husband when he ran for a second term?"

"Sure," Jenna lifted a shoulder. "Why not? What does she have to lose? My best guess would be that since she's not with either man now, things must have ended badly with Henry as well as with her ex-husband. Maybe she's angry with both men and has been waiting for the right time to get some payback. What?" she asked, when he continued to stare at her. "Women who are pushed too far can do some real damage if they're not treated right."

Tom's palms began to sweat. Was that a threat? Was she comparing her own situation to Lydia's? "Jenna—"

"I think she got what she wanted," Jenna said, standing. "Whether or not it was true, it's out there now. It hurt him."

"Wait," Tom said, scrambling to his feet. "Where are you going?"

"To tell Richard."

"No." He grabbed the evidence before she could reach for it. "Let me at least talk to Lydia first. Maybe she has an explanation."

Jenna looked at him like he'd lost his mind. "You have to be kidding."

He stuffed the papers and photos into a drawer and locked it. "She's one of our most important clients. She deserves the chance to explain herself first."

Jenna shook her head. "We need to tell Richard now. If he finds out we were sitting on this—"

"He won't find out." He walked out from behind the desk and surprised her by taking her hands. He had never been affectionate with her before, unless he was also trying to take her clothes off. "Let me handle this."

"Tom—"

"Trust me," he said, and watched her eyes soften. Lowering his mouth to hers, he silenced her with a kiss.

～

"HEY, BUDDY," Jake Haddaway said as he walked over to where Luke and Colin were standing outside the doors of the school at the end of the day. "Want to head over to the marina for a while? We could put a couple rods in the water, try to catch a few perch?"

"Sure!" Luke said, grabbing his backpack off the ground and slipping his arms through the orange straps. He looked up at Colin. "Want to come?"

The kid's expression was so hopeful, there was nothing Colin could do but nod and say yes. Courtney had arrived a little while ago to pick him up, but Shelley had caught her out in the parking lot and invited her in for a chat. Becca must have asked her father to keep Luke occupied so she and Shelley could have some time to talk to Courtney.

Crossing the street to the harbor, Colin felt a little better knowing that Shelley was handling the situation, at least on an administrative level. He was planning to handle the situation with Jimmy in a much less professional manner later this afternoon. But that could wait, at least for another hour. He wanted to talk to Will on the phone first, to find out exactly what had happened when his friend had located their contractor earlier that day.

"You like to fish?" Jake asked as they stepped onto the pier.

"I do," Colin said.

Their footsteps echoed over the wooden planks as they passed the row of workboats. Jake nodded to a middle-aged man in one of the boats before stepping into the back of his own boat. He opened a salt-crusted storage bin and pulled three fishing rods out. "You like to hunt?" he asked, climbing back up to the pier.

"I do."

Jake handed him one of the rods. "I hear you're a pretty good shot."

Colin smiled, taking the rod. "I am."

"You should come out with me sometime." Jake fell into step beside him as Luke ran ahead of them to the far end of the pier. "I wouldn't mind picking up a few tips from a sniper."

"I'd like that," Colin said, and he meant it. He'd only met Jake eight hours ago, but he already felt completely at ease around him. He could tell he didn't have to do anything or say anything to impress him. He could just be himself. It was incredibly refreshing.

Unhooking the lightweight lure from the circular guide in the rod, he cast the line out into the shallow water. Beside him, Jake patiently coached Luke on the best way to use the rod—casting underhanded to keep the hook away from the people on the dock, giving it enough time to let it sink to the bottom before slowly reeling it back in.

Leaning back against the piling, Colin took a moment to study Becca's father. He thought he'd met almost everyone on the island by now, but he'd never even laid eyes on Jake before today. He'd have thought he would have at least run into him at the café or at Rusty's from time to time. He must keep to himself.

Reeling his line in and casting it back out, Colin wondered what it would have been like to grow up with a father like Jake, one who wasn't always chasing the limelight, one who wasn't always pushing his children to exceed so he could look better, one who actually had time for his children—to teach them how to fish, to be there for them when they called, instead of always expecting them to be there for him.

"I got one!" Luke exclaimed when the tip of his rod twitched. He started to reel it in, but the line went slack again almost immediately. His face fell when he realized he'd lost it.

"You'll get him next time," Jake said patiently. "When you feel him bite, give the rod a good hard yank to hook him. Like this." He demonstrated by flicking his wrist with the sharp, practiced movement of someone who'd been doing it all his life.

Within minutes, Jake got a nibble on his line. He hooked the fish easily, pulling up their first catch of the day. The white perch was barely six inches long, with shiny silver scales and fins that gleamed in the sunlight. It flailed and flopped at the end of the line until he caught it gently in his hand and removed the hook, showing Luke how to do it properly so as not to tear the fish's mouth.

Luke grinned when Jake dropped it back into the water with a splash and it swam away. They fished in silence for a while, each of them catching several perch and tossing them back into the water. When one of the charter boat captains motored a fifty-foot powerboat into the harbor, Jake set his rod down and headed over to the largest slip to help the crew with the lines. Their voices echoed over the marina as they talked about the day's catch, what they'd been using as bait, where they'd had the most luck, and who else had been out on the water that day.

Reeling in a clump of grass, Luke untangled it from the hook and then cast his line back out into the water.

"Have you ever been out on one of the big boats?" Colin asked, nodding toward the powerboat.

Luke nodded. "My dad used to take me."

Of course, Colin thought. His dad. He'd only lost him a few months ago. It was probably strange for Luke to be out here with him and Jake now, instead of his father. "Did he like to fish?"

"He did," Luke said. An osprey cawed, gliding toward a nest perched on top of a red channel marker a few hundred yards away. "But not like this. He only liked to go after the big fish. Out there." He nodded toward the deeper water of the Bay. "There's a contest in the fall. Lots of people come to the island for it. We used to go out on Captain Billy's boat every year, help him with the lines and stuff for the tourists. He let me reel in a huge rockfish last year. My arms were so tired afterwards. It was huge. Like this." He held out his arms about a foot and a half apart.

Colin smiled, knowing the size of the fish always got bigger with each retelling, but he couldn't help thinking that it sounded like fun. Motoring out to the open Bay with a boat full of people, spending the day on the water, a bunch of guys ragging on each other as they tried to hook the massive rockfish that swam deep into the heart of the Chesapeake to spawn.

"Miss Haddaway caught the biggest fish last year," Luke went on, happily reeling in another tiny perch and then releasing it the way Jake had taught him.

Impressed, Colin glanced over. "Did she?"

Luke nodded, wiping his wet hand on the hem of his shirt. "She didn't enter the contest. Most of the locals don't. But I saw the picture. Her fish was a lot bigger than the winner's was."

"Maybe she should be out here giving us some pointers."

"She should," Luke said with complete seriousness.

"I guess she's a pretty good teacher, huh?" Colin asked, compelled to continue talking about her, even if it was only with one of her eight-year-old students.

"She's my favorite teacher," Luke said.

Colin looked back out at the water. He imagined she was a lot of her students' favorite teacher. Not that he'd had any doubt that she'd be great in the classroom. He'd seen her around Taylor and some of the other kids on the island enough times to know she was a natural with children. It was clear that she'd put a tremendous amount of time and energy into the day, creating activities that would engage both the parents and the students. It was obvious that she took her job seriously and worked hard at creating an environment that was both fun and encouraging for all different learning styles.

It hadn't been easy for him at first, knowing that he'd be in such close proximity to her all day and not be able to touch her. But with every hour that had ticked by, he'd grown to respect her more, to admire her more, to see her in a way that had gone way beyond mere physical attraction. He had found himself wondering what it would be like to come home to her every night, to hear about her day over dinner, to listen to her tell him stories about what had happened with each of the kids.

He'd been surprised to find her father in the classroom when he'd arrived that morning, and even more surprised at how much he'd wanted to be that person—the first person she'd called when she'd needed something. But it seemed like the more his feelings grew, the harder she tried to push him away.

They had spent six hours in the same room, but she had purposefully avoided looking at him, talking to him, even being near him. After her initial reaction to seeing him first thing that morning, she had managed to avoid him as much as possible.

He didn't know what to make of that.

He knew she was attracted to him. That much was obvious. But what if that was all it was? What if she regretted their kiss from the night before? What if she was just having cold feet about marrying Tom, and had only kissed him to have one last bit of fun before tying the knot?

What if, despite her misgivings, she decided to go through with the wedding anyway?

Spending the day with Luke and the other children had only reinforced his longing for a family of his own. All he wanted was to settle down, to start a family, and to raise a few kids on this island. But if he couldn't have that life with Becca, did he still want to live here? Did he really want to stick around and see her married to another man? Even if she was moving to D.C., she and Tom would come back to the island to visit. He wouldn't be able to avoid seeing them together.

"I think I'm stuck," Luke said, tugging on the line. The rod bent as he tilted it up, but the line wouldn't budge.

"Probably snagged something on the bottom," Colin said,

walking over to give the line a tug with his hand. When it still wouldn't come loose, he stepped back. "Try jiggling it a little."

Luke jiggled the rod, then twisted it from side to side. Colin started to reach for it, to take it from him and see if he could get it to unsnag, when the phone in his pocket began to buzz. Pausing, he slipped it out, checking the number on the screen in case it was Will returning his call. It wasn't Will. And it wasn't a contact he had saved in his phone, but he recognized the L.A. area code, and knew instantly that it was Austin Turner—the former SEAL who wanted to hire him as a consultant.

He was about to hit ignore and slip his phone back in his pocket. He still hadn't decided what he wanted to do about that yet. But when Luke gave his rod a hard yank, the line snapped free.

"I got it!" he said triumphantly, reeling it in as fast as he could so it wouldn't snag the bottom again.

The rod was still bent slightly and the line was still taut. There was definitely something attached to it, probably another clump of weeds or some eelgrass, but it was light enough that Luke could handle it on his own. Glancing over at Jake, Colin saw that he was still chatting with the guys unloading fish from the coolers in the charter boat. The phone continued to buzz in his hand, and he looked over at the school, spotting Courtney crossing the street and heading toward them.

Will's words from that morning floated back: *'You don't need to be here to run this place once we get it off the ground. I can take it from here.'*

It was true, Colin thought. Will didn't need him here. Maybe no one did. Even this morning, when he'd gone to the school to fill in for Jimmy, someone else had already been there.

Becca had her father. Annie and Taylor had Will. Luke had his mother, and after today, every other parent on the island would be watching out for him, too.

Looking back down at the phone, he set down his rod. "Luke?"

"Yeah?" the kid said distractedly.

"I'm going to head over to the parking lot and take this call."

"Okay," he said, not bothering to look up, still fixated on reeling in whatever he'd snagged on the bottom of the harbor.

Colin turned, walking back toward the parking lot, as he lifted the phone to his ear and picked up the call.

SIXTEEN

By the time Becca left work, it was after five o'clock. Late afternoon sunlight cast the village in a warm, golden glow. The rain from two days ago had intensified all the colors: the brilliant green of the leaves, the deep blue of the water, the vibrant pink, orange, and purple of the flowers blooming in her neighbors' window boxes and gardens. Even the grass looked thick and lush.

Walking slowly into town, she passed the street where she lived and kept walking. She wasn't sure where she was going yet, but she couldn't go home. She couldn't face what was waiting for her there—the reams of uncut lace on her kitchen table, the half-finished seating chart for the reception filled with names of too many people she didn't recognize, the notebook lying open on the coffee table where she'd been working on her vows, which she still couldn't seem to find the words to write.

Her fingers drifted to the charm hanging from the chain around her neck. She wished her mother were here. She wished she could talk to her. She wished she could ask her what to do. She rubbed the heel of her palm over the hollow ache in her chest, unconsciously following the faint sound of wind chimes to the café. She wasn't just attracted to Colin anymore. She was falling for him.

She was supposed to be walking down the aisle to marry Tom in two weeks and she was falling in love with another man—a man she barely knew. She had always thought that love should be based more on friendship, on stability. But nothing about her feelings for Colin felt safe. Whenever she was with him, she felt like a sail snapping loose from its riggings, whipping wildly in the wind.

If this was what falling in love felt like, she had never been in love before. She had never felt so restless, so panicky, so less like herself. As much as it scared her, she was beginning to crave it—the dizzying loss of control, the intensity of emotions that swept up as fast as the storms rolled over the water in the summertime, the blurry, rose-colored haze that scrambled all rational thoughts.

Pausing on the sidewalk in front of the café, she watched the chimes dance and sway, catching the fading sunlight and reflecting shoots of color across the underside of the roof. She could hear voices in the backyard—Taylor and Ryan tossing sticks for their dogs to retrieve. A child's laughter drifted toward her as the two labs barked and splashed into the shallow cove. She knew Ryan was keeping an eye on Annie and Taylor now that Will had left, and she knew that Annie was still mad at her. But she couldn't stand their friendship being strained any longer.

Walking up the path to the porch, she climbed the steps and let herself in. The café was closed, the chairs turned upside down on the tables, the day's specials wiped from the chalkboard menu hanging on the wall behind the register. Della had left and the kitchen was empty, but the lingering scent of butter and sugar still clung to the air.

She heard someone moving around upstairs, the old wooden floorboards creaking under a set of footsteps overhead, and she made her way slowly across the dining room and up the steps to the apartment.

Annie turned when Becca got to the landing. She had a basket of laundry in her hands, a dishtowel thrown over one shoulder, and her long red hair was pulled back in a messy ponytail. "Hey," she said.

Becca could tell she was exhausted, and not terribly happy to see her, but she didn't ask her to leave. That was progress, at least. Annie turned the laundry basket over, dumping the clean clothes onto the cushions as Becca walked over to the couch. "Need a hand?"

Annie hesitated, then nodded, accepting the small peace offering. "Sure."

Becca picked up a shirt, still warm from the dryer, and started to fold it. The simple motion of doing something with her hands made her feel a little bit better. Looking out the window, she had a clear view of Ryan and Taylor playing fetch with the dogs in the backyard. She watched Ryan's chocolate lab, Zoey, streak out of the cove with a stick in her mouth, followed by Riley, hot on her heels. Zoey dropped the stick at Taylor's feet and both dogs shook, spraying muddy water all over Taylor. Taylor squealed, and Ryan's easy, carefree laughter rippled over the water as he picked up the stick and launched it back into the cove. "Did Will get off okay this morning?"

Annie nodded. "He made it back to Virginia Beach around two."

Becca reached for a pair of black sweatpants, shaking them to smooth the wrinkles out of each leg. Behind the couch, she spied a row of cardboard boxes taped up and ready to be carried over to the inn. "When's the official move in day?"

"We haven't decided yet." Annie dug around the pile, searching for a match to the sock she was holding. "We drove a load of boxes over last night, and we only have one room left to paint in the new wing, but there isn't a whole lot more we can do to the main house until Jimmy finishes the renovations."

At the mention of Jimmy's name, Becca remembered the promise she'd made to her father earlier, that she would agree to steer clear of him for a few days. She wondered if he was at Rusty's now, finishing off his third pint in less than an hour, oblivious to the fact that everyone on the island was furious with him now. "I overheard someone mention earlier that Will was going to try and track down Jimmy before he left."

Annie nodded. "He found him passed out in his truck outside Rodney White's house in Sherwood."

Rodney White? Becca's hands stilled on the jeans she was folding. Rodney had been in her class in elementary school, but he'd dropped out after eighth grade. He was a notorious screw up and rarely held down a job for more than a few months at a time. He'd worked in the kitchen of almost every restaurant in the area, but his real income came from the drugs he sold to whoever was stupid enough to buy them. From what she'd heard, the people who bought from Rodney were into things a lot harder than pot.

If Jimmy was hanging around Rodney's house now, things were a lot worse than she'd thought.

Annie picked up one of Taylor's jumpers, folding it into thirds. "Will said Jimmy was so messed up when he found him this morning, he was barely coherent." She shook her head, her expression darkening. "He called one of the guys from the fire department to give him a ride home. He said there was no way he was going to bring him into the school like that."

"Don't worry," Becca said, picking up another pair of jeans and giving them a hard thwak to get the wrinkles out. "He won't be coming into the school anytime soon. Shelley and I met with Courtney this afternoon. We told her that Jimmy is no longer allowed to set foot in the school. As far as we're concerned, until he gets his drinking problem under control, he's a threat to Luke and the rest of the children."

"How did Courtney take that?"

"Not well." Becca set the jeans down. "I think she's still in denial. She had to pick up a second job after her husband passed away and she needs help taking care of Luke. If she can't count on Jimmy, she might have to drop the second job, and I don't think she can afford to right now."

Annie frowned. "If all she needs is help watching Luke when she's at work, I'm sure there are people on this island who'd be willing to help. I could even step in and watch him if she got in a bind."

"I know. Believe me. I've offered plenty of times. Lots of other people have offered. She refuses to accept help from anyone who's not family. The problem is that the only family she has now is Jimmy. And if she continues to let Luke stay at Jimmy's house, we're going to have to report the situation to Child Protective Services."

Annie winced.

"I know it's harsh," Becca said, "but we can't risk Luke running away again or accidentally crossing his uncle one night when he's been drinking and having him blow up. We've given her several options on the island—baby sitters who would charge almost nothing, other parents who've come forward and offered to look after Luke at no charge. Hopefully, the threat of the state's involvement will scare her enough to accept the help that's being offered. Filing a report is an absolute last resort."

Annie's gaze shifted back to the window, where she had a view of Taylor chasing Riley down to the end of the dock. "Do you want me to talk to her?"

Becca paused, surprised. "What do you mean?"

"I can relate to her not wanting to accept help," Annie said, as she continued to watch her daughter play in the yard. "As a single mother, I've been in her shoes. I can understand where she's coming from. Maybe I can get through to her."

"It's worth a try," Becca said.

Picking up the empty laundry basket, Annie carried it over to the closet beside the kitchen, setting it back on top of the dryer. "If the single mom card doesn't do the trick..." She lifted a shoulder. "My mother was an alcoholic. I can tell her a few stories about what it's like for a child to grow up in that environment."

Becca turned slowly, meeting Annie's eyes across the room. "Your mother was an alcoholic?"

Annie nodded.

"I didn't realize..." Becca said, trailing off.

Annie closed the door to the laundry closet. "It's not something I'm proud of, not something I particularly like to share with anyone. But if it'll help Courtney and Luke, I will."

Becca watched her friend walk into the kitchen. She thought about her own father, how she never talked about his alcoholism with anyone, how, when she'd been living through it, she had tried to hide it, desperate to pretend that everything was fine.

Looking back at what was left of the pile of laundry, she thought about how many times she'd spoken with Courtney over the winter about Luke, raising her concerns that he was withdrawing, that he wasn't getting the support he needed from her to cope with the death of his father. But she hadn't considered sharing her own experience. She hadn't considered opening up that part of herself. She hadn't realized that it might be the only thing that could get through to her.

Dishes clinked behind her as Annie stacked them in neat rows on the exposed shelves lining the walls above the sink. Folding the last T-shirt from the pile, Becca set it on the arm of the sofa. She thought about how badly she'd wanted to shield Annie from the news about the school. Her friend had been through so much in her life. She didn't need to be shielded from anything.

"Annie." Becca turned and walked over to the counter that offered the only separation between the kitchen and the living room in the apartment. "I know I've already apologized, but I'm sorry. Again. For everything. I should never have kept the news about the school from you. I should have told you right away."

"I know," Annie said, sighing. "I didn't mean to take it out on you the past few days. I was just so angry. I'm still angry. Taylor and I...we were finally good again. We were finally settled. Everything seemed to be going our way...and then...." She shook her head, wiping a rag over a frying pot and slipping it into the drawer on the other side of the counter. "For the first time in my life, I didn't want anything to change. I just wanted everything to stay the same."

Becca nodded. She understood. A week ago, she had felt the same way. Now...she didn't know what she wanted anymore.

Walking out from behind the counter, Annie scooped up the piles of laundry from the sofa, carried them into the bedrooms, and set them on the beds. When she came back out, she gestured for Becca to sit on one of the stools. "Do you want something to drink? Water? Iced tea? Soda?"

"Iced tea would be great," she said, grateful that they'd finally reconciled.

Annie poured two glasses of iced tea, and handed one to Becca.

Becca took a sip of the Southern-style recipe she had probably learned from Della—brewed with cloves, fresh mint leaves, lemon juice and gobs of sugar. "How did you think today went?"

"I thought you did a great job," Annie said. "I was impressed by how many parents showed up."

"I had to make a few calls last night, but it made a huge difference to have everyone there."

Annie nodded, putting another dish away. "I was surprised to see Colin there."

Becca picked up the spoon Annie had given her, stirring the tea so she wouldn't clench her hands together in her lap, so she wouldn't let the rush of nerves at the mere mention of his name give her away. "Me, too."

Annie wasn't fooled. She continued to watch her closely. "I didn't realize he knew Luke that well."

"He doesn't."

Annie put away a few more dishes, letting the silence stretch out. "Then why did he come?"

Becca poked at a clove floating beside one of the ice cubes with the tip of the spoon. "I don't know."

"Becca?" Annie said gently.

Becca glanced up.

"I saw the way you looked at him today." Annie's green eyes were filled with compassion and understanding. "And the way he looked at you. There wasn't a person in that room who couldn't see the chemistry between you."

Becca swallowed. What could she say? There was no denying it.

"Did something happen?" Annie asked. There was no judgment in her voice, no accusation in her eyes. It was a simple question.

Becca's hand curled around the glass as the memory of their kiss from the night before swam back. "I'm attracted to Colin," she said, letting the words out in a rush.

As soon as they left her mouth, she regretted them. She shouldn't be saying things like that out loud, not when she was still wearing Tom's ring, not until she'd made a decision about what to do.

Desperate to backtrack, she struggled to come up with an excuse for what she'd just said. She thought about what Grace had said out on the deck at Rusty's on Tuesday—that even if she were engaged, she'd have to be blind not to notice Colin. "Who isn't, though, right?"

"I'm not."

Becca glanced up. Her friend was dead serious. "Well," she said, attempting a breezy smile. "You have Will."

"And you have Tom," Annie said quietly.

Becca pulled in a breath.

"What's going on, Becca?"

"Nothing." *Everything.* A flutter of panic tapped at the base of her throat. She looked away. Part of her wanted to tell Annie. Part of her wanted to open the floodgates and let it all out. Wouldn't it be better if she told someone? If she got an outside perspective? But as badly as she wanted to tell someone, she didn't know if she was ready to admit it yet, not out loud. As soon as she said the words out loud, she would have to face them. She would have to face the truth—that she wasn't sure if she wanted to marry Tom anymore.

"Are you having second thoughts?" Annie asked gently.

The fluttering in the back of her throat turned into a lump. She took a sip of sugary tea, trying to force it back, but the cold drink did nothing to soothe the dryness in her throat, or the emptiness in the pit of her stomach whenever she thought about her upcoming wedding.

Becca set down the glass, looking away. She couldn't meet Annie's eyes as she shook her head, as she tried to pretend everything was fine. After all this time, after everything she'd invested in her relationship with Tom, she was two weeks away from finally getting everything she'd ever wanted. Tom had even agreed to start trying for a baby on their honeymoon. Now, *she* was the one who wanted to pull the plug?

How could she throw away everything they'd built over the past fifteen years for a man she barely knew? She didn't even know if Colin felt the same way about her. She knew he was attracted to her. She knew he wanted her physically. But what if that was all he wanted?

She had no interest in flings or meaningless sex. She wanted marriage. Children. Family.

She wanted commitment.

A man who kissed like Colin could make a woman think about doing crazy things, things she would never have imagined doing before he'd come into her life, like calling off the wedding she'd been planning for years, to a man she'd been with since she was a teenager.

What if what she was feeling for Colin *wasn't* love? What if it was lust? What if she didn't know the difference because she'd never been this attracted to someone before?

"I'm just nervous," Becca lied, tracing a groove in the worn wooden counters with her thumb. "You'll probably feel the same way right before you and Will get married." She glanced up, grasping onto the opportunity to change the subject. "Speaking of... Have you two gotten any closer to setting a date?"

Annie said nothing, continuing to study her for several more moments. Becca could tell she wanted to say something else, but couldn't decide whether or not it was her place. Finally deciding to let it go, Annie reached for the cluster of utensils in the drying rack, and started putting them away in a drawer at the far end of the counter. "Actually, no," she said. "Neither of us can afford a wedding right now."

"Oh," Becca said, immediately feeling badly for asking. She should have known better. With Annie just getting the café off the ground and Will funneling most of his savings into the veterans' center and the brand new wing at the inn, it was no wonder they couldn't afford a wedding right now. Having just gone through the process of planning one of her own, she knew how quickly the costs could add up.

Annie shrugged, as if it weren't that big of a deal. "To be honest, I would be perfectly happy to go to the courthouse. We almost did back in February, over Valentine's Day, when Will was home visiting. But when we told Della, she burst into tears."

Becca took another sip of iced tea, relieved that the discussion about weddings had shifted to Annie and Will and away from her and Tom. "I can imagine."

"She said she'd been dreaming about our wedding ever since we got engaged, that she'd pictured a beautiful sunset ceremony at the inn and a big party afterwards with everyone on the island. She said she'd already planned out the whole menu and had over a dozen cake recipes picked out for me to taste." Annie shook her head, blowing out a breath. "I understand where she's coming from, but a big wedding just feels like taking on a whole lot of work for everyone else." Her eyes widened when she realized what she'd said. "Sorry, I didn't mean..."

"It's okay," Becca said, her gaze drifting down to her engagement ring. She knew exactly how Annie felt. She had never wanted a big wedding either. She had never wanted all this stress. But, at the same time, she agreed with Della. The thought of Will and Annie going to the courthouse seemed so unromantic. Didn't they want a different memory to hold onto, if not for themselves, at least for Taylor? "Wouldn't you rather do something small on the island? Even if it was just here, in the backyard of the café, with a few close friends?"

"Of course," Annie said, a little wistfully, as she walked back over to the spot across from Becca at the counter. "But how would I decide who to invite? If Will and I got married on the island, everyone would want to come. We wouldn't be able to do something small."

Taking the dishrag off her shoulder, Annie draped it over the faucet. "I'm not going to pretend that I haven't had a vision of what my dream wedding would be like since I was a little girl.

But I guess I have a more realistic view of what really matters now, as opposed to what society expects me to do. I'm not a traditionalist. I got pregnant at seventeen. I've done everything backwards. Before Will came along, it was just me and Taylor for a long time, and I was okay with that."

Leaning her forearms on the counter, Annie gazed back out the window. "What matters now is that Taylor is taken care of. Since the day she was born, I have worried about what would happen to her if something happened to me. I know I don't have to worry about that anymore. I have Will now. I have Della. I have Joe. I have the Hadleys. But I want to make it official. Taylor belongs on this island and she belongs with Will. I want to make sure she would be able to stay here, with him, if anything ever happened to me."

Becca took in the circles under Annie's eyes, the already pale complexion that had lost even more color from worrying about Taylor's school situation this week. Becca had wanted to be a mother her whole life, but she had never really known the kind of worry Annie lived with every day—the constant worry every mother lived with. She wished she hadn't added to it this week. She wished she could do something to lift a little of the burden. "Maybe when Will gets back and you're both settled, we could plan a little ceremony with a few people and a dinner back here where Della can cook as much as she wants and everyone's invited. I'd be happy to help. I'm sure we could come up with a way to give you what you want without breaking your budget."

"I'd like that," Annie said, smiling. "But right now, let's focus on yours. What's the final count on the guest list."

"One hundred and seventy three."

Annie gaped at her. "I thought you were capping it at a hundred and fifty?"

"I was," Becca said, rubbing a hand over her eyes. "It's gotten completely out of control."

"Where are they all staying?"

"I rented houses for a lot of them on the island. Some of them are staying in hotels or B&Bs in St. Michaels."

"How many are staying at the inn?"

"Twenty," Becca said. "As long as it's ready by then. If not, I'll have to figure something else out."

"Are all three guest cottages booked?"

Becca nodded.

"Even the one Colin's been staying in?"

"No," Becca said. "I mean, I saved that one for Colin...and whoever he's bringing."

Annie looked up. "Colin's coming?"

"Yes."

"And he's bringing someone?"

Becca nodded. "That's what he said."

"Huh," Annie said.

"What?" Becca prodded, thinking about how she'd had to remind him the other night about his RSVP, how long it had taken him to finally commit. "Are you surprised he said yes?"

"Well..." Annie hesitated. She picked up the towel again, wiping at a few nonexistent crumbs on the counter. "I don't think Colin's a big fan of weddings these days."

Becca frowned. Despite whatever else had been growing between them over the past week, he'd been incredibly generous in accommodating her wedding, with all the guests and the issues with the construction. She hadn't felt like it had been a burden, even once. "Why not?"

Annie set down the towel, taking a deep breath. "I thought you knew."

"Knew what?"

"Colin was engaged not too long ago."

"Engaged?" Becca echoed, stunned. "When?"

"Before he came back from Afghanistan," Annie said. "He

was supposed to get married in San Diego last summer. Will was going to be his Best Man."

"But..." Becca trailed off, trying to wrap her head around it. "I don't understand. What happened? Did he call it off?"

"No," Annie said, shaking her head. "She did."

Becca's eyes widened. "I can't believe anyone would break off an engagement to Colin. He's..." *perfect*, she almost said, before she caught herself. Before she realized how easily the word could have slipped out of her mouth.

Annie lowered her voice when the door to the café opened downstairs and they heard Taylor and Ryan walk inside. "Will told me this in confidence, so please don't spread it around."

"Of course," Becca said. "But...what happened? Why did she call it off?"

"She gave him his ring back when she came to visit him at Walter Reed, when he was still in bed recovering from the surgery." Annie said. "She said she couldn't marry an amputee."

SEVENTEEN

Engaged? Walking away from the café half an hour later, Becca's head was still spinning over what Annie had told her. How could she not have known that Colin had been engaged? It wasn't like asking someone to spend the rest of her life with you was a small thing. And if it had only been a year since she'd broken up with him—had left him because he'd lost a leg fighting for his country—then the wound must still be fresh.

She gazed down at the sidewalk, at where a cluster of dandelion was breaking through a crack in the cement. No wonder he'd reacted so strongly when she'd seen his prosthesis for the first time. No wonder he'd gotten so angry when she'd stared. He must have thought she was turned off by it, like his fiancée had been. Nothing could have been farther from the truth.

For the first time since meeting Colin, she felt like she was finally starting to get a full picture of him. And he was nothing like what she'd originally thought. Nothing at all.

She reached out, letting her fingers trail over the velvety petals of a peach rose climbing riotously over a neighbor's white picket fence. The scent of the flower drifted into the air, almost dizzying in its sweetness. It wasn't just his fiancée that he'd lost. He'd lost two teammates on that mission. He'd lost his ability to walk without the help of a prosthesis. And he'd lost his career as a SEAL, which he'd told her he still missed every single day.

There had to be a lot more going on underneath the surface than anyone realized.

Was it possible, she wondered suddenly, that his decision to open the veterans' center on this island wasn't just because he wanted to do something to give back to his fellow wounded warriors? Was it possible that *he* needed what this island could provide, too—a place to heal?

She thought back to the night when she'd gone up to Annapolis for his father's fundraiser dinner, when he'd told her he wanted to buy a house on the island, that he wanted to spend the rest of his life here. She thought about the first night he'd come to her house, when he'd said it would be a good home for a family, and that he wanted three children one day.

Yes, he'd *said* all those things. But she hadn't really believed him. Even when he'd told her he loved it here, she had assumed he would tire of it eventually, that it wouldn't be enough for him, like it had never been enough for Tom. Since the first night she'd met him, she'd assumed that a man like Colin would never actually want to settle down. Not when he had so many women to choose from.

A barn swallow alighted from a sycamore tree, flapping its wings across the street toward the marina. What if all he wanted was the same thing she wanted—a house, a family, a quiet, simple life on this island?

She'd given up hope a long time ago that she could ever have that, because of who she'd chosen to be with, and because—as Colin had so bluntly put it last week—she'd never imagined, in her wildest dreams, that she would actually meet someone on this island. The thought that she could, that she could actually have everything she wanted, made her heart ache with longing.

When she got to her own street, she took in the familiar row of homes. Her gaze paused on her father's house, the house she'd grown up in. His truck was parked in the driveway and she could just make out the shadow of a man through the kitchen window.

She still owed him for stepping in at school today, for sacrificing a day of work to be there for Luke. Her gaze shifted back to the other side of Main Street, where Rusty's hugged the edge of the marina. She didn't feel like talking to anyone, but she could pick up some take-out and drop dinner off to her father before heading home.

The parking lot was already packed and she did a quick scan of the cars as she crossed the street. She felt a small thread of relief when she didn't see Jimmy's red F-250 anywhere. Her shoes crunched over the oyster shells scattered over the gravel as she wove through the parking spots marked by worn wooden pilings and thick strands of rope.

Walking through the front door of the restaurant, she inhaled the tangy aroma of fried food and draft beer. The sun was beginning to set, flooding the wooden interior in soft orange light. The outdoor deck was filled with people, not just locals, but a few out-of-towners, too—the first of the weekend boaters who would stop by on their way down the Bay for a sunset cocktail.

She recognized them instantly from their pastel polo shirts, aviator sunglasses, and pressed khaki shorts. Their return, like the ospreys and the blue crabs, and any other migrating species that left and came back every year when the weather warmed, gave her a small sense of comfort as she headed up to the bar to place her order.

"Hey, Becca," Dave Moore called over the baseball game blasting from the TV hanging over the bar. "What can I get you?"

"A crab cake sandwich and a rockfish platter to go."

"Coming right up," he said, moving over to the computer screen where he punched in the order. "Want something to drink while you wait?"

"Just a glass of water."

He filled up a pint glass, added a slice of lemon, a straw, and a friendly wink as he passed it over.

She smiled. "Thanks."

Beside her, Billy Sadler, one of her father's waterman friends started to get up off his stool. "Want to sit down?"

"No, thanks," she said, waving him off. She knew he was there to watch the game, as all of the other men on the barstools were. She glanced up at the TV. "Who's winning?"

"O's," Billy said, settling back onto the stool and looking up at the screen. "We're up by two. Bottom of the eighth."

She watched the game for a few minutes, then turned, leaning back against the bar to survey the dining room. Every table was filled with someone she knew. She waved to a few people who caught her eye, taking a sip of her water, and listening to the crack of balls from the pool table where a group of teenagers were playing a game in the far corner.

She spotted Luke and Courtney, sitting at a small table near the other side of the bar and walked over to say hi. It was unusual for Courtney to come into Rusty's for dinner, but maybe she was trying to do something nice for Luke to make up for missing the day at school. Luke seemed perfectly content, slurping down a soda, nibbling on a plate of fries, and sketching on his paper placemat.

"Hey, Courtney," she said, keeping her tone upbeat and friendly, hoping to ease some of the tension from their meeting this afternoon. "Hi, Luke."

"Hey, Becca," Courtney said, glancing up warily.

Luke's face broke into a grin when he spotted her. "Hi, Miss

Haddaway," he said excitedly. "Did you hear about all the fish we caught today?"

Becca smiled, shaking her head. "How many did you catch?"

"Seven!" he said triumphantly, popping another fry in his mouth.

"All perch?"

He nodded.

Some of the guys at the bar started to shout when one of the players on the TV hit a fly ball into the outfield with the bases loaded. She glanced over her shoulder, watching the runs come in, then looked back at Luke. She was about to ask him what kind of lures they'd used to catch the perch when the door to the restaurant swung open, smacking against the interior wall. She jumped, and knew instantly from the expression on Courtney's face who it was without having to look. Instinctively stepping between Luke and the door, she turned, watching Jimmy saunter up to the bar.

He was wearing a faded T-shirt and ripped jeans. His hair was limp and greasy. His beard was grizzled and unkempt from a week's worth of growth. His eyes were bloodshot, his skin sallow, and he looked like he was starting to lose weight—in a bad way.

"Give me a couple of Budweisers," he said, leaning on the bar to keep himself upright. "And make sure they're cold."

"Not tonight," Dave said quietly.

"What are you talking about?" Jimmy asked, slurring his words. He pulled out a few crumpled bills from his back pocket, tossing them onto the bar. "Just give me what I asked for."

"I think you've had enough," Dave said, keeping his tone calm, trying to diffuse the situation.

Everyone in the restaurant had gone quiet. Every eye was on Jimmy, except for a few teenage girls in the corner, their heads bent together whispering.

Oblivious, Jimmy looked over at where Becca stood, and a slow smile curved his lips. Pushing away from the bar, he walked over, his red-rimmed gaze combing up and down her body.

Becca was vaguely aware of several men pushing back their chairs, rising to their feet.

"Nice dress," Jimmy slurred, in reference to her modest, work appropriate, blue sweater dress.

"Go away, Jimmy," she said coldly, remembering not only her father's warning now, but Grace's from a few days ago. This wasn't the time or the place to confront him.

Undeterred, he looked past her at where Luke and Courtney were sitting, looking down at their plates, humiliated by his behavior. "Well, hey there, sis," he said, grinning.

"Go away, Jimmy," Courtney echoed.

He ignored her and looked down at Luke. "I heard you went crying to your mom about me not coming to school with you today." He laughed as Luke's face went white. "Real men don't go crying to their mamas. Didn't your daddy ever teach you that?"

"How dare you?" Becca snapped, her temper breaking as she stepped between him and Luke again.

"Becca," Dave warned, lifting the hatch from behind the bar.

"No," Courtney said shakily, pushing to her own feet. "She's right." She walked up until she was standing face-to-face with her brother-in-law, anger and protectiveness rippling off her in waves. "How dare you talk to my son that way?"

Jimmy's red-rimmed eyes narrowed. "Pull the stick out of your ass, sis." His gaze raked critically over Courtney's scrawny, overworked frame. "Maybe if you got laid, you'd chill out a bit."

"Hey," Billy barked, stepping between them. He put a hand on Jimmy's chest, pushing the contractor back a few steps. "That's enough."

"Fuck you," Jimmy said, batting his hand away.

Joe Dozier walked up—all six-foot-three-inches and two-hundred-and-seventy pounds of him. "Is there a problem?"

Jimmy started to laugh, as he stumbled backwards. "Look at you people. You're all pathetic. None of you would even know how to have a good time if it stared you in the face." He started to turn, head back to the truck, when his gaze zeroed in on Becca again. Lurching forward, his hand shot out, grabbing her arm.

"Why don't you come out for a ride with me, honey," he slurred, nodding to where his truck was idling outside the door. "I know I could show *you* a good time."

Becca's breath caught at the strength of his grip. It was so tight, she flinched in pain. She tried to wrench her arm free, but he pulled her against him, his whiskey-soured breath hot in her ear as he whispered what he'd like to do to her.

Several men stepped forward all at once, but before they could get to him, Becca drove her knee up, hard, into his groin.

Jimmy doubled-over in pain. "Fuck," he wheezed.

Joe grabbed him by the back of his shirt, hauling him upright. "I think it's time for you to leave."

Jimmy came up swinging, and Joe caught Jimmy's pathetic attempt at a punch in his hand. "I said," he repeated, lowering Jimmy's arm back to his side, "it's time for you to leave."

Jimmy's eyes narrowed, but he snatched his hand free and turned, weaving as he made his way back toward the door.

"Get the keys out of his truck," Dave murmured to Joe.

Joe nodded, walking after him.

As soon as Jimmy heard him coming, he scrambled into the driver's seat, threw the truck into gear, and gunned the engine out of the parking lot. Gravel spun out from under his tires as he turned the corner too sharply, ripping out a neighbor's fence post.

"Mom," Luke said shakily, clutching onto Courtney's side.

"It's okay, baby," Courtney said, fumbling through her purse for her phone. Becca watched, her heart still pounding, as Courtney punched in the number for 911. "Yes," she said when the first responder answered. "My name is Courtney Faulkner. I live on Heron Island. I need to report a drunk driver."

EIGHTEEN

Crossing the Chesapeake Bay Bridge to Maryland's Western Shore the next day, Becca glanced down at the phone in her lap. What was taking Tom so long to call her back? She'd left him three messages and he hadn't even bothered to send her a text. She'd waited around at home for as long as she could stand it that morning, hoping he'd call her back so they could set a time to meet. When she still hadn't heard from him by ten o'clock, she'd simply walked out the door, got in her car, and started to drive.

She needed to see him. She needed to talk to him. She needed to know if what they had was worth saving. If he told her he loved her, that he still felt the same way that he had when they were teenagers, she would put her feelings for Colin aside and go ahead with the wedding. But she couldn't keep pretending that everything was fine. She'd been letting too many things happen without taking action, without taking control, without facing the truth.

It was time that changed. It was time a lot of things changed.

What had happened at Rusty's the night before had rattled

her. Jimmy had been pulled over a few miles outside St. Michaels and charged with a DUI. The cops had confiscated his license, and she could only hope the reality of that, when it finally sank in, would be the wake up call he needed to clean up his act. But all she'd been able to think about after they'd gotten word on the island that he'd been picked up, was how much worse it could have been.

What if Luke had been in the car with him? What if they'd gotten in an accident? What if something had happened to one of them? She should never have let it go on so long without telling Courtney the truth, without sharing her own story. After what Annie had told her in the café yesterday, that her own mother had been an alcoholic, she couldn't help wondering, now, how many others were out there? How many others were hiding it? How many others were suffering through it alone, trying to protect the ones they loved by pretending everything was fine?

She was done hiding it, done trying to pretend it was fine.

She had spent several hours at Courtney's house last night, after Luke had gone to bed. She'd told her everything about what had happened the year after her mother's death. She'd given her the name of the rehab center her father had finally checked himself into to get clean. And she'd told her she could call, anytime, at any hour, if she needed anything.

The biggest mistake she'd made when she was in Courtney's shoes was trying to hide her father's problems from everyone else. She'd been embarrassed. She hadn't wanted anyone else to know how bad it had gotten. She had hoped—prayed, even—that one day she'd wake up and it would have just gone away. But alcoholism wasn't something that just went away. It took an enormous amount of strength from the person who was falling into that hole to pull themselves out. And she knew, as well as anyone who'd been down that road with a loved one, that waiting for that to happen was usually a lot harder for the one who was watching than the one who was doing the drinking.

Following a sedan full of teenage girls off the bridge and onto the first stretch of highway of Anne Arundel County, she thought back to the year she'd lost her mother—the year she'd almost lost both of her parents. Tom had been the one she'd called, the one she'd gone to when anything had happened, the one who'd helped her carry her father to bed when he was too heavy for her to lift. She had gone to him because he'd been grieving, too— because that shared tragedy had linked them together in a way she'd thought no one else would understand.

But what would have happened if she'd let more people in? If she'd asked for help? If she hadn't tried so hard to hide it?

Would it have ended sooner? Would it have been a little easier, just knowing she had the support?

When her phone buzzed and Tom's picture flashed on the screen, she reached for it, expecting to see the face of the boy she'd fallen in love with so long ago. But the face staring back at her was older...different. She felt the strangest sensation as she glanced back up at the road, almost as if she were seeing him for the first time. Shaking it off, she plugged in the earphones connected to her phone and answered the call. "Hey," she said, forcing an upbeat note into her voice. She didn't want him to know anything was wrong yet. She wanted to hash things out face-to-face, not over the phone.

"Hey," he said back, his tone not at all friendly.

She frowned, glancing in the rear view mirror as she switched back into the right lane after passing a tractor-trailer. "What's wrong?"

"Nothing. You called me."

She blinked, taken aback. She'd been waiting for Tom to return her call for hours. He didn't even have the courtesy to apologize, to explain why he hadn't gotten back to her yet? "Did you listen to my messages?"

"No. I haven't had time."

I haven't had time? It was Saturday. What could he possibly be doing that he couldn't take a two-minute break to listen to her messages? "I've been trying to reach you all morning."

"I know. I've been busy. What do you need?"

She didn't *need* anything, Becca thought, feeling the first pinch of frustration. She wanted to talk to him. She wanted to have a conversation with him and not be squeezed into a block of time like one of his clients. "I'm on my way to D.C.," she said, cutting to the chase. "I'd like to see you."

"Today?"

"Yes," she said, feeling her own patience begin to give. "Today."

"I'm busy today. I've got a million things going on at work."

Becca took a deep breath, counting to three. He always had a million things going on at work, but she needed to talk to him today. And she didn't want to begin a conversation this important on a bad foot. "How about lunch?" she suggested, searching for a compromise. "I could pick up some sandwiches and we could meet at one of the parks near your office?"

"I'm not in D.C. today."

"Where are you?" she asked, surprised.

"Baltimore. I'm meeting a client."

"Okay," she said, glancing up at the green sign over the highway. She was only a few miles from I-97, which would give her a straight shot up to Baltimore. "I could come there instead."

"No," he said quickly. "I mean...that's not necessary. I'll be back in D.C. tonight."

Tonight? Frustration shifted to irritation. She couldn't wait until tonight. "I need to talk to you today. Soon."

"About what?"

"I'd rather talk to you about it in person."

He sighed. "Is this about the wedding?"

Yes, Becca thought. It was about the wedding...and a lot more than that. But she didn't want to have this discussion over the phone. "Yes."

"Fine," he said, not bothering to mask the annoyance in his voice. "I'll be back in D.C. this afternoon. Meet me at home at four."

"*Four?*"

"Yes. That's the best I can do. I have to go. I'll talk to you later."

Becca's mouth fell open when he hung up on her. Was this how he'd been talking to her all along? Had she been so desperate to make things work between them that she'd let him believe it was okay to talk to her like this? To treat her like this?

Had she gotten so used to justifying his behavior as stress that she hadn't even noticed that it had become a habit?

Her fingers curled around the steering wheel. She wasn't just angry at Tom. She was angry at herself. She should never have let him think that it was okay to talk to her like that. She was his fiancée. She was the one person he should be willing to drop everything for. Instead, for the past several months, he had made her feel, over and over again, like a nuisance.

She had told herself it was the wedding, that he shouldn't have to be dragged into the planning when he had so much else to do. But he was the one who'd insisted on inviting everyone from his firm. He was the one who'd blown up the guest list. After everything she'd done over the years to accommodate him, after all the time she'd spent driving back and forth to D.C. so they could spend their weekends together, he didn't even have the decency to give her an hour for lunch on a Saturday? To listen to her messages before returning her call?

She saw the exit for I-97 a mile away and was tempted to take it. She didn't care if Tom was meeting with a client. She was tired of being nice, of being understanding, of always accommodating everyone else.

When was she going to learn to stand up for herself?

Veering toward the interstate, she felt the phone in her lap buzz with a text message. A tiny glimmer of hope lit up inside her. Maybe he'd realized what an ass he'd been after he'd hung up the phone. Maybe he was texting to apologize. She glanced down and shook her head as the last flicker of hope faded away. She should have known better. It wasn't Tom. It was Shelley.

Just stopped by your house. Where are you?

It was uncanny how Shelley always seemed to know when something was wrong. She wasn't even her real mother, but somewhere along the way she'd developed that same sixth sense that a mother would have for her biological child. There were times when Becca appreciated it and times when she wished she wouldn't try so hard to step into a role she'd never be able to fill. Right now, was one of the latter times, but she hadn't told anyone on the island where she was going, and she didn't want Shelley to worry her father if she started asking around. Checking the lanes behind her to make sure there was room to move over, she took the last exit before the interstate. As soon as she came to a stop at the traffic light at the bottom of the ramp, she sent her a message back.

In Annapolis...on my way to D.C.

To see Tom?

Yes.

Everything okay?

No, but I'm dealing with it.

Okay...

The light turned green and Becca prepared to make a U-turn to get back on the highway when another message came through.

I heard back from Lydia this morning.

Becca paused, her foot hovering over the gas pedal. Lydia, like Tom, hadn't bothered to return a single call she'd made over the past week. She and Shelley had both left multiple messages asking to set up an appointment to talk about the school, and specifically Taylor, and they'd gotten nothing, not even a hint of a response. Nor had Lydia bothered to reply to any of the emails they'd sent. Pulling into a gas station instead of continuing onto the highway, Becca slid into an empty parking spot and put the car in park.

What did she say?

She said if we have concerns, we should raise them at the public hearing on Friday.

Becca gazed down at the screen, waiting for Shelley to write more. When several moments passed and she didn't, Becca typed back:

That's it???

That's it.

Unbelievable, Becca thought as coils of anger sprouted inside her. She typed back another message:

Can you get me her address?

Why? What are you going to do?

What she should have done days ago, Becca thought, tossing the phone onto the passenger seat and throwing the car into reverse. Pay her a visit. She turned out of the parking lot, onto one of the heavily trafficked roads leading away from the mall. Colin had said his mother lived in Severna Park, so she'd head in that direction. If Shelley hadn't sent her Lydia's address by the time she got there, she would drive up and down every street and search every mailbox for the name, Vanzant, until she found it.

She wasn't going to sit back and let a woman who knew nothing about them, who hadn't even bothered to come out and visit their school, who wouldn't even afford them the respect of returning their phone calls, roll right over them. This was *her* school. This was *her* island. These were *her* friends.

Taylor and the rest of the children might not be old enough to speak for themselves yet. The islanders might not have the polish, or the money, or the academic degrees to earn the respect of the board members. But Becca could speak for them. She could speak for all the children and all the parents who wanted to send their children to that school, who wanted to build a life on that island. She had spent her entire professional life helping make Heron Island Elementary a place any parent would be proud to send their child to. She wasn't about to let it become another statistic in Lydia's portfolio.

Fighting stop-and-start traffic for the next thirty minutes only fueled her anger, and by the time she got to the affluent neighborhood skirting the Severn River, her temper was ready to break. She was vaguely aware of the homes getting bigger, the yards getting wider, and the cars getting fancier as she tracked the numbers on the mailboxes, searching for the address Shelley had sent her. When she found it, she turned into the long, paved driveway, took in the stately brick mansion and the familiar black Acura parked out front, and slowly hit the brakes.

Was that...Tom's car?

No. It couldn't be.

That wouldn't make any sense.

He'd said he was in Baltimore.

Easing off the brakes, she inched forward, but a niggling doubt crept in when she got close enough to see the plates. They were D.C. plates. Her gaze cut to the left fender, where a small L-shaped scratch was etched into the metal—the same L-shaped scratch Tom had gotten while parallel parking in Georgetown two weeks ago. She knew, because she'd been in the car with him when it had happened.

Slowly putting her own car in park, she sat in the driver's seat with her hands on the wheel, staring at the black car in front of her. What was Tom doing at Lydia's house? Why had he lied to her about being in Baltimore?

The front door to the house opened. Tom walked out, waved goodbye to the woman inside, and closed the door behind him. Becca got out of her car and Tom looked out at the driveway. He stopped short when their eyes met.

"Becca?"

She crossed her arms over her chest. "Baltimore, huh?"

His gaze shifted left, then right. "What are you doing here?"

"I could ask you the same thing."

He walked quickly down the steps. "I had to drop off some papers for a client. Did you...follow me?"

"How could I have followed you when I didn't even know

you were here?" she snapped, stalking toward him. "You said you were in Baltimore. What the hell's going on?"

Tom glanced back at the door, as if he were afraid Lydia might come out and see them arguing. God forbid they make a scene in front of one of his precious clients. Becca shook her head, wondering how she had never seen it before, how she could have stayed with someone for so long who didn't care about anyone or anything but himself.

Tom lowered his voice as he closed the rest of the distance between them. "Not all of our clients can go into the office during regular business hours. In some cases, special cases like Lydia's, we need to respect their privacy and come to them."

The lies came so easily to him, Becca realized. It was no wonder she'd been falling for them for so long. "What, *exactly*, are you doing for Lydia?"

"Just some basic contract work." He took her by the elbow and started to lead her back to her car. "It's not important."

It was obviously important enough that it needed to be hand delivered on a Saturday. How stupid did he think she was? Becca stopped walking, her eyes widening. "Oh my God," she breathed.

"What?"

"You're working together." She took a step back. "You're on her side."

"What are you talking about?"

How could she not have seen it before? How could she have missed this? "Richard Goldwater," she said, staring back at him— this man who she had spent half her life with, who she had almost walked down the aisle with, who she'd thought she'd known better than anyone.

She didn't know him at all. "He works at your firm."

"Of course he does," Tom said, and had the nerve to look baffled. "What does that have to do with anything?"

Becca turned, walking back toward the house.

"Becca, wait," Tom said. "What are you doing?"

She ignored him.

He jogged after her. "Is Lydia expecting you?"

What was he, her assistant now? "No."

"Becca." He caught her arm.

She winced when he grabbed her in the same spot where Jimmy had left a bruise from the night before. She stopped walking, looking down at where his fingers were wrapped around her forearm.

"Let it go," Tom ordered.

She looked up at him, at those blue-green eyes she had fallen for so many years ago, during the weakest time in her life.

She wasn't weak anymore. She wasn't grieving. And she wasn't going to let anyone tell her what to do.

"It's over," Tom said firmly. "You need to let it go, Becca—the school, the island, your father, everything. It's the only way you'll ever be able to move forward."

No, Becca thought, shaking her head. There was only one thing she was letting go of, and it wasn't the island, or the school, or her father, or her friends. She jerked her arm out of his grip and stalked passed him toward the door.

"Becca—"

She ignored him, not even bothering to look back. Taking the front steps two at a time, she thought back to the night Tom had come to the island, the night she had thought she'd finally gotten him back. He hadn't come down to comfort her. He'd come down to get information out of her for one of the partners at his firm.

He'd used her.

And she'd fallen for it.

How could she have been so blind?

She lifted her hand to knock on the door, and spotted the charm bracelet—the charm bracelet he'd said he'd been saving for their wedding night. Had he lied about that, too?

"I thought you wanted to talk?" Tom called after her.

She paused, looking back at him. Talk? What could they possibly have to talk about anymore?

"I have to get back to the office in Baltimore for another meeting," he said, checking his watch, "but I could probably squeeze in a quick lunch..."

"Go ahead," she said, and was amazed at the lack of emotion in her voice. "I wouldn't want to hold you up."

Tom hesitated for about three seconds, then turned, walked over to his car, slid behind the wheel, and drove away. She hadn't expected him to put up a fight. She knew now that he was too weak to stick around, to risk one of his clients seeing him in a less than favorable light.

Turning back to the door, she knocked—three loud raps.

A few moments later, she heard footsteps on the stairs. The muted click of a woman's heels came closer, until the mahogany door swung open and a tall woman with long, dark hair and pale green eyes stood on the other side. She was wearing gray slacks, a sleeveless white shell, and a necklace that looked like it was made of little bits of broken glass. "Can I help you?"

"Yes," Becca said, lifting her chin. "My name is Becca Haddaway. I'm a second grade teacher at Heron Island Elementary and I'd like to speak with you about your decision to close the school."

Lydia blinked, her gaze sweeping past Becca's shoulder to the driveway, probably trying to see if she'd brought any reporters with her. Once she was satisfied that it was only the two of them, she looked back at her. "I'm sorry, Ms. Haddaway," she said, her tone dismissive. "I was just on my way out. Now's not a good time."

"I'm sure you're very busy," Becca said, struggling to control her temper, "but I think I've earned a right to speak."

Lydia's expression grew cold. "This is highly unprofessional, coming to my house like this."

"So is refusing to call us back and ignoring all our emails."

"As I wrote *in an email* to your principal this morning, if you have any concerns, you should raise them at the public hearing this Friday. Situations like these need to be handled through the proper channels." Lydia stepped back, about to shut the door. "Now, if you'll excuse me—"

No, Becca thought. She would not excuse her. She would not be pushed aside. She caught the door before it swung shut and shoved it back open, stalking into the foyer. "Everyone knows the only reason you're doing this is to get back at your ex-husband. You already got what you wanted. You sabotaged the governor's announcement. You hurt his campaign. Can't you let the school go now?"

"This is completely inappropriate." Lydia reached for the cordless phone on the wall. "If you won't leave, I'll call the police."

"Go ahead," Becca shot back. "I can see the headline now. Retired public school administrator calls cops on second grade teacher intruder."

Lydia lowered the phone to her side, studying Becca for several long moments across the formal entranceway. "I don't know what kind of operation your principal runs, but you should know better than to get involved in decisions that are so far above your pay grade. The only thing you should be doing right now is looking for a new job."

No. Becca shook her head. As soon as she got home, the first thing she was going to do was ask Shelley to rip up her resignation letter. She wasn't leaving the island. She wasn't leaving the school. And she wasn't going to let Lydia shut them down.

She opened her mouth, about to tell her that, when a fragment of light in the living room caught her eye. She glanced over, at the beam reflected off a sterling silver frame, and trailed off when she saw the pictures. Dozens of them, in all shapes and sizes. They covered every surface, hung from every wall. It was the same person in every shot—a child, at various stages in his life.

"Is that...Colin?"

"No," Lydia said sharply.

She took a step closer, unable to look away. Did Colin have a brother? If so, they must not be close, because he'd never mentioned him. The skin on the back of her neck prickled when she realized, suddenly, that this room was a memorial. The boy in the pictures had never aged past eighteen.

In the hallway, a grandfather clock ticked, triggering some distant memory. She turned slowly back to face Lydia when she remembered that Colin *did* have a brother, a younger brother—one who'd enlisted in the military right out of high school, against his parents' wishes. She remembered hearing about it on the news, before Nick Foley had been elected governor, back when he'd been running for Mayor of Baltimore. A reporter had asked him how he'd felt about having two sons serving in the military when he'd been so outspoken about his opposition to the wars. She couldn't remember what his answer had been, but she did remember, now, that his youngest son—a helicopter pilot—had been shot down in Iraq a year later.

Gazing across the marble foyer at the woman still clutching the phone in her hand, Becca felt an overwhelming rush of sympathy. The only thing worse than losing a parent had to be losing a child. She could only imagine what Lydia must have gone through when she'd received that news.

She knew how hard it was to lose someone, how hard it was on those left behind. She started to say something to that effect, but then stopped...because something still didn't add up. If Lydia had lost one son to the war, wouldn't she be even closer with the only one she had left?

Thinking back to how upset Colin had been when he'd come to her house on Easter, Becca looked back at the living room, scanning the photos for a clue. But the only thing that stood out to her was the *lack* of photos of Colin anywhere in the house. She turned back to face Lydia. "Why don't you have any pictures of Colin?"

Lydia said nothing and her expression betrayed nothing—not even a hint of emotion.

"You hurt him, you know," Becca said. "By sabotaging your ex-husband's announcement, you hurt Colin, too. He worked really hard on that jobs program. He worked his butt off all winter to get the veterans' center ready to open by Memorial Day. He's doing everything he can to help his fellow service members, to give them a second chance."

"Not everyone deserves a second chance."

Becca took a step back. What was she saying? That she didn't think the people who'd fought for their freedom deserved to be taken care of when they came home?

Was she talking about Colin or veterans in general?

Becca had never supported the idea of going to war. She'd probably been as against it as both Colin's parents, but that didn't mean she thought any less of the men and women who'd served in it. Most of the people who went overseas had nothing to do with the decision to go to war. They had simply carried out an order that had been handed down to them. Now, over two million post 9/11 veterans were back home, many of them suffering from lingering physical and psychological wounds from a war their country had sent them to fight...and Lydia didn't believe they deserved a second chance? "More people got hurt in the wars than your youngest son. *Colin* got hurt. He lost a leg in Afghanistan."

"Colin got what he deserved."

Becca gaped at her. She couldn't possibly mean that. No one deserved to have a limb amputated. No one deserved to lose his fiancée when he came home because he wasn't whole anymore. No one deserved to lose two of his closest friends in a single day. She continued to stare at Lydia across the formal entranceway as, suddenly, everything clicked into place. "This was never just about the governor, was it? You came after the jobs program and the veterans' center on purpose? You *wanted* to hurt Colin?"

"If it wasn't for Colin," Lydia lashed out, her emotions finally snapping, "Hayden would still be here."

"What?" Becca asked, baffled.

"I begged Colin not to join the Navy. I offered him everything—money, a car, a full ride to any graduate program in the country. I offered him anything he could ever possibly want. But he wouldn't listen. No. He wanted to be a hero. He wanted to prove something. Even though he *knew* Hayden would follow in his footsteps."

Follow in his footsteps? Becca's head spun. Lydia couldn't possibly be implying...?

"Hayden died because of Colin's selfishness," Lydia said, her voice breaking.

Selfishness? Becca took another step back. The last word she would ever associate with Colin was selfish. The air conditioning clicked on, blowing a cold stream of air through the vents, despite the fact that the weather was perfect outside. Becca was vaguely aware of the tick of the grandfather clock again in the hallway, the only sound inside this cold, lonely house.

No wonder Colin had been so upset when he'd come to her house last weekend.

She knew what it was like to carry grief around, to have lost a family member at a young age. There was always a certain amount of guilt that snuck in when a loved one passed away. *Had you spent enough time with them? Had you told them you loved them often enough? Had your last conversation together been a good one?*

Her last conversation with her mother had been an argument. She'd been sixteen and desperate to go to a concert in Baltimore with some friends the following weekend. The rest of her friends' parents had all said they could go, but her mother wouldn't give in. She'd been against it from the moment Becca had first brought it up. But Becca hadn't been willing to let it go.

A part of her had always wondered if the words they'd exchanged that night had left her mother so angry that she hadn't been focusing when she'd been driving, if they'd caused her to lose control of the car on the slippery roads on the way to the restaurant. But her father had silenced her every time she'd brought it up. Even Tom had shot her down, vehemently, whenever she'd tried to take the blame. It hadn't made it any easier, but at least she'd always known that any guilt she carried was her own.

How would she have lived with herself if her father and Tom had blamed her? If they'd laid the same guilt on her that Lydia had laid on Colin?

The phone in the house rang, a shrill reminder of the outside world pealing through the silence.

"I want you to leave now," Lydia said coldly. Not waiting for a response, she turned, her heels clicking over the marble floor as she walked into the next room, stopping only when she came to the window overlooking the water.

Becca started to follow her, then paused when she spotted an envelope lying on a table in the foyer. It was mostly hidden under a pile of mail, but she could clearly make out the embossed logo belonging to Tom's firm on the seal. She looked back up at Lydia. The other woman's back was still turned as she picked up the phone call, as she gave her full attention to whoever was on the other line.

Slipping the envelope from the pile, Becca turned and walked quietly back out the front door. She walked down the steps, got in her car, and started to drive. She didn't stop until she'd made it to the stop sign at the intersection of Ritchie Highway a few miles away. Her hands shook as she picked up the envelope and pulled out the contents.

She took one look at the photos and knew instantly that they were pictures of Lydia with another man. She flipped through the financial statements. She didn't know why they were important, but she would find out. Sliding everything back into the envelope, she set the package on the passenger seat and reached for her phone, punching in one of the first numbers on automatic dial.

Grace picked up on the second ring. "What's up?"

"Where are you?" Becca asked.

"At my apartment. Why?"

"Stay there. I'm coming over."

"Now?" Grace said, surprised.

"Yes. I'll be there in an hour."

"I thought we were meeting in Annapolis this afternoon? For the practice run at the salon?"

"No," Becca said, turning onto the highway. "The wedding's off."

NINETEEN

*W*alking across the tarmac at Baltimore-Washington International Airport, Colin took in the sleek private jet idling at the end of the runway. "Nice ride," he said, holding out his hand to the man who'd insisted on picking him up and flying him out to Colorado as soon as he'd expressed the slightest bit of interest in his offer the day before.

Austin Turner returned his handshake. "Beats the birds we used to ride in."

Colin smiled, remembering the days of being strapped into the cargo holds of Black Hawk helicopters flying under the cover of night on the way to a mission. The tactical transport aircraft were designed for high-risk combat insertions and enemy engagement, not for their passengers' comfort. He had a feeling this plane had been designed with the exact opposite in mind. "Is it yours?"

Austin shook his head, releasing his hand. "It belongs to a client."

He said it like it was no big deal, like it was perfectly normal for a former SEAL to have access to a private jet. Colin had grown up with wealth, but this was another league entirely. He couldn't help being intrigued at the prospect of working with someone who had those kinds of connections, who could tap into that kind of money for vets.

He'd done a lot of thinking over the past twenty-four hours. It was time to refocus on the mission at hand. He'd gotten side-tracked, letting his feelings for Becca cloud his better judgment. He'd fallen for the romance of Heron Island—the idea of buying a home, of putting down roots, of belonging somewhere.

But Heron Island wasn't his home. It would never be his home. Not the way it was Will's, or Annie's, or Becca's.

Becca had been right when she'd assumed he'd only been passing through. He didn't belong there. He didn't belong anywhere.

"I've been following the news on your father," Austin said, gesturing for Colin to walk with him toward the stairs leading up to the jet. "He's denying everything. Who should I believe?"

"I don't know," Colin admitted. Frankly, he didn't care anymore. The only reason he'd agreed to work with his father when he'd come back from Afghanistan was because he hadn't known what else to do with his life.

He knew exactly what he wanted to do with his life now—help other veterans. If Will saw him as a liability because of his connection to his father, then it was time for him to leave. He needed to go where he was wanted, where he could make a differ-ence. Maybe Colorado would be that place, for the next few years, at least.

After that, who knew?

It didn't matter. If it was just going to be him, he could go anywhere. He could reinvent himself every few years if he had to.

Stepping into the cabin, Colin's gaze swept over the plush leather seats, the comfortable sofa and coffee table, the fully stocked wet bar. Austin had retired from the teams only a few years ago. Life as the CEO of a private security firm seemed to suit him just fine.

As if the picture weren't appealing enough already, an attractive woman with long auburn hair stepped out of a room in the back and offered him a chilled bottle of water. He took it and thanked her as the slow quiet whir of the stairs receded behind them.

"We'll be taking off in five minutes," she said, her voice soft and soothing. "Is there anything else I can get for either of you?"

"No. Thank you, Nicole," Austin said. "That'll be all."

She smiled at Austin and blushed before pressing a button on the wall and slipping into the cockpit with the pilot, disappearing with a quiet whoosh of the electric door.

Colin lifted a brow.

Austin smiled. "She's got a twin sister who lives in Crested Butte. It's a few towns over from where we're going, but they offered to meet us for a drink later, if you're interested."

I'm not, Colin thought, but he caught himself before he said the words out loud. There was no reason why he shouldn't be. There was nothing holding him back. Maybe a meaningless hookup was exactly what he needed to help him put things back in perspective. "Sounds good," he said, settling into one of the aisle seats and buckling the belt low across his hips.

The pilot came over the loud speaker, instructing them to prepare for takeoff. Colin took a sip of water and looked out the row of windows as the plane began to taxi, picking up speed down the runway. In moments, the nose tilted up and they were airborne, heading west.

Austin waited until the pilot came back on with word that they'd reached a comfortable elevation and they were free to move around the cabin. Leaning back in his seat and stretching out his legs, he turned his attention back to Colin. "Enough with the small talk. Tell me what I need to say to convince you to move to Colorado and work for me."

Not much, Colin thought as the fields and highways faded beneath them. He'd already made his decision.

BECCA PARKED on the street outside Grace's apartment in Capitol Hill. Grabbing the envelope, she got out of her car and dodged a trio of twenty-something girls giggling over a text one of them had just received on her phone. She let herself into her best friend's tiny front yard through a rusted wrought-iron gate, dialing Colin's number as she made her way up to the door. When the call went straight to voicemail, as it had every time she'd tried calling him since leaving Annapolis, she hung up, frustrated. Why wasn't he answering?

Shoving her phone back into her purse, she reached for the knob. The door swung open before she had a chance to touch it. Grace stood on the other side, her gray eyes filled with concern. "Hey," she said worriedly. "What's going on? Are you okay?"

"No." Becca handed her the envelope and strode into the turn of the century row house that had been converted into two separate apartments—one upstairs and one downstairs—and climbed the steps to the second floor.

Grace followed, the old wooden steps creaking under her bare feet as she peeled the flap open and pulled out the contents of the envelope. She stopped walking when she got to the landing and saw the photographs. "Is that Lydia?"

"Yeah," Becca said, turning back to face her.

Grace glanced up, her eyes widening. "Who's the guy with her?"

"I don't know. I was hoping you would."

Grace looked back down, flipping through the pictures more

slowly this time. "I'm not sure. His face seems vaguely familiar, but I can't place him." Walking into the living room, Grace set the photos on the coffee table and pulled out the rest of the papers inside the envelope. "Where did you get these?" she asked, thumbing through the financial statements.

"Lydia."

Grace looked back up. "Lydia gave you these?"

"Well, she didn't exactly *give* them to me," Becca admitted. "I took them from her house."

"When?"

"Just now. Right before I came here. I went to talk to her about the school—"

"Wait," Grace said, cutting her off. "Hang on. Back up." She set the financial statements on the coffee table with the photos. "What does this have to do with your wedding?"

Becca let out a long breath. Laying her hands on the back of the sofa, she told her friend everything.

After she'd finished, Grace stared at her for several long moments. "Are you sure?" she asked finally. "Are you sure it's over? It's really over?"

Becca nodded.

"You're not going to change your mind?"

"No." Becca looked down, picking at a thread coming loose from one of the sofa cushions. "You were right."

"About what?"

"Tom," she said. "I can't believe I didn't see it before."

"Hey." Grace walked over to where she stood and took her hands. "Don't be so hard on yourself. I knew you'd figure it out eventually. I'm just glad you did before the wedding, and not after."

The wedding. Becca looked up at her as the reality of the situation began to sink in. "All that planning," she said. "All those people. What am I going to tell everyone?"

"The truth," Grace said, leading her over to the sofa. "That the groom turned out to be a dick. Maybe some of the vendors will be willing to give you your deposit back."

Becca covered her face with her hands. How had she let this situation get so out of control? She needed some time to think, to process it all...and to officially tell Tom that it was over. But she didn't know how long it would take for Lydia to realize the envelope was missing. She lowered her hands back to her sides, looking at the papers on the table. "We need to find out who the man in the pictures is and what those financial statements mean."

Grace's eyes grew concerned again. "Are you sure you don't want to press pause for a few hours? We could get some lunch, split a bottle of wine, do a little shopping? You just called off your wedding. Maybe you need some time to breathe."

Becca shook her head. She didn't need time to breathe. She needed to find a way to save the school. And she needed to reach Colin. Fishing her phone back out of her purse, she checked the screen for a missed call. Nothing. "Do you know where Colin is? I've been trying to reach him since I left Annapolis."

Grace shook her head as she snagged her laptop from the kitchen counter and carried it over to the coffee table.

"I'm going to call Annie and see if she knows," Becca said.

"Okay," Grace said, already pulling up a search engine and starting to type.

Becca walked out onto Grace's small balcony. She could hear sirens in the distance and the steady whoosh of traffic from Pennsylvania Avenue a few blocks away. She dialed the number for the café, watching a robin hop over the pavement as she waited for Annie to pick up.

"Wind Chime Café. This is Annie."

"Hey, Annie. It's Becca."

"Hey, Becca. What's up?"

"I'm trying to find Colin and his phone keeps going straight to voicemail. Do you know where he is?"

"He's probably still in the air."

"In the air?"

"On his way to Colorado."

"Colorado?"

"To meet with Austin Turner," Annie explained, as if that was supposed to mean something to her.

"Who's Austin Turner?"

There was a pause on the other end of the line. "I thought he would have told you."

"Told me *what*?"

Becca heard voices in the background, two women speaking to each other in hushed tones—most likely Annie and Della. A few moments later, Annie came back on the line and it was quieter in the background.

"There's another SEAL who's launching a program for vets in Colorado," Annie explained. "He's got a ton of money behind him and he wants Colin to come out there and work for him."

Becca's mouth fell open. How was this the first time she'd heard about this? "But what about the inn? What about Will?"

There was another long pause. "Will's probably going to start looking for another partner soon."

Becca stared across the alley, at a telephone line dipping between two neighbors' homes. Colin couldn't leave. Not now. Not before she'd had a chance to tell him how she felt.

"Hey," Annie said gently. "Are you okay?"

"I have to go," Becca said, and hung up. Another siren wailed in the distance, closer this time. How long had he been planning this? How long had he been thinking about leaving? He'd told her only a week ago that he wanted to buy a house on Heron Island, that he loved it there, that he wanted to live there forever.

What had changed?

"Hey," Grace called from inside. "I think I found something."

Becca turned, slowly. What if Colin had left so that Lydia would leave them alone? What if he'd realized that if he took himself off the island, his mother would have no reason to come after them? What if he'd done this simply to protect them?

Even if they found a way to discredit Lydia, even if they found a way to save the school, and the veterans' center, and everything went back to the way it was before, life on Heron Island would never be the same.

Not if Colin wasn't there.

TWENTY

*T*wo days later, Becca woke to the sound of mourning doves cooing. Through a gap in the drapes, she spied the first hints of dawn breaking over the island. The faint blue light filtered into the room, revealing her grandmother's hand-made quilt lying on the floor, her cranberry-colored comforter a rumpled mass at the end of the bed, her white cotton sheets twisted and tangled around her feet.

She'd finally left Grace's apartment in D.C. after spending the past thirty-six hours uncovering enough dirt on Lydia to open an investigation into her entire professional career. It hadn't taken Grace long to identify the man in the pictures as Henry Cooper, and to realize that it must have been Lydia who'd made the promises to the casino owner, not Nick Foley. As soon as they'd known what to look for, they'd started digging into the financial records of every school district Lydia had managed.

They'd found dozens of inconsistencies—state grants that had been received but never dispersed, after-school programs that had been created and heavily funded but had never gotten off the ground, endowments that had come in from anonymous private donors and then mysteriously disappeared six months later. It hadn't been entirely clear where the money had gone at first, but in most cases, it hadn't gone back to the schools.

When it had, it had been funneled into the larger schools in the primarily white, wealthy communities, never the smaller schools in the lower-income communities that desperately need it. The smaller schools had been shut down, while the larger schools had received lavish remodels: a new set of LED lights for a football stadium at one of the high schools, a fancy equestrian center with an indoor ring at one of the elementary schools, a state of the art technology lab with heated floors and ergonomic chairs at one of the middle schools.

It wasn't a coincidence that the schools that had received the most extravagant upgrades were the same schools where the children of major political donors had gone.

For years, Lydia had been using her position of power as a politician's wife to collect huge donations into her school systems, making her look like an incredibly effective and efficient administrator, in exchange for favors that would be doled out later, once her husband was elected governor.

Becca had spent most of the past two days on the phone, calling every teacher who had ever worked with Lydia, including the ones in the Dominican Republic. Some of them had refused to speak with her when they'd found out why she was calling, but a few had cautiously offered bits and pieces to round out the story. The last piece of the puzzle had fallen into place when she'd reached a woman named Caroline Strang in New Hampshire, the same woman who'd given the photos to Tom's firm.

Caroline was an American who'd spent a few years teaching at the school in the Dominican Republic and had become friends with Lydia when she'd been down there. They had lost touch over the years, but she'd heard from some of teachers at the school that Lydia hadn't fulfilled any of her promises recently. Books hadn't been ordered. Teachers hadn't been paid. Repairs to the school hadn't been made. Despite the fact that there was plenty of money in the account, no support was being provided anymore.

Caroline had tried to contact Lydia to confront her about it, but despite leaving several messages, she'd never gotten a response. When she'd caught the clip on the news about Richard Goldwater accusing Nick Foley of corruption, she'd known it was a lie and had decided to come forward.

According to Caroline, Lydia had never planned to divorce Nick Foley. She'd been perfectly willing to remain part of a political power couple while continuing her affair with Henry Cooper, a man who had his own wife—a wealthy heiress—who he had no desire to divorce. Making frequent trips down to the island to "oversee the school" had been the perfect cover for both of them.

But when Hayden had been killed, everything had fallen apart. Within months, Lydia's marriage had crumbled. Henry had slowly withdrawn, and eventually ended the affair. Lydia had quit her job, giving the Maryland school system only a few days' notice, and she'd let the school in the Dominican Republic fall into disrepair as she'd retreated into a cloud of grief so thick she couldn't see anything but her own pain anymore.

Shifting onto her side, Becca watched the morning sky turn a paler shade of blue. There was a part of her, a small part, that felt bad for Lydia. Losing her son had destroyed her. But instead of seeking help, of trying to find a way to deal with the grief, she had searched for someone to blame.

There was a point at which you had to take ownership of your grief. You couldn't let it hold you back, crippling you in the past forever. No matter how much tragedy or trauma you'd suffered, there was always a choice, every day, to stay in that place of sorrow, or to get out of bed, put one foot in front of the other, and move forward.

You could bury your pain in work or alcohol or drugs or even focusing all your attention on helping others instead of yourself, but at some point you had to face it. You had to deal with it. You had to let it work its way through you and then find the strength to release it.

You weren't doing the person you lost any good by living in the past. You weren't honoring them. You weren't serving anyone but yourself and your own selfish need to cling onto their memory.

Easing her feet over the side of the bed, she felt the cool wooden floorboards brush against the soles of her feet. It was way past time she let some of her memories go.

She had seen a small glimpse of herself in Lydia two days ago, and she hadn't liked what she'd seen. She hadn't liked it at all. She might not have pinned the blame for what had happened to her mother and Tom's mother on anyone else, but she had been harboring her own guilt for that accident for far too long.

She had carried that guilt around for so long that the lines between love and obligation had begun to blur. Somewhere along the way, she had lost all sight of what she really wanted.

All she had ever wanted was a simple life on this island. She wanted to wake up every day and walk to the elementary school and make her living teaching at the same school her mother had taught at. She wanted to raise her children in this neighborhood, a place where they could ride their bikes without worrying about traffic, a place where they could spend their weekends exploring the shoreline and marshes instead of going to the mall.

As much as she'd hoped that one day Tom would change his mind, she had always known, deep down, that he had no desire to ever come back to this island. He had turned his back on it years ago. For some reason, he had held onto her—a bridge to a past he desperately wanted to forget.

A warm breeze blew into the room through the open window, teasing the curtains in a gentle dance over the sill. Lifting her left hand slowly, she gazed down at the tear-shaped diamond still glittering from her ring finger. She'd been so focused on helping Grace, she'd forgotten to take it off. She hadn't even had a chance to cancel a single vendor yet, or tell anyone besides Grace, Tom, and Shelley that the wedding was off.

Rising, she walked over to the wooden bureau to pull out some clothes. She dressed in a pair of faded jeans and a lightweight sweater and headed out to the living room. She would start boxing everything up and making a list of everyone she needed to call after breakfast. But, first, there was someone else she needed to talk to.

Slipping her feet into a pair of flip-flops from the pile of shoes by the door, she quietly let herself out of the house. A soft mist rose over the marshes, tinged with pink. Workboats threaded through the still waters and she could hear the deep voices of several watermen calling out to each other in greeting as they laid their morning traps. She reached down, snapping off the stems of a few purple irises growing along the side of the road as she started down a dirt path she could walk with her eyes closed.

When she came to the small white chapel overlooking the water, she made her way to the familiar resting place behind it. Streaks of pink bloomed in the sky as she laid the flowers on her mother's grave. Stepping back slowly, she lowered herself to the cool stone bench facing the headstone.

"Hi, mom," she whispered.

The marshes rustled. An egret high-stepped through the shallow waters. In the distance, a bald eagle glided toward a solitary oak tree clinging to a sinking finger of land.

"I think I made a mistake," she said, twisting her engagement ring slowly around her finger. "I think I was too scared to see it before, but I'm..." She looked down at the diamond, testing the words out loud for the first time. "I'm not in love with Tom."

Bluebirds sang from the branches of a weeping willow. The faintest scent of roses drifted through the air as a pink sunrise bled over the horizon. "I'm not sure I've ever been in love with him."

She twisted the ring again, round and around her finger. The mists rose, curling over the surface of the water like smoke. "All I ever wanted was to follow in your footsteps, to have what you and dad had. I think I always knew, deep down, that I didn't love Tom. Not the way you're supposed to love someone. But I thought that was okay, because I didn't want to love anyone that much. I thought it would be safer to be with someone who I could never give my whole heart to, because if I ever lost him, it wouldn't destroy me."

She looked back at the flowers lying at the base of the headstone. "After the accident, I almost lost both of you. I think...there were times when Dad wanted to die, when he wished that the alcohol would just take him and numb the pain forever. And I think I've been afraid of a love that strong my whole life—a love that could kill me if it ended. I thought it was something I could protect myself from."

She looked back down at the ring as a single tear rolled down her cheek. "But you can't protect yourself from it, can you? You can't stop yourself from falling in love when you meet the person you're supposed to be with. There's nothing that can stop that, is there?"

She twisted the ring around one more time, then slowly eased it off her finger. Laying it on the bench beside her, she felt a weight—a weight she'd been carrying for years—begin to lift. She looked back out at the water, breathing in the scent of spring flowers, of morning dew, of new beginnings. She sat for several minutes in silence, watching a workboat motor slowly through the mists until the sound of the engine faded, and there was nothing but the songs of the birds and the whisper of wind playing through the marsh grasses.

She didn't hear the footsteps of the man walking up behind her until he was only a few feet away. She glanced over her shoulder and froze when she caught sight of her father. "Dad," she said, looking away and quickly swiping at the tears on her cheeks before he could see them. "What are you doing here? I thought you were out on the water."

He walked around to the front of the bench, sitting down beside her. "The hydraulics are leaking again."

"Again?"

He nodded. "I thought I had a few extra gaskets in the truck, but I couldn't find any. I was heading home to check the garage when I saw you walking this way."

If he'd seen her walking from home and followed her, how long had he been here? How much had he heard?

Slowly, answering her question before she had to ask it out loud, he reached for her hand. "Have you told Tom?"

Becca let out a shaky breath. He'd heard everything. "I told him yesterday."

"How did he take it?"

"Not well." She looked back out at the water. Tom had been furious, not because she'd broken his heart, but by how the partners at his firm might react to the news. He was sure they would see him as unstable now, unfit to be a part of the family at the firm because he couldn't get his own fiancée to walk down the aisle.

He'd told her she was selfish, that she was making a huge mistake. When she'd offered to come over and get her things, he'd told her to wait until later this week when he was at work, so he wouldn't have to see her.

Her father looked down at the ring on the bench between them, his gaze lingering on the diamond glittering in the soft morning light. When he looked back up, his eyes were sad. "I thought you loved Tom, that he was what you wanted. I didn't realize you never really loved him. I'm sorry if I ever made you feel like that's what your mother and I would have wanted. Just because we were high school sweethearts doesn't mean that everyone will meet their true love in high school. All your mother and I ever wanted was for you to be happy."

"Are *you* happy, Dad?" she asked. "You've never remarried. You've never even dated anybody since Mom. Haven't you ever wanted to at least try to move on?"

"I've never had any interest in anyone but your mother."

"But aren't you lonely? Don't you wish—"

"I *wish*," he said gently, "that you would stop trying so hard to make everyone else happy and start thinking about yourself for once."

She looked down at their joined hands. Was it possible they had both spent all these years trying to make up for what they thought they'd done—she inadvertently causing the accident and he falling apart afterwards—that they hadn't taken the time to consider what they needed individually?

What would happen if she opened up to him? If she told him the truth? If she didn't try so hard to be the strong one? If she let him be her father again?

"You're falling for Colin, aren't you?" he asked quietly.

She nodded as another tear slipped free. She brushed it away, but she didn't try to hide her face from him anymore. "He's leaving, Dad. He got a job offer in Colorado. I can't ask him to stay here for me. I don't want to hold him back. I don't want to make the same mistake I made with Tom."

"Colin's not Tom," her father said. "You need to tell him how you feel. If you don't, you'll always wonder."

"I'm scared," she whispered.

"I know," he said, squeezing her hand.

"What I feel for Colin... It's..." She shook her head, unable to put it into words. "I've never felt this way about anyone. What if he doesn't feel the same way?"

"All love is risk, Becca," her father said gently. "It's true that losing your mother almost killed me, and I will always regret how I handled things after the accident. But I would never have taken back one moment of my life with her." His brown eyes softened, reflecting the memories that no one would ever be able to take away from him. "I would rather have a love as strong as I had with your mother for a single day than a lukewarm love that lasted a lifetime."

WALKING HOME A HALF HOUR LATER, Becca thought about what her father had said—that all love was risk. She had never considered herself much of a risk taker. She had spent most of her life choosing the paths that were safe, the ones that would result in the least possibility of getting hurt.

But was that any way to live? Without taking risks, how would you ever know what you were truly capable of? How would you ever know how happy you could be? How would you ever know if someone you loved felt the same way about you, unless you found the courage to tell him?

She thought about the risk Annie had taken in going after Will six months ago. After spending five weeks on the island—the first time he'd been home in over ten years—Will had left abruptly when his SEAL team had been called up for a mission, without any plans to ever return. Becca had been one of the first people who'd encouraged Annie to go after him. She'd been the one to purchase the plane ticket and put it in her friend's hand.

With Grace, Ryan and Della's help, she'd practically forced Annie onto that flight to San Diego.

But Annie and Will's situation had been so different. Will had been in love with Annie. Anyone who'd seen them together had known that. And the bond between Will and Taylor had grown so strong in those five short weeks, that if Annie hadn't gone after him, the rest of the islanders would have gone for her.

Following the thin path that skirted the edge of the marshes, Becca thought back to what Annie had said to her a few days ago, when they'd been talking in her kitchen: *I saw the way you looked at Colin today. And the way he looked at you. There wasn't a person in that room who couldn't see the chemistry between you.*

Letting her fingertips trail along the tops of the grasses, Becca knew it was true. There was no question there had been chemistry between them since the first night they'd met. But was it fair of her to ask him to stay—to turn down a job offer he was obviously interested in if he'd flown all the way out to Colorado to interview for it—when they hadn't even gone on a single date yet?

The soft ground gave way to pavement and she was back on her street. A few neighbors were waking up, sipping coffee on their porches or wandering out to the sidewalk to retrieve the morning paper. Randy Cole's black lab was outside, chasing bunnies through Gladys Schaefer's flowerbeds, her tail wagging, her nose wet with dew. She could hear children running around inside some of the houses, their squeals and laughter drifting out the windows, into the street.

What if Colin had finally realized that Heron Island wasn't big enough for him? That he needed more out of life? That he was destined for greater things?

Who was she to hold him back from that?

Turning up the path to her house, she glanced up at the porch, and stopped dead in her tracks. Her heart jumped, thumping against her rib cage as she took in the man sitting on her steps.

Colin rose slowly.

"I-I thought you were in Colorado," Becca stammered.

"I was."

Becca's heart beat faster. What was he doing here? Had he come back to say goodbye? To tell her that he was leaving? That he needed to start his new job right away? She forced herself to remain calm, to put one foot in front of the other as she started toward him. "Annie told me about Austin...about the job."

Colin nodded, never taking his eyes off hers as she slowly closed the distance between them. "It was a tempting offer."

She paused, looking up at him, her heart in her throat. "You're not taking it?"

"No."

A seed of hope sprouted inside her, stretching up toward the sun. "Why not?"

"Because it wasn't on Heron Island," he said, reaching for her hand, "and you weren't there."

Petals unfurled, blooming inside her.

"I saw Grace's article," Colin said quietly. "I called her afterwards, to thank her." His fingers curled around Becca's—safe, warm, secure. "She told me you were the one who gave her the pictures."

Becca nodded.

He turned her hand over slowly, gazing down at her bare fingers. "And that you weren't engaged anymore."

"I'm not," she said softly.

He lifted his eyes back to hers, brushing his thumb over the spot where her ring had been. All around them, birds chirped from the branches of the trees. Down the street, a neighbor's sprinkler clicked on, shooting a cheerful spray of water into the flowerbeds.

"Are you sure this is what you want?" Becca asked. "Are you sure this island, and the inn, will be enough for you?"

Colin smiled. "I'm not taking the job in Colorado because Austin and I came to a different arrangement, one that's much more appealing to both of us."

Becca waited for him to go on.

"We both want to expand on what we're doing, to open more of these centers all over the country," Colin explained. "We're going to use Will's inn and the center in Colorado as models. As soon as both places are up and running, we're going to reach out to everyone we know and see how many people we can recruit who might be willing to open similar places in their hometowns. We're going into business together. Austin will run the West Coast side of the operations from L.A., and I'll head up the East Coast side from here."

Becca held her breath. "Here?"

He nodded. "I'm going to keep my apartment in Annapolis. I'll probably be back and forth a fair amount, at least in the beginning, but I'll spend most of my time on Heron Island."

Risk, Becca thought as early morning sunlight slanted into the yard, bathing them both in a warm golden glow. If this wasn't worth risking everything for, then what was? "Colin, I—"

His mouth was on hers before she could finish her sentence, before she could even say the words out loud.

And what was there to say, really? Hadn't they talked enough?

He had come back. He had decided to stay. That was all the answer she'd needed.

Melting into him, she surrendered to the kiss. She gave into the feeling of falling, of losing control, of letting everything go but the two of them and this moment. His arms came around her and she felt something shift, like rocks tumbling from a stone wall. The base crumbled, washing away, until there was nothing but grass and flowers—row after row of beautiful flowers swaying in the wind.

Colin pulled back slowly, laying his forehead against hers. "I want to spend the day with you, Becca," he murmured, touching her cheek. "Just you."

"I'd like that," she whispered.

"And then," he said, his hand skimming down her arm, reaching for her hand, "I'd like to take you out. On a date. Somewhere nice. Somewhere quiet. Somewhere in St. Michaels or Easton where we can talk and get to know each other, without everyone on the island watching us."

She glanced up at him, surprised. He'd never seemed like the kind of person who cared what other people thought.

He nodded over her shoulder and she turned, following his gaze to where several of her neighbors were standing in their front yards dressed only in their robes and pajamas, gaping at them.

She turned back, stifling a laugh. "I haven't had a chance to tell everyone that the wedding's off."

Colin's lips curved as he went in for another longer, deeper kiss. "Maybe you won't have to now."

No, Becca thought, laughing. She knew how fast gossip traveled on this island. She pulled back, smiling, and gave her neighbors a friendly wave, as if it were perfectly normal for her to be kissing Colin when she was supposed to be marrying Tom in two weeks.

She had no doubt that the entire village would know that the wedding was off in less than an hour.

Turning, together, they started to walk up to the porch. They were almost to the top step when a flash of light caught her eye. Becca looked up at a tiny wind chime that Taylor had made for her months ago. It hung from one of the beams, spinning slowly as rays of light bounced off the pieces of a mirror Taylor had salvaged from a garage sale.

Becca reached up, touching one of the small reflective pieces, as a crazy thought began to take shape.

"Colin?"

"Yes?"

"How would you like to be my date at a wedding in two weeks?"

He looked back at her. "Whose?"

"Well..." she said, letting her hand fall away from the chime. "I don't know if they're going to go for it yet, but I have an idea..."

TWENTY-ONE

TWO WEEKS LATER...

*T*winkle lights shimmered through the leaves of every tree in the backyard at the inn. Wind chimes dangled from the branches, filling the air with their soft, lilting melodies as they swayed in the breezes blowing off the Bay. Mason jars filled with white candles flickered from the lawn, leading over two hundred guests on meandering paths between the inn, the pier, the picnic areas, the buffet, and the dessert table—which was where Colin was headed now, in search of a slice of that famous Smith Island Cake everyone kept talking about.

Skirting the edge of the dance floor, where a local band was getting ready to play, he waved to a group of people walking out of the inn. Most of the islanders had been in for a tour by now, eager to see the transformation. The construction had wrapped up a few days ago, and Annie, Will and Taylor would be moving into the brand new wing this weekend.

He'd been surprised at how many people had come up to him

this evening to tell him how good it looked, how happy they were that he'd brought this place back to life. He'd expected most of the praise to have gone to Will, since the place technically belonged to him, but maybe some of the islanders were actually starting to accept Colin as one of them.

It hadn't hurt that Grace's article had destroyed his mother's professional reputation and the board had subsequently fired her and dropped the threat to close the elementary school. With Taylor's grandfather's generous contribution, they had approved the renovations to the gym for that summer and found a way to fund the rest of the operating expenses with state money. All the teachers and staff would get to keep their jobs, and since Shelley hadn't found a replacement for Becca yet, Becca had gladly accepted her old position back.

He looked across the lawn, at where Becca was talking with Grace by the water. He'd been concerned when she'd first come up with the idea of handing her entire wedding over to Annie and Will that it might be difficult for her to attend as a guest. But as far as he could tell, the fact that this event was supposed to have been hers didn't seem to be fazing her at all. In a blue sundress, with a glass of pink champagne in her hand, she had never looked happier and more beautiful to him than she did tonight.

Passing by the old hackberry tree, he lifted his own glass in a silent toast to Will, who was chatting with Ryan and Jake, his arms wrapped securely around his bride. It was hard to believe that next weekend, the inn would officially open for business. A bunch of guys from their former team were flying out from San Diego to be here for the event on Memorial Day, as well as close to three hundred people he'd met working in Annapolis and volunteering at Walter Reed over the past year.

The next day, the first eleven veterans who were coming to stay with them would arrive. He already had jobs lined up for most of them on the island. Five of the men and two of the women would be working on Ryan's father's oyster farm. It would be hard work and it wouldn't pay much at first, but they wouldn't have any living expenses, and it would at least get their hands moving and their heads back in the right place. The ones who'd been too badly injured to do the heavy manual labor could work on the public relations side—marketing, branding, website development, building relationships with chefs, distributors, and other professionals who worked in the local seafood industry.

The whole thing was an experiment, and he knew they'd hit a few bumps along the way, but he couldn't wait to get started.

He'd officially stepped down from his position at the State House the week before. He felt confident that the jobs program was in good hands with the rest of the team who'd helped him make it a reality. After getting off to a wobbly start, it was slowly starting to pick up traction again.

Richard Goldwater's party was still scrambling to try to find more instances of corruption related to his father, but so far they hadn't had any luck. He and his father had had a long talk after Grace's article had come out, about a lot of things—things they probably should have talked about years ago.

His father wasn't perfect. He'd made some mistakes in his life. But who hadn't?

What mattered now was that they were back on good terms. They had both agreed that Colin wouldn't have anything to do with the rest of the campaign. For the first time ever, they were going to try to have a normal father-son relationship—one that didn't have anything to do with politics.

Spotting Luke and Courtney at the far end of the dessert table, he walked over to them. Della had outdone herself, baking around the clock for the past several days to create a mouthwatering spread of meringue pies, berry tarts, lemon bars, iced sugar cookies cut out in the shape of wedding bells, and of course, those famous Smith Island Cakes—a local specialty that featured ten layers of rich, buttery cake, each separated by a layer of icing.

"Which one should I try first?" he asked, when Courtney handed him a plate.

"Coconut," Luke said quickly, then hesitated. "No. Wait... chocolate!" He came over to stand beside Colin, peering down at the cakes. "Or caramel," he said, pointing at one in the middle. He looked up at Colin and grinned, his mouth covered in icing. "I like them all."

"You should try the traditional one first," Courtney said, cutting him a slice. "It's yellow cake with chocolate fudge icing." She lifted the serving knife, sliding a piece onto his plate.

Colin took a bite and let out a groan. "That's insanely good."

Courtney smiled. "Della had a great-aunt who lived on Smith Island. She learned how to make them from her."

Colin took a few more bites, then picked up the serving knife Courtney had set down. He cut a generous slice of red velvet and added it to his plate.

Beside him, Luke's eyes widened. "What kind is *that*?"

"I think it's red velvet." He broke off a small piece with his fingers, popping it into his mouth. "Yep," he nodded. "With cream cheese icing." He looked down at Luke. "You want a piece?"

Luke nodded, grabbing a new plate.

Colin started to cut another slice, then glanced up at Courtney for approval. "Is that okay?"

"You're going to make yourself sick," Courtney said to her son, but she nodded her consent to Colin.

Colin laid the cake on Luke's plate. The kid was already gobbling it up with his fingers before Colin had set the knife back down on the table.

"Here," Courtney said, wiping at Luke's mouth with a napkin

and then stuffing a few clean napkins in his pocket. "At least take a few of these with you."

Luke finished the cake and grinned up at his mother as he wiped fingers covered in icing all over his shirt.

Courtney shook her head and sighed. "You're hopeless," she said, but there was a small smile twitching at the corners of her mouth.

"Luke!" Taylor ran over, holding a fistful of unlit sparklers. "Look what Uncle Joe gave me!" She pushed half of them into his hand. "He said if we light them, they'll sparkle!"

"Cool!" Luke dropped his plate on the table and ran after her as she raced to the nearest Mason jar and dipped the first sparkler into the flame.

Colin and Courtney watched them chase each other around the yard, laughing as little bits of fire shot out of the top of the sticks. "Luke seems happy tonight," Colin said.

Courtney nodded, but her smile faded as she turned and began tidying up the dessert table. He'd heard that she'd started leaning on some of the other mothers recently, letting them help out by watching Luke when she was at work. The kid was obviously doing a lot better, but something must still be upsetting her.

He knew she was still working two jobs. She still had permanent circles under her eyes, but despite how tired she looked, he couldn't help noticing how much effort she'd put into her appearance tonight. She was wearing a black cocktail dress that complemented her slim frame perfectly. Her hair was swept back from her face in a simple, classy knot, and she'd even taken the time to curl a few pieces around her face.

He'd gotten used to seeing her in her work clothes—an old T-shirt and a pair of baggy sweatpants and beat-up sneakers—whenever he'd stopped by to check in on Luke, as he had a few times over the past couple weeks. But the first thing that had struck him the moment he'd walked in her door was how impeccably clean and organized her home was. The second thing that had struck him were the pictures of her with her late husband all over the house. In every shot, she'd been dressed up sharp and looking good.

She may not have come from money, but she had style and class and she obviously took pride in keeping up her both appearance and her home—when she had the time to devote to them.

Turning around to face her, an idea began to stir inside him. "You cut hair, right?"

"Yes," she said, glancing up and giving him a brief once over. "You look like you could use a trim."

He smiled. "I wasn't thinking about myself. But some of the people who are going to be staying with us might need some help getting cleaned up."

"I'm always open to taking on new clients," she said, still tidying up the table, which really hadn't needed any tidying up in the first place. "Just give them my number."

"Actually, I was thinking more along the lines of you coming here, instead of them going to you."

She glanced up. "What do you mean?"

"Well," Colin said, leaning back against the table. "Most of the people coming to stay with us have never been on a real interview before. I know at least five of them enlisted straight out of high school. They might not know how to dress, how to present themselves professionally. Will and I will be working with them on how to answer questions and build a decent résumé, but we could use someone to help with shopping for clothes, finding outfits that'll look good on them. I'm thinking mostly consignment and second hand stuff. We don't have a big budget, but we've got some funds to play around with. Think you'd be interested in something like that?"

He caught the flash of interest before the shield went up. "I already have two jobs," she said, shifting a cake platter an inch to the left that had looked perfectly fine where it had been before.

"How much do you make?"

She paused, taken aback by the bluntness of his question. "Excuse me?"

"How much do you make at the hotel?"

She straightened her shoulders, turning to face him, too proud to be embarrassed. "Eight dollars an hour."

"We can double that."

She blinked. "Double it?"

Colin nodded. "We're still looking for someone to clean once a week, too, if you have any interest in that. You could pick the day, set your own hours. You'd still have plenty of time for your regular hair clients. You do most of your appointments out of your house anyway, right?"

She nodded slowly.

"We're only a mile down the road, so it'd be an easy commute, and you could bring Luke with you whenever you came to work." He nodded back out to the kids, who were still chasing each other around the yard. "It looks like he and Taylor get along pretty well. They could do their homework together in the evenings if you wanted to fit in a few hours of work at the end of the day."

She looked up at him, like it was too good to be true. "I'm not looking for a handout."

"You're a hard worker, Courtney. You'll earn every penny we pay you." He watched the wheels turning in that sharp, efficient mind of hers. He had a feeling she could be an asset in a lot of ways, if she'd agree to the job. "But you should know—the people who are coming here next week, they're coming to heal. They've likely fallen on hard times. Some of them are going to be pretty rough around the edges."

Courtney lifted her chin. "I can handle rough."

"I don't doubt it." He smiled. "Why don't you stop by on Monday? We'll work out the details, then."

Courtney looked back out at the yard and was silent for several minutes as she watched her son light his last sparkler. "Thank you," she said finally, the words so soft he could barely hear them.

"You're welcome." He turned his attention back to the dance floor as the band started strumming a few introductory notes. He spotted Jimmy standing nearby with several members of his crew, without a drink in his hand. As far as he knew, he'd been sober since the night he'd been pulled over.

"How's he doing?" Colin asked, nodding toward the contractor.

"Better," Courtney said. "I think he had a pretty big wake up call when the cops took away his license. He can't get around to the sites like he used to and he's missed out on a few big jobs that came up when people in the area found out about what happened. The hearing's in a few weeks from now, so I think he's motivated to stay clean. Jake's been a big help. He's been taking him to AA meetings, coming over to his house each night to make sure he has someone to talk to or watch the game with so he won't be tempted to go to Rusty's."

Colin looked over at Becca, who was slowly walking up from the pier with Grace. He knew, now, that her father had been an alcoholic. He knew a lot of things about her now that he hadn't known before. They'd spent almost every night together since he'd come back from Colorado, and everything he'd learned had only made him love her more.

"I'm happy for you," Courtney said softly, her gaze following his to where Becca had paused at the edge of the dance floor. "It's hard for me to imagine it now, but, maybe one day..." She trailed off, and was quiet for a long time. "I don't think I'll ever love anyone the way I loved Rob, but I'd like to think there might be someone else out there like me—someone who lost the person they loved and might be willing to take a second chance."

The chords of a love song floated into the air as they watched Will lead Annie out to the dance floor for their first dance as husband and wife. "I'm sorry I didn't get a chance to know your husband," Colin said. "I bet I would have liked him."

Courtney looked away, but not before he caught the sheen of tears glistening in her eyes. "He would have liked you, too."

THE PARTY WAS in full swing by the time Becca spotted her father making his way toward her to claim the dance she'd promised him earlier. Excusing herself from the group of teachers she'd been chatting with, she smiled and walked across the grass, meeting him halfway. Night had fallen and a spray of stars winked overhead. White candles flickered from every picnic table, illuminating the hundreds of frosted milk jars that she, Grace, and Gladys had spent all day filling with white roses, pink tulips and Baby's Breath.

It was amazing how much more fun the preparations had become the moment she'd started putting this wedding together for someone else. Maybe it hadn't been the wedding planning that had been stressing her out before. Maybe it had simply been the fact that she'd been planning a wedding for herself to the wrong man.

Slipping her hand into her father's as he led her onto the dance floor, she let him guide her around in a simple two-step to an old country song that had always been one of his favorites. She had thought she might feel a touch of sadness, maybe even a hint of regret at some point during the ceremony earlier that evening. But how could she have felt anything but pure joy as she'd watched two of her best friends, two people who deserved happiness more than anyone she'd ever known, commit their lives to each other.

Will and Annie had been married at sunset, just like Della had wanted, under a driftwood arch covered in roses as the sun sank into the water behind them, painting the sky in a thousand shades of pink. Annie had worn a short, lace dress that she'd sewn herself from vintage fabric. She'd left her long red hair loose and flowing, with a single white tea rose tucked behind her ear. Will had looked stunning in his black suit, but it was the love in his eyes for the woman beside him when he'd recited his vows that had ensured that there hadn't been a single dry eye in the audience.

Annie had been right when she'd said there was no way she and Will could get married on this island without inviting everyone. And they hadn't had to. Once they'd removed all Tom's co-workers from the guest list, there had been plenty of room to extend the invitation to the rest of the islanders. Everything about this night had turned out differently than the way she'd planned it. But, in the end, it had turned out exactly the way it was supposed to.

Gazing across the lawn, she spotted Colin leaning against an ash tree, his hands in his pockets, his tie loosened around his neck, the top button of his dress shirt already unbuttoned. The moment their eyes met, a slow, lazy smile curved his lips. She would have thought she'd have gotten better control of her reaction to him by now. After spending almost every night together over the past two weeks, she had expected at least some of her nerves to calm down.

If anything, they'd gotten stronger. She still felt slightly out of breath every time he looked at her. She still got tongue-tied every time he touched her. And whenever he left the island, even if it was only for a few hours, a strange ache settled deep in her chest

—an uncomfortable longing that gripped her until the moment she saw him again.

When her father's gaze followed hers across the yard, and he saw who she was looking at, he smiled. "Colin's been watching you all night."

"Dad," Becca said, blushing. "That's embarrassing."

"No, honey," he said quietly. "It's not." Her father's expression sobered as he turned her around slowly. "Because the way he looks at you is the same way I used to look at your mother."

Becca felt the familiar lump begin to form in her throat, but instead of wishing her mother was there with them, that she was the one dancing with her father right now, she focused instead on the other couples dancing—all of the other people smiling and laughing and twirling each other around. When she spotted Shelley walking over to the tent, a glass of champagne in her hand, she waved. But the other woman didn't wave back. Shelley paused, alone, by the edge of the dance floor with the strangest, most wistful expression on her face.

Becca frowned. She could have sworn Shelley had been looking straight at them. She waved again, but the other woman didn't even seem to notice. Shelley continued to watch them, and Becca slowly began to realize that it wasn't her she was looking at...it was her father.

Becca stared at the woman who'd been like a second mother to her all these years, who had been a fixture in her life for so long now it was impossible to imagine what a single day would be like without her. Was it possible that she had been secretly hoping, all this time...? "Dad," she said slowly, pulling back as the song ended and the band switched to a slower tune. "Maybe you should ask Shelley to dance."

"Shelley?" he asked, as if the thought would have never occurred to him. "Why?"

Becca glanced back at Shelley, just to be sure. The other

woman was still watching her father with that same expression of longing on her face. She couldn't believe she had never noticed it before. She looked back at her father. "Have you ever thought that Shelley might be interested in being more than just friends?"

"No." Her father was shocked.

"Well." She took a deep breath and gave him a little nudge toward the woman standing at the edge of the dance floor. "Maybe it's time we both stopped living in the past."

She smiled as she left him standing awkwardly in the middle of a crowd of people, trying to get up the courage to approach a woman he'd probably never thought twice about before tonight. She walked across the lawn to where Colin was still standing under the tree. In the flickering candlelight, his hair was so black it gleamed. The slightest hint of stubble darkened the line of his jaw, and the pale blue eyes that stared back at hers reflected the same rush of emotions that coursed through her every time she laid eyes on him.

When he opened his arms, she walked into them, pressed up on her toes, and laid her lips on his.

"Have I told you how beautiful you look tonight?" he murmured, when she finally pulled back.

She nodded, blushing. She still hadn't gotten used to his compliments, the way he never missed the slightest change in her appearance, or a single detail in the stories she told him each night about the kids at school. She had been with a man who thought only about himself for so long that she had assumed that was how all men were.

She knew better now.

Shifting in his arms so her back was against his chest, so he could continue to hold her while they both watched the party swirl around them, she took in the scene of over two hundred and fifty of their friends and neighbors milling around the yard. A few yards away, Luke and Taylor were blowing bubbles at Riley, as the dog barked and nipped at them until they popped. Hundreds of wind chimes swung from the branches of the trees, sparkling in the soft glow of the twinkle lights.

When she heard the faint sound of her mother's charm bracelet, she almost didn't bother to look up. She'd been hearing it more and more now, whenever she and Colin were together. She'd stopped trying to understand it, and had simply accepted it as a sign that her mother was there, watching over her.

In the east, a thumbnail moon was rising, its silver curve visible through the low-hanging branches of the ash tree. Pale green leaves shivered in the salty breezes overhead, drawing her eyes up to where a tiny, hidden wind chime dangled from a thin branch. She blinked when she saw a familiar shape spinning slowly at the end of one of the strings. "Oh my God," she breathed.

"What's wrong?" Colin asked.

Pulling out of his arms, she took a step closer and spotted more familiar shapes through the leaves. Lifting up on her toes, until she could just barely reach it, her fingertips brushed over one of the charms. Most of them were rusted, corroded from years of being underwater, of being constantly lashed by salt and tide. A few of them had lost their shape completely. But there was no question that this was her mother's charm bracelet—the one she had lost in the harbor so many years ago.

"Taylor," she whispered.

Taylor paused in the middle of blowing more bubbles, glancing up at her teacher. "Yes?"

"Where did this come from?" Becca asked, struggling to find her voice.

Taylor pushed to her feet, walking over. She looked up at the chime Becca was holding. "I made it," she answered simply. "From an old charm bracelet."

"But...where did you find it?"

"Luke gave it to me." Taylor looked over at Luke, who'd walked over to stand beside her. "You said you found it in the harbor, right?"

Luke nodded. "I caught it," he said, looking from Becca to Colin. "That day we went fishing after school. That's what the hook got stuck on."

Colin reached up, touching the rusted pieces that had been hidden underwater for so long. He found the matching mourning dove to the one Becca still wore on the chain around her neck and smiled down at her. "I think," he said, letting go of the charm and drawing her back into his arms, "that your mom just gave us her blessing."

THE END

A NOTE FROM THE AUTHOR

Dear Reader,

I hope you enjoyed *Wind Chime Wedding*. The Wind Chime series continues with Ryan and Izzy's story, *Wind Chime Summer*, which is available now. Read on for a special preview. For updates on future books, please sign up for my newsletter at sophiemossauthor.com.

In each of the Wind Chime Novels, I feature a Chesapeake Bay recipe at the end of the story. On the next page, you'll find a recipe for a ten-layer Smith Island Cake. I have only baked this recipe once, and while I promise it's worth the effort, it's definitely a labor of love.

If you want to try a Smith Island Cake without having to spend an entire day in the kitchen, check out the Smith Island Baking Company at smithislandcake.com. They specialize in authentic Smith Island Cakes—Maryland's State Dessert—and they ship their products around the world. I have tried several of their cakes, and they're fantastic.

Lastly, I have a small request. If you enjoyed *Wind Chime Wedding*, it would mean so much to me if you would consider leaving a brief review. Reviews are so important. They help a book stand out in the crowd, and they help other readers find authors like me.

Thank you so much for reading *Wind Chime Wedding*!
Sincerely,
Sophie Moss

SMITH ISLAND CAKE

Ingredients for the cake:
2 sticks unsalted butter, cut into chunks
3 cups flour
¼ teaspoon salt
1 heaping teaspoon baking powder
2 cups sugar
5 eggs
1 cup evaporated milk
2 teaspoons vanilla extract
½ cup water

To make the cake:

Preheat the oven to 350 degrees. Lightly grease 10 nine-inch round cake pans. Sift together the flour, salt and baking powder. Combine the butter and sugar and beat until light and creamy. Add the eggs one at a time and continue to beat. Add the dry ingredients. Add the evaporated milk. Add the vanilla and water. Beat until smooth. Place about 2/3 cup of batter in each of the cake pans and spread out evenly with the back of a spoon. Bake 2 to 3 layers at a time on the middle oven rack for 8 to 9 minutes.

Ingredients for the icing:
- 3 cups sugar
- 1 large can evaporated milk
- 1 stick butter
- 2 heaping tablespoons unsweetened cocoa
- ¼ teaspoon salt
- ½ teaspoon vanilla

To make the icing:

Bring all the ingredients except the vanilla to a boil. Continue to simmer on low while stirring until the chocolate thickens (about 15-20 minutes). Take off the heat. Add the vanilla. Mix by hand until the chocolate is thick enough to spread (about 15-20 minutes). The icing will thicken and turn into fudge so you have to be ready to ice the layers as soon as it thickens to the point where it won't just drip down the sides. Ice each layer as you stack it on top of the next one and then cover the sides and the top with icing, too.

Cake recipe used with permission from "Mrs. Kitching's Smith Island Cookbook" by Frances Kitching and Susan Stiles Dowell, courtesy of Schiffer Publ., Ltd. The icing recipe is my own.

For more *Wind Chime Café* recipes, visit my website at sophiemossauthor.com.

ACKNOWLEDGMENTS

Thank you to my mom and dad for your constant support and encouragement. Thank you to my editor, Martha Paley Francescato, for helping me bring this story to life. Thank you to my first readers—Audra Trosper, Melissa Hladik Meyer, Patricia Paris, Hannah Steenbock, Christine Fitzner-LeBlanc, and Tracy Hewitt Meyer—for taking the time to read early drafts and provide valuable feedback. Lastly, thank you to all the men and women who have served in our military. I am so grateful for your sacrifice and for everything you do to keep this country safe.

ABOUT THE AUTHOR

Sophie Moss is a *USA Today* bestselling and multi-award winning author. She is known for her captivating Irish fantasy romances and heartwarming contemporary romances with realistic characters and unique island settings. As a former journalist, Sophie has been writing professionally for over ten years. She lives in Maryland, where she's working on her next novel. When she's not writing, she's testing out a new dessert recipe, exploring the Chesapeake Bay, or fiddling in her garden. Sophie loves to hear from readers. Email her at sophiemossauthor@gmail.com or visit her website sophiemossauthor.com to sign up for her newsletter.

WIND CHIME SUMMER

CHAPTER ONE

Izzy Rivera didn't notice the marshes. She didn't notice the tall reedy grasses that swayed into the beams of her headlights with every gust of wind. She didn't notice the wildflowers that lined the narrow strip of road through her rain-streaked windshield, or the way her whole car shook with each thunderclap from a storm that only seemed to grow worse the closer she came to this place at the end of the earth.

What she noticed were the pine trees. Or what was left of them. Hollow, broken stumps of pine trees glowing ghostly white in the strobes of lightning that splintered the sky.

That was how she felt now.

Dead. Broken. Empty inside.

She reached for her worn, Army-issue handkerchief and pressed the cloth to the back of her neck. It was already damp. Cold from the sweat she'd soaked up a few minutes ago.

She'd had to pull over three times since crossing the drawbridge to Heron Island. She'd passed through the tiny village about a mile ago, spied a blurry outline of an ice cream shop, a bookstore, a café, a school...and then nothing. There was nothing at all out here.

Nothing but her and those trees.

The memories crept in, threatening to swallow her whole. She forced them back as another flash of lightning lit up the sky and she spotted a lone structure in the distance, an old yellow farmhouse rising up from the end of this soggy, sinking spit of land.

She nearly stopped the car again, nearly turned around. But she wasn't a coward.

Broken? Yes.

A coward? No.

She willed her foot to stay on the gas pedal, to keep pushing the car forward. The wiper blades scraped sheets of rain from the glass, providing intermittent glimpses of a circular driveway filled with cars, a wide front porch covered in potted plants, and a waterlogged garden edging the base of the house.

There were lights on in the downstairs windows. She could see people moving around in the rooms. She eased her car into the last empty spot in the driveway and sat with her foot on the brake, watching them.

She wasn't good with people anymore. She didn't like the way they looked at her, the questions they asked. The smallest exchange of pleasantries—*How's it going? How are you today?*—could set her off now.

She wanted to scream, to throw things, to break things.

I'm fine, was all she ever said, but she wasn't fine. She was as far from fine as she'd ever been in her life.

Shifting the car into park, she cut the headlights and felt a moment of panic when the darkness closed in around her. It was the kind of darkness that could seep through your skin, sink into your bones, spread through your mind until there was nothing left but madness.

Her hand shook as she reached for her water bottle. Somehow, she managed to unscrew the cap. She drank until the dryness in her throat gave way to the familiar pulsing knot of rage that lived inside her.

It was the only thing that kept her going now.

Tossing the empty bottle onto the floor, she lifted her gaze to the yellow house. The colors dripped and melted, the image distorted through the wet glass, until the corners warped and the roof tilted. She was supposed to spend the next three months here. Three months with people like her—people who needed to heal.

As if there were any hope.

She'd read the mission statement on the website. She understood the purpose of this program. Will Dozier and Colin Foley weren't the first Navy SEALs to start rehab programs for down-and-out veterans. It seemed like a perfectly noble goal from the outside. But she'd encountered her share of SEALs overseas. Most of them were arrogant pricks who thought they were better than everyone and knew everything.

They probably thought fixing her would be a breeze.

Sliding the key out of the ignition, she grabbed her pack, flipped the hood of her raincoat up to cover her tangled mass of black curls, and opened the door. An unfamiliar scent rushed toward her. It was muddy, tangy, and smelled faintly of saltwater.

The Chesapeake Bay, she mused. She'd read about that on the website, too. The big body of water that surrounded this island was supposed to help with the healing process. Their fearless leaders were probably going to take them out kayaking and bird watching. Maybe they could hold hands and skip afterwards.

Stepping out of the car, she slammed the door and made her way to the porch. If they even mentioned the words 'group therapy' later, she was going to lose it. Mentally preparing herself for one of those big, cocky SEALs to answer, she knocked on the door. She was pretty sure she'd read somewhere that one of them was the son of the Governor of Maryland.

She could only imagine how big his head must be.

The door swung open, she took one look at the person on the other side, and the speech she'd rehearsed in the car froze on her lips.

He wasn't military.

He was...

A dog barked, slipping out of the gap in the open door and launching itself at her. She sucked in a breath as seventy pounds of wet dog wrapped around her legs in a sniffing, wiggling mass of brown fur.

"Sorry." The man grabbed the dog's collar, pulling the animal back to his side. "She's usually more polite than that." He glanced down at the dog, gave her a scolding look. "Sit."

The dog sat immediately, her tail thumping on the floorboards, her whole body quivering with excitement.

The man looked up at Izzy and offered her a sheepish smile. "This is Zoey. She's part of the welcoming committee."

No, Izzy thought as her heart rate struggled to return to normal. He was definitely not military. His stance was far too casual, far too relaxed. His build was tall and lanky, more like a long distance runner's, and he wore a faded T-shirt and jeans, both of which were streaked with mud.

"You must be Isabella." He smiled and held out his hand. "You're the last to arrive."

"It's Izzy," she corrected, glancing up at his face again. There was a small smudge of something that looked like white paint along his left cheekbone. His hair was a thick, tousled mess of sun-streaked blond. And his eyes were the palest shade of gray she'd ever seen.

Not the gray of storm clouds; they were lighter than that. Like the calm after the storm, the calm leftover as the last of the clouds blew away.

She took his hand. A warm, pulsing sensation spread up her arm. Not sparks of electricity, not wild currents of sexual energy, just warmth and peace and complete and utter calm.

"I'm Ryan," he said, releasing her hand. "Can I help you with the rest of your bags?"

"No," she said, mentally shaking herself. What was wrong with her? She held up her backpack. "This is everything."

His gaze lingered on her small pack and an unspoken question swam into his eyes. But he kept his thoughts to himself. "Come on in," he said, nodding for her to follow him into the house. "Everyone else is in the kitchen."

The moment Izzy stepped inside, the feeling of home wrapped around her like a hug. She tried to fight it, but it was impossible not to feel the love and attention that had gone into every detail of the renovation of this centuries-old farmhouse. She took in the collection of black and white photographs that lined the hallway leading into the next room—family portraits, children at various ages, people from all walks of life.

To the left of the entranceway, a cozy sitting room was filled with overstuffed armchairs and floor-to-ceiling bookshelves. To the right, a polished oak stairwell led up to the second story. The floors were wood as well, thick planks that felt strong and sturdy under her feet.

Ryan took her wet coat, hung it on one of the hooks by the door, and snagged a towel off one of the tables, handing it to her to dry off with. It was big and plush and cozy and made her want to weep.

Stop, she told herself. She didn't need comfort. She didn't want comfort. Comfort would make her soft, would make her face things she'd locked up deep inside. The fact that those things were starting to leak out through the cracks didn't matter. She could patch herself together. At least for the next three months. At least until she could return to Baltimore. She could fall apart there. Where no one could see her.

She handed the towel back.

Ryan dropped it into a hamper. "How was the drive?"

"Fine."

"You didn't run into too much water on the roads?"

There had been a few bends in the road where the water had reached the underside of her car, but she'd powered through them, as she did with everything in life now. "I managed."

"Summer storms can be rough out here. We had one a few years ago that washed out the road completely."

Izzy didn't doubt it, and wondered why anyone would choose to live here, in this place that looked like the next high tide could wash it away. A jingle of dog tags drew her gaze down to the chocolate lab, who had unearthed a tennis ball from beneath one of the tables in the hallway and was looking terribly pleased with herself.

"Ready?" Ryan asked, gesturing for her to follow him into the kitchen.

Izzy nodded, but her throat tightened when she spotted the crowd gathered in the next room. There had to be at least fifteen to twenty people in there. She forced her shoulders back and her spine straight as the first few curious eyes swung her way. *Don't let them see any weakness. Don't ever let anyone know that you're afraid.*

She stepped into the room and her own gaze automatically gravitated to the stove, where steam rose from the top of a large cast-iron pot filled with something that smelled amazing—earthy and spicy with a rich tomato and beef broth. Her fingers curled around the straps of her pack as she struggled against the urge to walk over and see what was inside.

"Are you hungry?" Ryan asked.

"No."

"I'll let Colin and Will know you're here," he said, slipping into the crowd.

Izzy took in the gleaming stainless steel appliances, wide chopping block counter, oversized farmhouse sink, and impressive collection of copper pots hanging from an iron rack mounted to the ceiling. It was the kind of kitchen that was made for cooking big meals that took all day to prepare and inviting everyone you knew over to enjoy them.

There was a time when she would have dreamed of having a kitchen like this in her own home.

She looked past the bar, where a few burly guys in their late-twenties were wolfing down big bowls of soup, and took a quick inventory of the rest of the people in the room. Besides the middle-aged woman tending to the soup on the stove, there were only two other women. One was in a wheelchair. The other was missing the lower half of her right arm.

She was the only female veteran still in one piece.

That should make her feel better, right? She didn't look broken, so she must be fine. That's what everyone else thought. Most of the time, it was easier to let them.

One of the women offered her a tentative smile, a small offer of friendship. Izzy looked away. She didn't want friends. She didn't need friends.

They wouldn't want to be friends with her anyway once they found out the truth—that she wasn't a real soldier.

She was just a cook. A woman who'd worked in the kitchen.

And now she couldn't even do that.

"Hey," Ryan Callahan said, putting his hand on Will Dozier's shoulder. His best friend from childhood turned. "Izzy's here." He nodded across the room to where the woman stood, looking like she was ready to bolt.

"Thanks," Will said, extracting himself from a conversation with an ex-Marine. "I know Colin's been anxious to get started. He was hoping to be halfway through the introductions by now." He walked away, heading toward Izzy.

Ryan's gaze followed his friend's path across the room. He couldn't help it. It was impossible not to look at the woman again. Izzy Rivera was captivating in a rough-around-the-edges, mistrustful-like-a-cat kind of way. Her thick black hair was pulled back in a ponytail, but a few wet curls had slipped loose, framing an exotic, golden-skinned face of either Spanish or Latina descent. Her body was all female, with soft round curves that had drawn the attention of more than one man when she'd walked into the room.

But it was those eyes—big and amber and filled with emotion —that made him unable to look away.

Jesus. Those eyes. He'd never seen a pair of eyes like that.

A sudden hand on his arm startled him and he flinched.

"Somebody's jumpy tonight," Della Dozier commented.

Reluctantly dragging his gaze away from Izzy's face, Ryan looked down at Will's aunt.

"That's not like you," Della said, her blue eyes concerned. "Is everything all right?"

That was a good question, Ryan thought. He hadn't expected to be attracted to any of the women who'd enrolled in this program, especially not one who would be working for him. Obviously, it went without saying that any woman on his payroll was strictly off limits. She had come here to heal, *not* get hit on.

Ryan's gaze swept over the rest of the faces in the room. When he'd offered to provide temporary employment to some of the veterans in this program, he'd been so focused on the mutual benefits—he needed the workforce to help his new business succeed, and they needed something to do with their hands to get their confidence back—that he hadn't really considered the full impact of what he was taking on.

Every person in this room had something in common that he didn't—they'd served in the military. He didn't have a clue what it felt like to be shot at, to put on a uniform, to be shipped overseas and spend years away from your friends and family. He had no idea what it felt like to come home after multiple tours and try to fit in with the people you'd left behind.

What if he couldn't relate? What if he couldn't offer them what they needed?

He looked at Della. "I guess it just hit me—what's at stake. I don't want to mess up."

"You're not going to mess up," Della said, giving his arm a squeeze. "I have faith in you, in *all* of you. And I know that you haven't eaten anything tonight, so I fixed up a container of soup for you to take home afterwards. It's in the fridge, on the top shelf."

"Thank you," Ryan said, and felt some of the tension dissolve. Della had never had any children of her own, but she'd been like a mother to a lot of people on this island. People on Heron Island took care of each other. They looked out for each other. Now that these eleven veterans were staying here for the next twelve weeks, they would look out for them, too.

"Welcome, everyone," Colin's deep voice cut through the room, silencing all conversation. "I think I've gotten to meet most of you by now. We'll go around the room in a minute and let you all introduce yourselves, but I'd like to point out a few key people first. Most of you have probably met Will Dozier. He and his wife, Annie, and their daughter, Taylor, live in the private wing on the north side of the house."

From their spot by the fireplace, Annie and Taylor smiled and waved to everyone.

"Della?" Colin asked.

"Over here." Della waved an arm, her short frame dwarfed by a wall of taller men who parted to let her through.

Colin smiled warmly at the gray-haired woman wearing an apron with the words *Kiss the Cook* embroidered across it. "Everyone, this is Della Dozier, Will's aunt and the best cook on Heron Island. Let's give her a round of applause for making this incredible batch of Maryland crab soup for us tonight."

Everyone applauded and Della beamed.

"Della wanted to be here tonight to personally welcome you all to the inn," Colin continued, "but she works at the Wind Chime Café in town, which Annie owns. From now on, you'll be responsible for preparing the meals we eat together." He motioned to a large chalkboard hanging on the wall. "Every week, we'll assign new jobs to each of you. You can see the first week's breakdown here. We'll go into this in more detail after the introductions, but as you can see it's all the basic housekeeping chores: cooking, cleaning, laundry, grocery shopping."

Colin looked out at the crowd. "For those of you still recovering from injuries, we have a physical therapist who will be meeting with you at her office in St. Michaels. We'll arrange the transportation, so let us know when you've worked out a schedule with your employer and we'll make sure you get there on time. We also have a social worker on call twenty-four seven. She'll be reaching out to each of you individually to set up your first appointment. These sessions will be private and completely confidential between the two of you, but we expect you to attend a minimum of at least one a week."

Ryan saw a few guys wince and figured most of them weren't too excited about the prospect of talking about their feelings. He understood why it was a mandatory part of the program, but he didn't blame them.

"For those of you who are interested—and we expect everyone who is physically capable to participate—Will has put together a rigorous exercise program that he'll be leading twice a day." Colin glanced up, catching Will's eye across the room. "And I can tell you from personal experience that it won't be a walk in the park." The two former SEAL teammates smiled, sharing an inside joke.

"Lastly, over the next few weeks, we'll both be meeting with each of you individually to go over your résumés, skillsets, and employment interests so we can find you a permanent position closer to your families and hometowns. As for your jobs on the island, we've secured temporary employment for each of you at a local business, which you'll be starting first thing tomorrow."

Colin glanced down at his notes, reviewing the list of assignments. "Troy," he said, looking back up and meeting the eyes of a short, stocky veteran near the front of the room, "you'll be working with Don Fluharty at The Tackle Box."

Troy nodded, as if he remembered seeing the small general store at the foot of the drawbridge when he'd driven by it earlier that night.

"Zach." Colin's gaze swept through the crowd, landing on a tall, brown-haired man near the middle of the room. "You'll be working on Bob Hargrove's charter boat as his first mate."

Zach lit up. "I get to work on a fishing boat?"

Colin nodded and glanced down at his notes again. "Megan, you'll be working with Lou Ann Sadler at Clipper Books."

Megan's face broke into a smile. The pretty brunette in the wheelchair was pleased with her assignment as well.

"Kade," Colin continued, "you'll be working with Gladys Schaefer at The Flower Shoppe."

A few people snorted as they tried to stifle their laughter, but most failed, and even Ryan's brows lifted at that one.

Kade McCafferty was the second tallest person in the room after Colin, which put him somewhere around six-foot-three. He was built like a linebacker, probably weighing close to three hundred pounds, and he was completely bald, like one day he'd just woken up and said 'screw it' to his hair and shaved it all off. Dark tattoos covered both arms and another huge tattoo on his left calf spelled out the word, 'MARINES.' He'd been one of the first to arrive at the inn that night and Ryan had spent some time talking to him earlier. He'd served five tours overseas as an infantryman. Front lines.

The Flower Shoppe?

That just seemed wrong.

But Colin was already forging ahead. "I know some of you have already met Ryan Callahan." Colin nodded to where Ryan stood and everyone turned to look at him. "Ryan is a marine biologist whose research has transformed the field of coastal ecology. He has a Ph.D. from MIT's joint program with Woods Hole Oceanographic Institution, and he's spent the past ten years fighting to mitigate the effects of climate change and pollution on our most endangered waterways. Last year, he moved back to this island to open a nonprofit to educate the public on how to become better stewards of the Chesapeake Bay and help his father, a fourth-generation waterman, expand his oyster farm. They've recently combined the two operations into a single company with a big vision and they're going to need a lot of help to get where they want to go."

"What's an oyster farm?" one of the women asked.

Colin looked at Ryan. "Go ahead."

"It's an environmentally sustainable process of growing and harvesting oysters," Ryan explained. "They start out as seeds, which we purchase from a hatchery, and then we plant them in the water like a regular farmer would plant seeds in the ground. It takes about a year-and-a-half for a farmed oyster to grow to market size, which is when we pull them out and sell them to restaurants, seafood markets, and wholesalers."

"Don't oysters grow in the wild?" one of the guys asked. "Why do you need to farm them?"

"The wild oyster population in the Bay was almost completely wiped out twenty years ago," Ryan said. "Right now, it's at about one percent of historic levels. There have been efforts to reestablish it, and it's starting to make a very small comeback, but it still has a long way to go. Oyster farming is a way of continuing a centuries-old tradition of harvesting seafood from these waters without affecting one of our most important natural resources. We don't take anything out that we don't put there ourselves."

"Which brings us to our last two groups of people," Colin said, segueing easily back to the point. "Hailey and Ethan, you'll be working on the nonprofit side of Ryan's operation. Paul, Jeff, Wesley, Matt, and Izzy, you'll be working on the farm."

"No," Izzy said.

Seventeen heads turned to face her, and Izzy's eyes widened, as if she hadn't realized she'd said it out loud.

Colin glanced over at her, surprised. "Is there a problem?"

She looked like she wanted to shrink into the wall, to disappear completely, but knew it was too late. "I'd rather not work... on a farm."

"Why not?"

She straightened her spine, visibly mustering her courage. "I would like to request to switch with someone."

"I'll switch with her," Kade said.

A few people laughed.

"I appreciate the team spirit," Colin said dryly, "but we put everyone in each position for a reason. If something changes over the next few weeks, we can make adjustments. Right now, we're confident that everyone is where he or she is supposed to be. Let's move on with the rest of the introductions and the tour so that those of you who are working with Ryan can make it an early night. You'll be leaving here before sunrise tomorrow to get to the farm by 0500." Colin looked over at Ryan, making it clear that the discussion was closed. "Is there anything else your staff should know?"

Ryan watched Izzy squeeze the straps of her pack. He caught the flash of fear in her eyes, and then something else, something that looked like anger, as if she were somehow offended by the assignment.

What could she possibly have against working on an oyster farm?

Suppressing the urge to speak up, to tell Colin that they should give her another job, he reminded himself that he wasn't in charge of this program. He was just one of the employers. He had to trust that Will and Colin knew what they were doing.

They were the ones who had served. They were the ones who could relate.

A wet nose brushed against his fingertips and he looked down as Zoey, his chocolate lab, nuzzled his hand. "Wear gym clothes," he said, "because you're going to get dirty."

19802323R00182

Made in the USA
Middletown, DE
07 December 2018